Volume Eight

Airship 27 Productions

Sherlock Holmes: Consulting Detective, Vol. 8

Editor: Ron Fortier
Associate Editor: Charles Saunders
Production and design by Rob Davis
Promotion and marketing by Michael Vance

Published by
Airship 27 Productions
www.airship27.com
www.airship27hangar.com

ISBN-13: 978-0692685150 (Airship 27)
ISBN-10: 0692685154

Printed in the United States of America

10 9 8 7 6 5 4 3 2 1

Sherlock Holmes
Consulting Detective
Volume VIII

TABLE OF CONTENTS

Sherlock Holmes

in

"Mysteries of the Buried God"

By

I.A. Watson

My regular readers will know that Mr Sherlock Holmes much prefers to see murder scenes undisturbed and as soon as possible after the crime has taken place. The great detective can become rather irritable when he is called in late and vital evidence has been destroyed by the curious or incompetent.

"You can hardly hold Professor Melville responsible for this one," I told my friend as we looked at the dead men in our latest case.

Young Appledore was quick to apologise for his mentor's absence. "I'm sorry the Professor could not be here to guide you himself. He gives private lectures at the College on a Monday morning, even during the vac. He will travel down by train and join us as quickly as he can. In the meantime we are all hoping that you can shed some light on our extraordinary discovery."

"Anything you can tell us would be most helpful," chimed in Reverend Endicott. "We were most excited when the diggers discovered the chamber – until this!"

Holmes and I stood in the crypt of St Edith-in-the-Field, an obscure medieval church in one of the tangled back-roads off bustling Fleet Street. The floor of the undercroft had been carefully lifted, the great flags stacked at one end of the crypt. Piles of London clay and some ancient bricks were heaped against the walls. Half a dozen workmen's lanterns lit the hole dug to a hidden level below.

We followed Appledore into the lower area. Only a few feet below the flooring of the church vault was the barrel-roof of another, even older chamber. The air smelled damp and ancient, befouled worse by the trickle of an inch-deep stream along the length of the compartment.

"Mind the water," Reverend Endicott called down to us; he was of advancing years and could not lightly manage ladders. "Some of us believe that channel to be some stray tributary of the lost River Fleet, long built over and turned into a sewer."[1]

1 The Thames' largest London tributary rises on Hampstead Heath and formerly terminated in a marshy river valley. A navigable tidal course in Roman times, the Fleet was canalled during the rebuilding of London after the Great Fire of 1666 and by the 18th century had been reduced to a sewer ditch. Between 1737 and 1880 portions of the river were covered over and built upon, so that now the waterway goes underground on the edge of Hampstead Heath and passes without ever seeing light beneath Kentish Town, Camden Town, and Kings Cross, then beneath Farringdon Road and Farringdon Street. It joins the Thames under Blackfriars Bridge, where its effusion can still be seen in heavy rains and low tide.

I could believe it from the unpleasant odour. It was also clear from crusted marks on the lower room's walls that the water levels had risen considerably higher at other times.

Appledore waited for Holmes and I to reach the floor before he shone his lamp around to show where we had come. The chamber beneath St Edith was some twenty feet wide and a little over forty feet long. The low barrelled roof curved to an apex some ten feet up. Stone benches lined the long sides. At one short end was a sealed apse doorway that must have been the original access. Down the room's length opposite was a carved stone pedestal containing a chipped bust, flanked by the remains of half a dozen shattered votive statues. The semicircular apse beyond was obscured by a grubby blanket hung as a curtain.

"Amazing, isn't it?" Professor Melville's student enthused to us. "It's lain hidden down here under the church for so long. Nobody had any idea it was here. If it had not been for the subsidence in the undercroft caused by the digging of our modern London sewer system, nobody would have suspected there was anything down here."

"You mentioned a dead man," Holmes interrupted. His keen eye had already fallen upon the alcove behind the religious statues. He swept past defaced graven images of Roman deities that I could not immediately recognise, pushed the dirty sheet aside, and shone his light into the low arch beyond.

That was where the dead man sat. Holmes regarded the fragile skeleton and said, in his most neutral tones, "I fear you may not be able to revive him, Watson."

This was true. The skeleton was ancient, held together only by centuries of wet dust that had clotted the components of his bones. Already one arm had disintegrated into separate parts and time had done away with the extremities of fingers and toes. The rest of him remained in the sitting position where he had been left who knows how many centuries earlier, bound at wrist and ankle by rusted metal fetters that held him on his stone throne.

His skull had fallen loose and lay on his lap, staring at us. The rusty metal short-sword that had probably ended his life still rested between his ribs.

"That is just how we found him on Saturday," Appledore insisted. "The Professor ordered that nothing be disturbed until drawings and measurements could be taken and everything recorded. Our agreement with the church is that no site work be done on Sundays, so today is our first opportunity for a proper inspection."

"Why did Professor Melville feel the need for a consulting detective?" I wondered. "Holmes is usually brought in on more... recent... activity."

"It... seemed like a good idea when the suggestion was made," Appledore answered haltingly.

"Is it not obvious, Watson?" Holmes demanded of me. "Look around you. This ancient place was constructed with care and skill. The stonework is Roman, if I am not mistaken, and the mortar is constructed with local ingredients. The doorway was blocked up a significant time after construction, for the mixture used to seal those bricks in place is of a different formulation using the coarser sand from the Limehouse area. You see the enigma?"

I looked at the gloomy underground chamber. It seemed to me a morbid, unearthly place, sinister even before finding a dead man shackled to a chair with a blade in his chest. I could not discern any reason why Holmes might believe there to be a case.

"The doorway, man!" he chided me. "Come, Watson, you observe that at some time the arch was bricked up to seal this place away. Look carefully at the mortar. What do you see?"

I trotted over to examine the original entrance in more detail. In better light at close quarters I realised what Holmes had observed. "This brickwork has been pointed from the inside. It was sealed from in here. And yet..."

"The man who laid the bricks must have been in this chamber," Appledore summarised. "He must have. He bricked himself in. But the only man we found in this place was bolted hand and foot into a stone chair and was murdered with a sword through his heart. If he was the bricklayer, then how was he locked up and how could he stab himself? If he was not, then where is the man who did it?"

"Not only a locked room mystery," I gasped, "but a bricked-up room mystery!"

"That is why Professor Abbot suggested that Mr Holmes be asked to comment," Appledore explained.

"Now you are being evasive," Holmes told the academic's protégé. "Come now, the full reasons."

Appledore looked a little apologetic. "This dig is a little bit controversial," he admitted. "It required special permission from the diocese and from the Church Commissioners, and even consent from the government – all archaeology under churches does.[2] The trustees of St Edith were not all convinced; we were granted leave only after a bitter row between them. A whiff of unpleasantness, the hint of unsavoury doings under their church, even many centuries ago, might be sufficient for them to revoke their licence. Furthermore, Professor Melville was not the only archaeologist eager to fathom this site. Be sure his rivals will latch on any anomaly to rubbish his work and to blacken his reputation."

"And an impossible body in a sealed tomb might offer them the chance," Holmes surmised. "Well, a murder is a murder. I warn you that the chance of bringing this killer before the magistrates is somewhat minimal."

"The Professor will be grateful for anything you might discern about what happened. Anything that might explain…"

"I'm sure he would," Holmes interrupted. He examined the dilapidated remains for a long while then stepped aside and prompted me to look also. "Doctor Watson, your observations as a medical man, if you please."

I held my light close to see the body. "It's remarkably preserved if it is Roman," I began. "The sealed chamber, the cold and the moisture are probably responsible. If he had been interred he would be nothing more than flakes by now."

"He is male, then?" Appledore checked.

"Judging by his pelvic bone and the shape of his jaw, yes," I agreed. "A man of middle years. His teeth are somewhat worn down. The porous crumbly nature of some of his remaining joints suggests the onset of osteoporosis." I checked his ribcage. "Whoever struck the fatal blow knew what he was doing. The blade avoided the ribs entirely."

Holmes made a noise in the back of his throat that might have been agreement or could have been his usual scorn at my well-meaning detec-

2 All planning permissions on Church of England property are covered by ecclesiastical laws that long predate modern building and planning regulation; indeed, modern legislation was modelled upon that already established for holy ground. Permissions are granted first at local level by the incumbent cleric, churchwardens, and parochial church council; at diocesan level by the Consistory Court of the Church or by chancellors; and appeals at national level by the Court of Arches or the Chancery Court, depending on whether the diocese falls under the Archbishop of Canterbury or York. Final authority rests with the Supreme Governor of the Church of England, the monarch, who retains *Fidei Defensor* (Defender of the Faith) as one of his or her ancient titles; in practice this responsibility is usually devolved to the Prime Minister and Parliament.

The Church of England, being a state religion, retains the power through its legislative body the General Synod to make English law. It can create *Measures,* which must be ratified by the Houses of Parliament but which Parliament may not amend, and which then become statute, or *Canons* that require Royal License and Royal Assent but are church (canon) law only. Twenty-six archbishops and bishops sit by right in the House of Lords.

tions. "Give us some background, Mr Appledore," he demanded of the student. "Begin with the history of the site and how you came to excavate this place."

"Mr Holmes, the Professor will be here soon and..."

"And we are here now. Surely a man whom the Professor delegated to receive us in his absence, a Grant Prize scholar and an enthusiastic historian who has lately consulted the parish rolls must be able to brief us on the background."

Appledore stared at Holmes dumbfounded. "How...?"

"He has observed the small pin in your lapel, signal of the academic award," I revealed for the stunned student. "He also noticed the granular smudges on your collar, where you ran your fingers over old faded ink on some crumbling parchment then touched your neck. This is Sherlock Holmes. To him such observations are so everyday that he scarcely realises that he is doing it."

"Your account, Appledore," Holmes demanded abruptly.

The student nodded nervously; Holmes' gaze can do that to people. "Er, yes, well... St Edith in the Field was built in 1577, the reign of Queen Elizabeth, as a chapel of ease for the poor of the parish, on land donated by Sir Francis Drake as he prepared for his expedition against the Spanish that became the second circumnavigation of the globe. There is no record of an earlier foundation here, although we know that late Roman Londinum extended as far as the Fleet.[3]

"The recent problems with subsidence in the vault were attributed to the excavations of the Bazalgette sewers.[4] A number of gravestones that had

---

3 Victorian antiquarian Roach Smith estimated that Roman London had been founded about A.D. 50 with a perimeter that ran from the Tower of London to Ludgate (St Paul's) and from the Thames to London Wall, an area of about 350 acres. The River Fleet was just outside the bounded city on its eastern side, and was then an active tidal river suitable for harbouring ships. Londinum was rebuilt after its sack and destruction by Queen Boudica's (Boadicea's) Icini rebellion in A.D. 60 and became the largest Roman city in Britain.

4 After "the Great Stink" of 1858, when a hot summer and raw effluent in the Thames brought London to a stop, Parliament urgently commissioned a series of modern sewers for the capital. These works were carried out by Sir Edward Bazalgette, Chief Engineer of the Metropolitan Board of Works, who oversaw the laying of 550 miles of sewers under London between 1858 and 1865. Such was the visionary scope and redundancy incorporated into his works that his sewers still have the capacity to serve modern London with its massively increased population density.

There is no conclusive evidence that either the sewer excavations or the underground railways installed from the 1860s onward were responsible for much subsidence, but their drilling was often held culpable by popular opinion. It is however true to say that what London is mostly built upon is older London.

been reused as floor materials sank unevenly, requiring them to be lifted and the ground beneath them shored. During that renovation, some ten years ago now, a range of artefacts were recovered from the ground beneath. Roman coins, pottery shards, and most interestingly a tiny votive effigy of Venus and several lead-scroll curse tablets."

"Curse tablets?" I interjected.

"Common at Roman religious sites, Dr Watson. Someone would take a scrap of lead or a fragment of stone, carve out the name of the person who had wronged them and sometimes a charge or a prayer for vengeance, then bury it close to a temple or holy statue. 'Furies take Fenix who stole money from me', 'Hekate shrivel Antus who betrayed my love', that kind of thing. The folded lead marker discovered here was just somebody's name written in mirror script, a less common kind of magical invocation but not unknown."

"And from this somebody concluded there was a Roman ruin beneath the church," I surmised.

"It is not unknown. St Martin, by the Tower of London, has a Roman pavement beneath it. There are classical ruins beneath the Guildhall. And the oldest remnant stretches of London's wall were built by the legions, of course. When the discoveries were made here, one of the parishioners alerted the College and Professor Melville took an interest."

Holmes gestured for Melville's apprentice to continue. My friend was busy scraping surface dust from the stone chair itself, carefully harvesting it into a twist of paper so that he could chemically examine it later.

"We began to dig two weeks ago," Appledore explained. "It took a long time to convince ecclesiastical authorities and the local churchgoers to grant permission, but at last we were able to lift the grave slab flooring and remove the material used to shore the foundations – carefully, of course.

"We discovered a few more items like the ones I described, but all the pottery and statuary was shattered, not worth retaining.[5] Then last

5 The most constant criticism by modern archaeologists of Victorian archaeology was their forebears' prioritisation of intact and impressive artefacts, which were removed from sites with scant regard to their positioning or context, often without accurate information about their source; treasure-hunting rather than scientific investigation. "Less valuable" strata of deposits were often stripped away and discarded to get to more "significant", that is good-looking or financially valuable, items.

The modern framework of legislation that protects British historical sites was mostly not in place at Holmes' time. The 1882 *Ancient Monuments Protection Act*, whilst groundbreaking (but not literally), covered only sixty-two named sites. Subsequent 1900 and 1910 Acts were eventually replaced by the comprehensive *Ancient Monuments and Archaeological Areas Act* 1979.

Much older are the English, Scottish, Welsh and Irish common laws of Treasure Trove, which gives rulers rights to all discovered hordes, so long as the treasure is judged

Holmes was busy scraping surface dust from the stone chair itself.

Friday we hit the top of this chamber's roof. It collapsed, in fact, dropping Garrison and Levizad right down into the chamber. Garrison broke his leg. You can imagine how excited we were."

"I imagine Garrison was very excited," I murmured.

"It was late in the day but the Professor insisted we carry on. As per our agreement with the church we sent for Reverend Endicott to observe, and then we proceeded down into the sanctuary."

"I hope that someone thought to hoist the unfortunate Garrison out and get him to a doctor," I suggested.

"Oh, yes. Although he really wanted to stay and look around," Appledore enthused. "Poor chap had been stretchered away before we shone our lights to the sacred alcove there and discovered Charlie."

"Charlie." He meant the cadaver, of course. Undergrad humour. How well I remembered medical school.

"Charlie was something of a shock, I can tell you," Appledore confessed. "We were just slapping each other on the back, telling ourselves we had found a genuine Mithraeum, and then suddenly there's a skeleton shackled to a throne."

"Mithraeum?" I echoed. "From... the Roman god Mithras?"

"An Eastern god really," the young scholar supplied. "A sort of solar deity of life and rebirth, an avatar of light.[6] Crept into the Roman Empire about the same time as Christianity. Was Christianity's main competitor for a while. Mystery religion, secret handshakes, secret initiation rites and all that. Popular with soldiers and so on. But no women allowed; perhaps that's why it never really made it."

"And their faith included locking people into chairs and stabbing them?"

---

to have been concealed with intent to retrieve it and the concealer is unknown or long since dead without heir. These rights are still upheld by the Crown.

6 The Persian god Mithra was adopted by Romans as Mithras during the 1st-3rd centuries A.D. and his cult spread across the Roman Empire, centred on Rome itself. Around 420 sites have now offered evidence about the faith. Many depict Mithras' birth from a stone, his slaughtering of a bull, and his feasting with the god Sol. Some sources argue that Mithras' birthday was 25th December and that for this reason the early Christian church placed the celebration of Christ's nativity on that day to replace his mythos; other experts disagree.

As a mystery religion with seven degrees of initiation, almost no liturgy or religious ceremony of Mithraism is now preserved. Archaeological evidence suggests the importance of feasting and of a solar calendar. Temples of Mithras were typically small, cheaply made, sunken or underground, windowless, and close by a stream or river. They were quite different from traditional Roman temples, consisting mostly of a single long thin chamber with benches along the sides and a number of altars and friezes, including a relief of the Tauroctony, the killing of the sacred bull.

"Not that we know of, no. Of course, we know so little about them.[7] They apparently did this unpleasant thing where they sealed their initiated into a dark hole and sacrificed a bull over them so that the blood drenched the candidate, but... not what we have here.[8] There are examples of Mithraea at the basilica of San Clemente in Rome and at the Circus Maximus, the Carnuntum Mithraeum at Bad Deutsch-Altenburg, the Aquincum Mithraeum of Victorinus near Budapest, a few other places. But in England we have only the site at the Roman fort at Rudchester. You can't imagine how excited we are to have found another."[9]

"And then you fathomed your sealed room dilemma," Holmes prompted, impatient with the history lesson.

"Why yes. It was the Professor himself who worked out that the apse entrance had been sealed up with mortar on the inside. We all looked pretty carefully at that. Even Reverend Endicott agreed that the signs of the wall being built from the inside were pretty definite. What with that, and a dead victim fastened to his chair with an ancient Roman soldier's sword sticking between his ribs, it was... pretty disturbing."

The whole chamber was eerie to me. The mournful flow of Fleet wash

---

7 The prevailing theory in the late 1800s came from K.B. Stark's "Die Mithrasstein von Dormagen" in *Jahrbücher des Vereins von Altertumsfrerunden im Rheinlande* vol 46 (1869), which argued an astrological interpretation of the subterranean temples and practices of the cult. Franz Cumont's opposing and determinantly influential view in *Texts and Illustrated Monuments Relating to the Mysteries of Mithra* was published in 1894-1900 and first translated into English in 1903, but had not yet changed the tide of scholarly opinion at the time of our present narrative.

8 Most Mithraea are impractical for the bull-blood washing traditionally ascribed to the cult. Many academics now offer differing interpretations. The statements in our narrative were typical of the understandings of Victorian scholarship.

Rudyard Kipling imagined "A Song For Mithras, hymn of the XXX Legion" in "On the Wall" in *Puck of Pook's Hill*, 1906. The late, great Lewis Carroll scholar Kate Lyon (1957-2007) believed there were Mithraic influences in the *Alice* stories and was working on a thesis about it at the time of her death.

9 Four Mithraea are now rediscovered in England and Wales. In addition to the 1844 find at Rudchester (Roman Vindobala), there are remains at another military site on Hadrian's Wall, Carrawburg (Roman Brocolitia), at Caernarfon, and most significantly for our story, at Walbrook, London, in the very heart of the oldest part of the city.

The London Mithraeum was discovered during construction works in 1954 and proved to be a major find. Originally located near the now-submerged River Walbrook, the rediscovered site was preserved from destruction by public demand and relocated whole before a modern office block was built where it had been. Its superb statuary is now displayed at the British Museum. The details of the purely fictional Mithraeum of our present narrative are largely drawn from the actual details of this real discovery, although the Walbrook site was in considerably better condition. A long-running proposal to return the temple to its original location continues to face financial and legal challenges.

trickling along the guttered length of the sanctuary to vanish under a carved stone, the way the ruined statues cast jerking shadows in our flickering lamplight, the separated skull glaring malevolently at us, had a cumulative effect that was most unpleasant.

"You have not located the mystery bricklayer," Holmes understood. "There are only two possibilities, of course."

"We have thought about every feasible means, Mr Holmes," Appledore assured my friend. "But the Professor hoped that you might spot something that we have missed."

The great detective snorted. "There are a good number of things suggested by the evidence of this room, trampled as it has been by some score of well-meaning gawkers in a range of footwear. Your Professor, I deem, wears size nine brogues and favours his left leg due to incipient arthritis. Reverent Endicott prefers an eight and a half boot and spent his time down here hovering at the edges, uncertain how much it was appropriate to participate. Your injured Garrison wore a size ten half-boot with a square heel and smokes Venables' tobacco. All easily evident to anyone who applies a little observation."

Appledore blinked.

"Have you a theory to share with us, Holmes?" I asked to ease the moment along.

"A few minor conclusions," my friend replied. "Firstly, this dead man is not Roman, nor of that era. Note the dentistry, Watson. Different ages pulled rotten teeth in different ways. This man was of medieval vintage, though I would have to consult my books to offer a more precise date. Likewise the brackets and bolts on this stone chair are of middle ages construction."

Appledore rushed forward to look more closely at the evidence. "I'd... have to call experts to check, but... yes, I've never seen Roman construction that uses bolts of that kind. How did we miss that? We were all so excited..."

"Likewise the sealed door that so perplexed you was bricked up using different mortar and different techniques than was applied to building this place," Holmes went on. "The bricks are of a similar age to the rest, presumably reused since they were on site, but some are weathered where they have previously been exposed to the elements while others laid next to them are not. I posit that the re-sealing of the apse was also medieval."

"It must have been before St Edith-in-the-Field was founded," Appledore reasoned.

"It was probably at that time when the Mithraeum was looted," Holmes went on.

The young archaeologist looked up sharply, aghast. "Looted?"

"Most likely. You discovered several items in your spoil heap as you dug down here, but no material in the temple itself? Yet there are wall-niches for devotional items, brackets to hang lamps. Where are the items they contained? It is possible that the contents were removed long before the apse was sealed, of course, but I do not perceive the weathering around the doorway that suggested it was exposed for long periods of time. More likely the entrance was uncovered at some moment in the middle ages, the temple despoiled of its riches, and then sealed again; with at least one unfortunate left inside."

Appledore looked around. "Where might any other man go? And why bring a victim in here and drill shackles into a stone chair?" He thought again. "No other Mithraeum has contained a stone chair."

"That too might be a medieval modification," Holmes allowed. "Clearly there was much superstition and skulduggery at work in the days before the entrance was reblocked. You observe the damage done to the remaining votive statuary? Attempts were made first to break it free and remove it, and when that failed to destroy it in situ. Attempts that were then abandoned."

"Can we know that was done at that time, Holmes?" I challenged. "Many pagan sites were destroyed by the early Christians."

"A useful point, Watson. We must not run ahead of the evidence. Let us say for now that it is likely that this chamber was concealed from Roman times, exposed for a while sometime before 1577, used to contain the unfortunate fellow we see sitting here, and then sealed again in a very particular way. A pretty mystery." He turned suddenly to Appledore. "The rubble from the floor here. What happened to it?"

The scholar shied back from Holmes's accusatory question. "We... there was a lot of fragments when we broke through. As you can see, a part of the roof caved in. We swept up all the stones and carted them away."

"Only the stones, or everything on the floor?"

"Everything. You can't imagine how much detritus had accumulated over the years, dirt and cobwebs and... worse filth from the Fleet discharge."

"I can well imagine," Holmes insisted. "Were there plaster shards amongst the debris? You'll observe that the interior of the sealed door was once covered with the stuff, and probably all the interior walls too? It must have crumbled away over the centuries. What became of those shards?"

Appledore blanched. "The Professor wanted the site cleaned up. We sacked up the refuse and lifted it out. The bags are probably still stacked outside awaiting disposal."

"Do not dispose of them," Holmes commanded. "I can see that the science of archaeology has much yet to learn from the science of detection! Those plaster shards can tell us much."

"But a second man, Holmes?" I interjected, eager to hear some solution to our present enigma. "How can a labourer seal a room with himself inside – *plaster* himself in if you're right about the evidence – possibly execute a shackled captive, then vanish into thin air?"

"Patently he cannot, Watson. A second man must go somewhere. There are two possibilities. The rubble that Professor Melville so foolishly discarded may offer us a lead on one of them. The other option lies at your feet."

I looked down at the trickling rivulet that flowed between my boots. I followed its course to where it disappeared beneath an etched stone. "Where does it go?" I wondered out loud.

Holmes clapped me on the back. "Exactly, Watson! What lies beneath that flag?"

Appledore began to get excited again. "There might be another chamber beneath! That might be where the missing man went! There may be more to this Mithraeum than we have so far discovered!" He turned away to the ladder and shouted up to the vault above. "Reverend Endicott? Have any of my colleagues arrived yet? Could you send them down with block and tackle?"

"The water must drain away somewhere," I admitted.

"The floor level has been raised since the site was originally constructed," Holmes pointed out. "Doubtless the proximity of the Fleet caused serious damp problems. The whole building has settled since that time; hence the small stream that now intrudes along the floor."

There was a bustling at the roof entrance. A pair of Appledore's fellow students clambered down, carrying between them a hoist and pulley. Appledore introduced them as Evans and Levizad.

"Any sign of the Prof yet?" he asked them.

"His train's due at King's Cross[10] at 12.41," Levizad answered. "About two hours?"

---

10 From this evidence we may infer that Professor Melville was attached to a Cambridge college. If he were travelling from Oxford he would have arrived at Paddington.

"Do we wait for him?" Evans worried. "He'd want to be here when we lift that stone."

"I have no intention of waiting two hours on the Professor," Holmes assured them. "Kindly attach the tackle and raise the slab." He pointed to a pair of worn indents on one edge of the stone. "You will note that some kind of ring or handle was once present here to assist in raising this hatch. The floor-groove there at the rear edge was intended to allow the cover to hinge up."

I noticed there were other floor grooves too, to help channel the water; except that Holmes had suggested that no water flowed here when this was a working place of worship.

Appledore had a theory. "Um, the Romans, that is the followers of Mithras, they believed that their god had slain a sacred bull. Like on that carving on the wall behind the throne. It's written that part of their religious rites was the sacrificing of a bull, its exsanguination. The blood was poured down atop a new initiate, a sort of baptism if you like. It must have been pretty grisly. He was sealed in utter darkness in a tight underground chamber, a grave really, and inundated with bull's blood."

"There could be such a chamber under that stone?" I recognised.

"Perhaps. There is so much we don't know about the Mithraics. Too little work has been done," Appledore admitted.

"They call it a mystery religion for a reason," Levizad pointed out.

The pulley was attached. The stone lifted easily. Below was a five-foot wide well, descending into darkness.

"Shine a light," Appledore demanded of his fellows. "Where's a bullseye lantern?"

Sufficient illumination was found to reach the base of the shaft some fifteen feet below. We all saw the second body.

It was not the man who had bricked up the Mithraeum. It was not a skeleton. The corpse that sprawled in two feet of run-off water at the pit bottom was fleshed, dressed in modern tweed jacket and Oxford bags. He lay crumpled in a corner, the exposed parts of him covered in blood as if a sacrificed bull had showered him.

Appledore gasped. "That… is Professor Melville!"

❊❊❊

The dig at St Edith's had been agreed on condition that there was a minimum of fuss and disturbance, and no publicity. That was now impossible.

"I suppose you have already solved this," Inspector Gregson asked Sherlock Holmes as police constables lifted Melville's body from the Mithraeum well.

"You have surely apprehended by now that I do not theorise ahead of my data," Holmes told the Scotland Yard detective. "Had you adopted the same rigour it would have saved you the embarrassment of arresting then releasing Fred Porlock[11] regarding the Dawson mail robbery. There is still a considerably body of evidence to sift before I am comfortable to draw a conclusion."

"So you're baffled as well," Gregson sneered. "I don't get this place anyhow. They reckon some bloke managed to wall it up and him inside, and then just vanish. There has to be a secret door or something, stands to reason. That'll be how the murderer did for this Professor, you mark my words."

I left Holmes wrestling with the detective and went to examine the body that had been raised from the well.

"What do you make of it, sir?" asked young Jones, who was newly appointed to the detective branch and still earning his spurs.[12]

I ran a practiced eye over the dead man. "Well, I'm no coroner but I'd say he died of a major wound to the chest from some piercing object. He might have been in a tussle before that judging by his clothes, but there was no time for bruises to form. I fancy his fall into that pit might have broken some of his bones, including his neck, but he was alive at the time he was stabbed. Look for a broad blade, perhaps two inches wide, and quite long. Not that sharp. Something like..."

"Like the rusty gladius currently decorating the skeleton our archaeologists have dubbed Charlie," Holmes supplied, appearing behind me to check my observations. "I will presently analyse that weapon for traces of

---

11 Porlock was eventually revealed to be Holmes' informer inside Professor Moriarty's organisation in *The Valley of Fear* – and died for it.

12 Tobias Gregson, "Lestrade's great rival" and "the smartest of the Scotland Yarders", investigates in *A Study in Scarlet*, "The Greek Interpreter", "Wisteria Lodge" and "The Red Circle". Holmes spoke well of Athelney Jones in *The Sign of Four* but then the officer vanishes from the Canon, many Holmes scholars have concluded that Gregson may have eventually retired from the force. Holmes spoke well of Althelney Jones in *The Sign of Four* but then the promising young officer vanishes from the Canon. W.S. Baring-Gould's seminal biography *Sherlock Holmes* suggests Jones proved to be Jack the Ripper and was secretly dealt with by the Great Detective, but this is unsupported by any Canon evidence.

modern blood, but it would certainly have left a wound similar to the one that ended Professor Melville's tenure and his life."

"He was dead before he was hurled into that pit," I reported. "The fall injuries he sustained would have left different traces on a man clinging to life. The stream along the Mithraeum floor would have sluiced any blood shed up here."

"Indeed, my dear Watson. Furthermore, he was able enough to try and protect himself from his attacker. See the gashes on his palms where he tried to catch the blade that killed him."

"Can you guess the time of death?" Jones asked, receiving a fish-eyed glare from his superior Gregson at his encouragement of Holmes.

"Difficult to be precise, given the low temperature here and the presence of water at the bottom of the shaft, but I would judge that Melville laid here since yesterday evening. Doctor?"

"Rigor mortis is passing and there is considerable clotting. I agree."

Gregson bustled in. "We will need a full list of all the suspects," he demanded of Jones. "Everybody who has been down here. Whoever has a key to the church crypt. Anybody who disliked the dead man."

Holmes snorted. "You clearly do not know academe, Inspector. We have already heard that this was a controversial excavation. Many did not want it to take place. Others wished to conduct the dig themselves. If you arrest every scholar who had reason to object to Professor Melville you will need to considerably expand your holding cells at Scotland Yard."

"We will investigate by routine," Gregson insisted. "That is how modern policing works, Mr Holmes. We may not get showy results for newspaper headlines but we generally get our man."

"Or some man," sniffed the great detective. "Perhaps then I could direct your enquiries in three areas? The first is why and how the Professor came to be here. What reason had he for creeping in on a Sunday evening without word to anyone? That is if he came here of his own volition. Either way, his movements are paramount. Secondly, assuming that this was the location of his murder, and I believe by faint traces between the floorstones here that it was, how was he concealed in the hidden pit? That requires the murderer to first know of it and then to have the equipment to raise it. As we have seen, a block and tackle was required, and two strong students to haul."

"And thirdly?" Gregson asked sullenly.

"What became of the small container that lay in this niche in the stone chair, between the feet of the skeleton?" Holmes demanded.

All of us had the same question. "What container?"

Sherlock Holmes showed us the small rectangular hole close to the base of the throne, between the rotted stumps of the old corpse's legs. It was the size of a letterbox and penetrated six inches back into the carved seat. A rusty discolouration on the slimy stone indicated something iron had resided there for a long while. Scrape marks showed where it had recently been lifted out.

"Something was concealed here. Its base was seven inches by four inches, its height three inches. A chest, perhaps, or some kind of box anyhow. Metal with reinforced corners, judging by the rust marks on the floor slab. The condition of the exposed stone where it rested attests to its recent extraction. Appledore claims that no great finds were removed, only rubble. So where did that container go, and when?"

"So the murderer is also a thief!" Gregson decided.

"I cannot yet confirm that assertion." Holmes lost interest in the Scotland Yard officer. "I have given you my advice. Whether you make good use of it is up to you. Come, Watson, I believe our time is best spent elsewhere."

"And the original purpose of our visit?" I asked him. "The sealed temple with the impossible execution?"

"That is simple," my friend assured me. "I shall leave you to puzzle out the solution yourself for a while. For now we must discern how a three hundred year old murder has led to a modern one."

❁❁❁

Inspector Gregson may have assumed that Holmes had left the church. Instead my friend paused to ask pertinent questions of the students who huddled in the nave wondering what to do.

"Some background on your late Professor, if you please," Holmes asked the worried young scholars who clustered around Appledore.

Under my friend's expert questioning he drew a picture of the deceased man. Melville was a confirmed bachelor; he lived alone in the faculty; his specialism was Anglo-Roman history, on which he had written a number of standard texts; he was of sedentary habits, famous for disliking open air even on his occasional archaeological expeditions; he favoured his left leg after a bad dog bite in his youth; he did not suffer fools gladly, nor academic opponents.

From Appledore and Evans we learned that Melville had departed Town on Saturday evening on the 18.42 from King's Cross; Appledore had bought the ticket for him. Melville parted from his protégés at the railway terminus gate, having instructed them on preparations to make on Monday morning in readiness for his arrival after he had discharged his lecture duties. None of the students had travelled with their tutor. Levizod had taken the earlier train to be able to attend the University's debating society. Evans took a shorter journey to check on the recovering Garrison in Greenwich and returned to College on the first Sunday train service. Appledore had remained in London visiting relatives at Highgate. None of L. J. Melville's students could suggest any reason why the Professor might secretly return to the site on Sunday. None of them had particularly noticed a filled niche in the stone chair, being rather distracted by the skeleton that occupied the seat. None could say where its mysterious container might have gone.

"It's that skull I dislike the most," owned Evans. "I don't know how eyeless sockets can glare at you, follow you round the chamber, but they do."

"What disturbs me is that they killed him so elaborately," Levizad admitted. "Bolted to a chair for execution? And left there afterwards, sealed up, to rot in the darkness? I don't mind confessing it gives me the shudders."

"That place is cursed. Look what it did to the Professor," Appledore added, close to weeping.

On the question of who might want to do Professor Melville harm his students had plenty to say. "E.P. Sauter," Levizad answered decisively. "The Reader in Early British History from B------- College. *He* wanted to undertake this dig very badly. There were open rows in the University Council."

"And Dr Bedderforth," remembered Evans. "He argued bitterly against the Church Commissioners' decision. He was convinced there was a plague pit beneath the site. He and the Professor had a stand up argument on Magdalene Street. Forsythe saw it. He thought they'd come to blows." He glanced back at us, remembering that we were outsiders. "Bedderforth's the chap who wrote the textbook on London's Roman boundaries," he explained belatedly.

"There was Rose of Trinity and A.C. Gadder at Oriel too," Appledore considered. "But although all those dotty academics got plenty worked up, umbrella-waving cross, I can't see any of them stabbing the Prof. Dr Sauter probably couldn't even climb down a ladder."

"His students might, though," Levizad answered darkly.

"Is there any reason other than their opposition to or jealousy for the dig to believe any of these men might be involved?" I checked.

"Dr Sauter told Professor Melville that the day would come when he would rue ever opening 'that hole'," Levizad reported. "He shouted it at the Prof right across the crowded dining commons."

We were interrupted from our window into the jealous work of scholarship by raised voices from the vestry. Holmes swivelled round without a word and stalked over there.

"...closed down entirely," an angry bearded chap was snarling. "The Bishop agrees with me. He should have listened in the first place. Now we have scandal and infamy blackening the good name of St Edith's!"

"Mr Steadfast, nobody could have foreseen the tragedy that is unfolding today," Reverend Endicott answered bitterly.

"So *you* say. A murdered man, on our very premises! And that... horror in the chair that is the gossip of the neighbourhood! Policemen everywhere! How long before the wretched press finds out and makes us a byword? *You* brought this down upon us, you and those meddling scholars. I warned you!"

"You warned about a chained skeleton and a lurking murderer?" Sherlock Holmes asked, bursting upon the tense scene. "Please, outline whatever information you possess in a brief and organised manner."

A red-faced black-bearded man of fifty or so stood across from the vicar of St Edith's, one finger outstretched in accusation at the unfortunate clergyman. He looked astounded at our entrance, unable to understand why anyone might intrude on his tirade. "And who the devil are you, sirs?"

"This is Sherlock Holmes. I am Dr Watson," I introduced us. "And you, sir?" I was perhaps somewhat curt. I do not appreciate being addressed in such abrupt tones.

"Sherlock Holmes? The meddler from the broadsheets!"

"A consultant on difficult problems of detection," I defended my friend.

"Who we are matters little," Holmes declared. "I am intrigued, however, as to why the chairman of the Parish Council is upbraiding his vicar in such a manner, why your comments required you to leave your work at the post office to come down here to state your piece, and what warning you offered that is pertinent to current events. Pray enlighten us."

The churchman stared at Holmes, baffled and unhappy. "How did you know about...?" he began.

Holmes waved his fingers dismissively. "The wear on your jacket elbows and ink on your thumb indicate office work. Linear smudges suggest the use of a rubber stamp. The emblem on your fob-chain is the winged Mercury of the postal workers guild. That you are here during opening hours, that you splashed and stamped heedless through the mud of the streets to get here, and that you did not wash your hands before leaving work all suggest an urgent haste. Your general bearing and bellicosity indicate that you feel you have information or opinion of importance. All trivial deductions. Now be so good as to answer my enquiries."

"This is Mr Steadfast, one of our parishioners," Reverend Endicott offered.

"A life-long parishioner," the angry bearded man corrected him. "I was christened in this very church. My parents were married and buried here. I am not some newcomer with high-church ideas and a desire to make a fuss. I told you at church council that it was a bad idea to disturb the vault. I told you!"

"Perhaps you could repeat that warning for us, Mr Steadfast," I ventured.

"It is well known to those of us in the parish for more than a *brief* time," —he sneered across at Endicott, whom the painted placard of incumbents on the wall indicated had been in post for five years—"that there is evil buried beneath this church. It is our oldest tradition."

"What kind of evil?" Holmes sought clarification.

Steadfast sighed. "Who knows? Or knew, until today. It has simply always been held that St Edith was erected on this spot to consecrate a terrible wrong, to guard against a great evil that lay below. I said as much and was laughed at by these new men who know *nothing* of this church or its history, or the feelings of its long-term congregants."

"Many churches are founded on older pagan sacred sites," Endicott argued. "It is evident now that this is the case here. If there is any substance at all to the tradition to which Mr Steadfast alludes then its origins lie in that."

It occurred to me that the oldest parish records might offer some reason for the foundation of a house of worship on this spot. When I said as much it trigged another explosion from the outraged congregant. "Hah! Well, you won't be able to look that up here. Reverend Endicott is too *modern* to retain records in the parish as they have been for over three hundred years. He has sent them away, for *conserving*, to the National Record Bureau where they are lost to us."

"Six hundred and eighty-three volumes of wormy, rotting, births, deaths, and marriages!" Endicott argued. "Many of the oldest rendered unreadable by this damp vestry. Better they are somewhere they can be preserved as best they may. The parish council agreed with me."

"The parish council may think again about the things they agreed with you on," Steadfast warned. "Do you know how I heard about this? About the policemen, and pressmen at our door, and idle gossip in the street about some fettered skeleton and of murder in our holy precincts? Do you? Two women chattering in line at the common counter queue! We are the stuff of scandal, Reverend Endicott! Of course I came at once."

Holmes had little patience for the recrimination drama that was unfolding. "Some pertinent questions, then," he insisted. "Is the crypt usually locked? If so who has keys?"

Vicar and church council chair were so at loggerheads that they were reluctant to agree even on factual information, but eventually they reached a consensus. "We each have one, of course, and the verger. Mrs Cleshop who cleans for us has one too. She keeps some of her supplies down there. A spare key was loaned to Professor Melville, and I believe he passed that to one of his students so that work could begin before he arrived."

Holmes asked for, and received, confirmation that both men were still in possession of their own keys. He checked timings of the church being unlocked on Sunday; the verger Troper had opened up at 7.30am, lighting the floor-stoves to warm the nave before the congregation attended to 10am service. The building was closed at 12.35pm and reopened at 5 for evensong. "We used to leave it open but we had trouble with tramps," Steadfast explained. The verger was also responsible for locking up when devotions were finished, but had been delayed until 7.40 by a conversation with Mr Steadfast who was unhappy at the state in which the archaeologists had left the undercroft.

"You were down there last night then," Holmes observed to the church elder,

Steadfast glowered at him. "And if I was? I have a perfect right, even a duty, to keep an eye on what these academic vandals are up to. I went down after evening service to check on them. I saw great bags and piles of rubble, badly stacked all along the vault. Tools scattered everywhere. A complete mess, and hardly in keeping with the dignity and solemnity of our church. I said as much to Troper. I'd have had a sharp with Reverend Endicott too but he had scurried off home by the time I was done."

"I was here until the last parishioner left, Mr Steadfast," the clergyman protested. "I had no idea you had crept down to the undercroft to spy on the scholars' work."

Holmes was impatient with their bickering. "A man is dead!" he snapped. "Kindly focus your statement on those matters which might be useful in determining his killer. Mr Steadfast, did you observe anything other than signs of excavation that you deemed unusual when you searched the vault? Did you also enter the uncovered chamber below?"

"I saw nothing but the mess," Steadfast answered sullenly. "I could not look down into the room of which you speak. There was no ladder to enable descent."

"No ladder?" I interjected. I glanced at Holmes "Then where was it?"

The detective waved a long sensitive finger to indicate we should hold that conversation for another time; but Endicott took up the thread.

"There was a ladder," the vicar objected. "I used it myself, about ten minutes past five o'clock, and almost killed myself on it." He looked apologetic. "I am not so spry as I once was. I thought I could manage the climb without difficulty. As it was I almost fell."

"Why were you there?" I wondered.

Steadfast smiled faintly and sadly. "I hoped to see again for myself what had got the diggers so excited, I suppose. I had scarcely seen anything when I was there before, with all those young men milling about and the labourers hauling stacks of bricks away and so much shouting and chaos. I thought perhaps I might allude to the discovery from the pulpit. There had been enquiries from parishioners yesterday morning and I had fobbed them off with generalities, knowing that the discovery was intended to be confidential. I was considering whether to include in my homily some reference to finding the chamber."

"You said nothing in your sermon," Steadfast accused.

"I did not. When I reached that gloomy underground place, scarcely uninjured after almost missing my step, heart pounding in an unhealthy manner, its atmosphere did not comfort me. There is a brooding pagan malevolence there, do you not think? It is not a place that was built to welcome, nor to glorify God. Its whole aspect, its shape and dimensions, the echoes it makes, the mournful trickle of that foul stream, those chipped, vicious statues and ancient friezes..." Endicott shuddered. "It is an unpleasant, unhelpful place, even without that long-dead victim, even before I knew of Professor Melville's demise. I did not linger long." He looked curiously at Steadfast. "But the ladder was there."

We called in Troper. The verger attested that he had not been into the undercroft, having been instructed by Reverend Endicott and Professor Melville to avoid the place whilst the dig was underway. He complained of the muddy boot-tracks that had to be constantly cleaned where students and labourers had tramped from cellar steps to east porch, but otherwise

"There was no ladder to enable descent."

offered no insight into the impact the dig had made upon St Edith's.

Athelney Jones came out to join us in the choir. "Still here? Old Gregson believes you have gone where you will no longer trouble him."

"The Inspector has his own lines of investigation," I suggested, somewhat sceptically.

"Inspector Gregson is of the opinion that the missing casket contained some valuable treasure, an historic artefact that has been stolen for greed and profit. His idea is that one of the labourers employed by Professor Melville crept back here to steal the thing by night and was discovered by the Professor who was here for his own obscure scholarly satisfaction. This murderer then slew Melville, concealed the body in the pit, and flew away with his booty. We are to bring in every workman who shifted soil and stone here and question them closely to wring out a confession."

Holmes sighed. "I will be sending labourers of my own, Jones," he instructed. "They will be bringing certain portions of plasterwork from the spoil-heaps here and from those stacked to the side of the west buttress. I trust that will not interfere with Inspector Gregson's investigation?"

"Not if he doesn't know about it," the younger Scotland Yard man grinned.

"That would be most helpful," my friend agreed. By way of reward for Jones' affable complicity he added, "I draw your attention to the ladder problem that Dr Watson mentioned earlier. If Steadfast speaks the truth and could not find a ladder to descend into the Mithraeum after the service last night there is only one likely explanation for it."

"The ladder was down in the chamber!" Jones understood; he was sharp. "Somebody was in the Mithraeum. He heard Steadfast unfastening the vault door, so he pulled the ladder down into the temple to prevent access and covered any light. Someone was *there* when Steadfast made his inspection!"

On that minor revelation Holmes made his departure. We had more to do to uncover the truth of two similar murders separated by three hundred years.

❋❋❋

The Public Record Office's white turreted neo-gothic frontage dominates Chancery Lane. Behind those elegant walls lie nine hundred years of government and legal records, accounts, wills, land deeds, and the whole body of English documentation, gathered under the judicial eye of the

Master of the Rolls.[13] It was to there that I repaired to untangle the knotty history of the Mithraeum beneath St Edith-in-the-Field.

"Ah, this again," the clerk who had received Holmes' telegram began. He appeared as crumbling and ancient as the manuscripts he handled. We retreated into the fusty lamp-lit vastness of the Rolls Chapel,[14] where he had already laid out a number of legers and letters for my inspection.

"You consulted with Professor Melville on this question, I understand, Mr Hickory."

"I answered some impertinent questions from his ill-disciplined students," the archivist sniffed.

"I would be grateful to hear what your researches pitched up."

Hickory tottered to the table, where a faded, brittle street plan of Temple Bar and Fleet Street depicted various coloured and numbered land plots. Beside it were tax rolls indicating ownership and value of properties.

"We shall work back," Hickory lectured. "St Edith was founded in 1577, though not completed and consecrated until the next year. You see the parcel of land marked here. It was a rather small and insufficient plot, but deemed adequate enough for a chapel of ease for the poor of the city."[15]

"I understand the land was donated by the famous Sir Francis Drake."

"That's so. It was awarded him along with several other parcels of royal

13 The Public Record Office was from 1838 the supreme repository of British government and court records. From 1852 these records were open to public inspection. The collection includes many documents formerly housed at the Tower of London and the chapter house of Westminster Abbey, and a copy of the *Magna Carta*. The Public Record Office merged with the Historical Manuscripts Commission in 2003 to form the National Archives. It has moved from the Victorian site designed by Sir James Pennethorne that Watson describes here and is now based in a modern building in Kew. The elegant edifice that formerly housed the records is now King's College London's Maughan Library.

The Master of the Rolls is the third most senior judge in England and Wales (after the President of the Supreme Court of the United Kingdom and the Lord Chief Justice). His duties since at least 1286 are to maintain "the rolls", the records of the Court of Chancery, and occasionally for holding the Grand Seal of the Realm by which legislation is authorised. His responsibility for maintaining national records, which were traditionally lodged in the Rolls Chapel at Chancery Lane, continued through to the 1958 *Public Records Act* which transferred the duty to the Lord Chancellor.

14 This places Watson's narrative before 1895, when the medieval Rolls Chapel was deemed structurally unsound and was demolished for the Public Record Office to be extended over the site.

15 A chapel of ease is a subordinate church built within the boundaries of an existing parish so that worshippers who cannot easily reach the parish church can still attend services. In some rich city parishes, chapels of ease were sometimes used as a means of diverting unsavoury lower class congregants from more exclusive and richer places of worship.

land after the triumph of his Panama isthmus raid against the Spanish. He was then making preparations for another sea foray, having been once thwarted by bad weather in November of 1577 that had caused his entire fleet to seek shelter and refit at Falmouth. He doubtless felt he needed a little more divine support and hence made a number of religious bequests, mostly of surplus odds of estate he could easily afford to lose. He finally sailed in mid December and did not return until he had traversed the world."[16]

"What stood on the site of St Edith's before the church?" I asked.

"It was a number of leased workshops," Hickory answered. "Nothing very solid or prestigious, judging by the pitiful rents the Crown received. Trades that required easy access to the Fleet, to draw water or to dump refuse."

"It was royal land, then?"

"Not for very long. The estate was seized — for a second time, as it happens — by the Crown in 1557, in the dying days of Queen Mary's reign. You will recall that 'Bloody Mary' burned upwards of three hundred Anglican religious dissenters during her reign and attained the lands of many more. One such was Edmund Wizot, a merchant who owned the parcel of land about which you are enquiring. But there is no evidence of Wizot being executed. Indeed, he was almost certainly not a Protestant."

"You know something of him?"

"Perhaps. At the time those turbulent young academics descended upon me I had not had opportunity to examine all the documentation relevant to the case. I will return to this point after finishing my history, if I may, Dr Watson."

Duly chastised, I allowed the archivist to unfold his story the way he preferred.

"Wizot acquired the land from the Crown in 1545, the year after King Henry VIII's ruinously expensive foreign wars, the so-called 'rough wooing' of Mary Queen of Scots to wed Henry's son, that near bankrupted England and France alike for no firm conclusion. The site had previously

16 Edith of Wilton (961-984), daughter of English King Edgar the Peaceful, lived her short life as a nun at her mother Wilfrida's convent in Wilton Abbey, Wiltshire. Her hagiography by Goscelin describes her appearing after her death in visions to her mother and later to St Dunstan. She was elevated to sainthood at her family's urging and was especially revered by King Cnut the Great (995-1035; also known as Canute) who attributed his fleet's survival of a storm at sea to her intervention.

Few churches are definitely dedicated to St Edith of Wilton; only two remain for certain, although a few others are named St Edith but may refer to other saints of the same name. Drake's choice of patroness was likely to do with her renowned ability to calm sea-tempests for English heroes.

been property of the Black Friars, the Dominicans, and had been taken by the Crown under Henry's *Dissolution of the Lesser Monasteries Act* 1536. The Black Friars held the land as part of their estates within the City at least as far back as the middle of the thirteenth century. Before that the records are obscure."

I was jotting notes in my pocket-book. "So, it was church land, then Crown land, then bought up by this Wizot, then taken back by the Crown, awarded to Drake, and donated back to the church," I summarised. "Nothing major was built on the site until St Edith was founded."

"Perhaps." The ancient archivist seemed amused for the first time. He almost smiled and disturbed the dandruff that covered his shoulders like academic dust. "Perhaps. But then there is Edmund Wizot. And another document."

He shifted aside the tax rolls and opened up a thin folio that contained a number of loose leaves of manuscript. He indicated the top one, tracing his fingers over a crabbed clerical Latin script almost too tiny to read. The ink was very faint, scarcely still legible.

"This is a letter from one Johen, priest of St Andrew's near Holebourn Bridge - we would say Holborn – to his confessor Canon Anselm. There is no date but the internal evidence suggests around 1557. Certainly the Catholic faith was in ascendance at the time he wrote, which places it before Protestant Elizabeth replaced Mary on the throne the year after that." Hickory stared at me triumphantly, proffering the text.

"Might I trouble you to translate for me?" I asked, unhappy to be exposed as so lacking in scholarship. I had been a shockingly bad Latin scholar at school and even now baulk at anything much more than medical terms.

I noted down the remarkable document as Hickory read it out:

'Your Grace, it has come to my attention that a strange and ungodly thing has happened which brooks proper investigation. My parishioners inform me of one Edmund or Edward, whom they call the Wizard or Wizot, for he is deemed to possess supernatural gifts. He is known for summoning and consorting with spirits and devils. Men are afraid to cross him.

'This Edmund has land taken from the Black Friars, hard by the Fleet or River of Wells. He has caused to be dug open an ancient tumulus that was formerly beneath a fuller's cot, and has uncovered therein a pagan temple. I have seen silver coins taken from this place, stamped with the head of a

Caesar. Evidently there are many statues of pagan gods and devils inside this underground room.

'My parishioners hold that Edmund keeps court in this evil den, surrounded by wicked followers who cavort with demons. He is wont to call to him young women of the town to slake his lusts, and if they go not he will curse their homes and slight them. Some say he sacrifices animals to the Devil, splashing their blood on his servants in black mockery of baptism. Other clergy must know of his actions but fear to cross so terrible a sinner.

'Reverend sir, after much prayer and thought I feel I must draw this before you. Your counsel and instruction on this would relieve my mind. I would act, but with authority. I have sturdy men who will defend the True Faith against all the snares and sins of Satan. I await your word and remain your humble servant, Johan.'

I looked across at Hickory. "Remarkable. And this is genuine?"

"A perceptive question, Dr Watson," the archivist congratulated me. "There is some possibility that the letter may be a contrivance to justify arresting a man or confiscating his assets. Queen Mary was not above tweaking the evidence when she wanted to accomplish some enemy's downfall. At this distance of time we cannot know."

He shifted back to the legal records that were the heart of his collection. "Here is the warrant by which Wizot's estate was distrained. There is no mention of wizardry here, only religious dissidence. Moreover, it is clear that the man was already deceased. See here, where it is mentioned that he died intestate. That was another common reason for the Crown claiming lands, where no surviving heir or clear covenant existed to determine who should inherit."

I considered what I had learned. Was Edmund Wizot the skeleton in the chair? By what means he had discovered the buried Mithraeum we could never now know. Certainly it had been open during Wizot's lifetime. Was it reasonable to surmise that Canon Anselm had commanded Father Johan to address the problem he had raised? Had that led to Wizot's unusual death and confinement in his underground lair and the subsequent resealing and loss of the Mithraeum? Was that why St Edith's had been raised over the mound, to cover 'a great evil' as tradition suggested?

I thanked the fussy archivist and returned to see what Holmes had to say on the matter.

❁❁❁

"Speak to him," complained Mrs Hudson. "Plaster dust everywhere, every floor covered in bits of old rubble, and who has to side it all up afterwards, you tell me that!"

Our redoubtable Baker Street landlady was often distressed by Holmes' Bohemian habits. Today he had pushed her too far. "I will see what I can do," I promised her.

"And the smell!" she vented further. "All them chemicals. The maid has had to go to her mothers to stop feeling sick. I'm getting complaints from the neighbours."

"I'll go up now and see what Holmes is up to, Mrs Hudson. I do apologise for the nuisance."

"It's not that I don't know as his work is important," the landlady insisted, "but there has to be limits, Dr Watson."

I passed upstairs to the landing outside our chambers. The rug there was indeed covered in laid-out pieces of mottled broken plaster and a few selected Roman building stones. The door to our sitting room was propped open so the display of shards could run uninterrupted across the whole carpet of our living space.

Holmes was on all fours, sorting out the fragments as a child might assemble a jig-saw puzzle. Both our windows were open, helping to dissipate the fumes from the chemical workbench.

"There is a pile of bricks on your bed," my friend apologised. "I shall see it removed shortly."

"Thank you." What else could I reply? "Mrs Hudson is distressed."

"Yes. I fear her priorities skew towards domestic order over murder."

"She seemed ready enough to contemplate murder to me, Holmes. Am I to assume that you have discovered something relevant in the discarded rubble of the archaeologist's dig?"

Holmes rose and brushed off his knees. I saw that the fragments he had been assembling just now showed a much-faded painted image.

"The archangel Michael, unless I am much mistaken," Holmes suggested. "The image was somewhat crudely painted and glazed on plaster that was then fresh and absorbent, on the inside of the brickwork blocking the Mithraeum apse. A warding against evil, perhaps? In Christian lore it was Michael who cast Lucifer from heaven, was it not?"

I agreed that it was so. "This coincides with a remarkable document on file at the National Record Office," I ventured, and appraised my friend of the fruits of my researches.

Holmes pressed his index fingers to his lips. "Hmm. Your theory is an attractive one, Watson. Those chemical tests that have so put Mrs Hudson out of sorts have established two very different formulae for the mortar fixing the ancient Mithraeum and its sealed entrance. Likewise the plaster that once lined the main walls of that chamber is unlike the varnished skim on which this religious image was rendered."

"Time and damp peeled the plaster from the bricks," I reasoned. "Professor Melville had the shards carted away with the debris where he had broken through the roof."

"And the whole matches with the possibility that this Wizot was seized by religious men outraged at his activity and killed for it in some manner that seemed good to them at the time. The Mithraeum was looted, accounting for the discards that were discovered by builders addressing subsidence and the damage done to fixed Mithraic iconography, although one can only guess why the iconoclasts hesitated to finish their work. In the end Wizot's bound body was entombed in his so-called lair and the whole site was damned to memory."

"I do not see that we can offer a better explanation than that," I owned. "You have clearly gone to significant effort to clear up a killing some three centuries old. What though of the present murder of Professor Melville?"

Holmes hopped over the fragment-strewn floor to achieve his writing desk. "We have a little more on that, too," he advised me. "Jones happened in just before your return, with the coroner's initial examination and the statements of those interviewed by Gregson's officers. I have also had some replies to a series of wires I sent seeking additional clarifications on some points about the case."

I lifted a sack of rubble from my armchair and sat down. "What have you learned?" I asked; not respect for others' personal furniture, for certain.

"First off, it appears that Professor Melville was not seen since he said farewell to his students on Saturday evening. He told them he intended to catch the late train back to College, to work on his notes on Sunday and to discharge his Monday lecture duties. It is the holidays, of course, but the Professor gave a remedial class to fee-paying scholars. He parted with Appledore and Evans at the Euston Road entrance to King's Cross. Jones can find no one who saw Melville board a train or disembark. No College staff noted him over the weekend."

"Melville may have stayed in London, then? Or been waylaid on his way home and confined in that pit?"

"You are allowing your imagination to run away with you, Watson.

Leaving the Professor in the Mithraeum would have been a very risky form of incarceration. Who could be sure that curious eyes might not have come to see what was discovered there? Mr Steadfast might have intruded, perhaps, or some rival scholar bribing his way past the verger. But there is a mystery about Melville's whereabouts before his fatal encounter in that temple."

"I imagine you have your street-lads talking to cabbies and the like."

"Of course; but one tweedy scholar loose in London may be difficult to trace. Meanwhile I have applied scientific principles to the tangible evidence of the case." Holmes gestured to his malodorous chemical bench. "The antique gladius was the weapon that stabbed Melville," he began. "It has been cleaned, but minute traces of blood remain in the rust-cracks upon the joint between blade and hilt. Medical experts accord with our findings that the Professor's other injuries were received shortly post-mortem from being cast into the 'bull-pit'."

"Might we think there was some confrontation which turned violent?" I suggested. "The murderer seized the weapon that presented itself, the sword laying loose in that skeleton's ribcage, and plunged it into the Professor? An unplanned death?"

"I am not so certain, Watson," Holmes frowned. "There are elements that suggest... but I am running ahead again. Thanks to your sterling work at the archive and some correspondence with various specialists in the field I am confident that your identification of Wizot is likely the correct one. The murder weapon was part of the original hoard sealed on the site when it was originally buried. We can never know the reasons that the Mithraeum was covered away by the Romans intact and unlooted. Likewise one can only speculate on what strange instincts allowed the people of the middle ages to plunder the temple but leave the murder sword behind."

"Unless we can locate the missing coffer that they also left untouched in the throne," I speculated.

"That may have been concealed, plastered over. Its covering had suffered like all the other plasterwork in the chamber, exposing to us what would have been invisible to the marauders of the Middle Ages. Yet someone wanted it very badly yesterday."

"You clearly suspect that historical events have some bearing upon the modern murder, Holmes."

"It is suggestive." Holmes turned suddenly, reaching for his coat. "We must go to Melville's college. We must see his chambers. We must understand his reasons for unexpectedly appearing at St Edith's on Sunday night."

"Now?" I still hadn't had dinner.

"Justice must not be made to wait, doctor! Come. We shall just catch the 7.11 from King's Cross and be there before the porter locks the gates. Mrs Hudson, I am done with these plaster fragments and bricks. Be so good as to tidy them away while we are gone. They are cluttering up our home!"

❋❋❋

"Hold," Holmes cautioned the College porter. He held Mr Shelley back from entering the late Professor's rooms. "There has been a visitor before us, I fancy."

He indicated the jamb where the lock had been broken by brute force.

"An intruder!" I realised. "Might he still be here?" I wished I had equipped my service revolver. It has not seemed necessary for a quiet visit to the University.

"I think not," Holmes answered me, "but let us be cautious all the same."

"A break-in!" Shelley wheezed, shocked at the blasphemy within his hallowed halls. "I must h'inform the Dean. I must summon the p'lice."

"In due time," Holmes told him. "Let us first establish the facts." He gestured for me to take position on the other side of the door and nudged it open with his toe.

The room inside was a shambles, strewn with papers and books from a desperate search. Even Mrs Hudson had not needed to face mess this bad in her service to Sherlock Holmes.

"I take it that Inspector Gregson's men didn't leave things like this?" I asked Shelley.

"The p'lice from London? They ain't been down 'ere h'yet. I'm h'expecting them tomorrow morning, sir. But the local constable, 'e came and 'ad a quick look to see h'all was well first thing today. I unlocked the door for 'im and it were nothing like this."

Holmes looked around the landing. "Who else occupies this floor?"

"Dr Hartness and Mr Benson, sir, but with it being h'out o' term they're both away from College. There's no-one on this landing to 'ear a door being kicked."

"The rooms could be accessed without you knowing?" I checked.

"There's h'always a porter when the outer doors is h'unlocked, from seven a.m. to ten o' night. But it might be we gets called h'away if one of the gentleman rings for us. And there's the connecting door through to the dining 'all, of course. People h'aren't supposed to 'ave keys for that, but a lot do."

"So anyone could get up here unnoticed," I realised, dismayed.

"Anyone who knows college procedures and layout," Holmes corrected me.

He ventured inside the Professor's chambers and looked around with a practiced eye. He snorted.

"You have apprehended something?" I guessed.

"The pattern of scatter of books and papers interests me. See how wide and random the spread is. A searcher, flicking through documents and shelved volumes, will work to a method. He might carelessly discard material he has dismissed, but would not fling it across the room. It is a waste of time and effort, and when repeated so constantly would become exhausting. The only reason for a squalor such as this is that it was not caused by a search. It was caused to disguise a search."

I understood. "We are to suppose that a burglar combed the entire place, seeking something. In fact he took what he came for and then laid a false trail to suggest a much wider and more comprehensive hunt."

"Precisely, Watson. Kindly also observe that amongst the piles hurled on the floor are several manuscripts borrowed from the University libraries, of considerable age and venerability. Despite their fragility, none is damaged. Although each of these lies as if it were hurled like the rest, each has in fact been carefully positioned to approximate such use. This betokens an intruder with a scholar's absolute respect for antiquity."

"A tutor or student, then," I recognised. "One of Melville's rivals or one of his pupils?"

"Now note these discarded drawers, upturned on the floor. The contents of two of them have simply been spilled out. But this topmost one, the only drawer to have a forced lock, which means the only one that was actually locked, that was emptied more carefully and probably first."

"How can you know that?"

"Consider the things a man keeps in his locked drawer. Here are Melville's bank book and cheque book, a pass-port, a set of keys for his country home, some long-kept personal correspondence; all of it at the very bottom of the pile of searched goods. These things were removed from their drawer before the rest was tossed about. Whatever else was in that locked compartment has been removed. It is what the thief came to take. All the other is misdirection."

"A thief who knew where to look right off," I recognised.

"Exactly."

Holmes returned to his examination of the room, The Professor's chambers consisted of a sitting room that doubled as a study, stuffed with old leather couches for student tutorials, and a small bedroom. The mattress and pillows of the single bed had been slit open; feathers were everywhere. Amongst the debris on the floor were dozens of framed wall-photographs depicting year after year of graduating students. A few splintered portraits of favoured postgrads were shattered on the rug.

The whole apartment smelled of strong pipe tobacco of a type that Holmes could undoubtedly name. The great detective located Melville's silver tobacco box and checked the contents. I bit my tongue and stifled comment about eccentrics who stuff their smoking leaf in a Persian slipper. Holmes flipped open the box, nodded to himself, and said, "Leonard."

"I beg your pardon?"

Holmes had already moved on, returning to the stitched pad of Bank of England form cheques discarded from the locked drawer. All the sheets were used in this old booklet. He brushed his fingers through the stubs where a record of payments had been left.

He swung round on Shelley. "You may notify your Dean now. When Gregson and Jones arrive in the morning direct their attention to the Professor's desk diary. It is discarded there beside the window under the overturned plant pot. I am certain they will pick up the thread from there. Eventually."

"Am I to understand that you have discovered something of value?" I asked Holmes.

"I have discovered where the Professor likely stayed when he visited Town. There are several payments here to the Convent House Hotel, Piccadilly."

"Gregson has not yet discovered Melville's London lodgings," I noted. "His students did not know where it was." That was odd, now I considered it.

"We must go there at once," Holmes insisted. "There is some urgency to the matter. A life may be at risk"

We hastened for the station.

❀❀❀

As we steamed back to London, Holmes revealed some of his thinking. "Review what we know of Professor Melville's movements, Watson. The man paid off the day labourer diggers and parted from his students on Saturday evening. He expressed an intent to return to the University but may never have taken his train. His movements are unaccounted for until he died sometime on Sunday night."

"There was someone in the Mithraeum after Sabbath evensong," I contributed. "Steadfast could not find the ladder because someone had drawn it down into the chamber to prevent access."

"At some time after the dig was shut up on Saturday, the metal container hidden at the base of the stone chair was removed and the slab covering the pit was opened. Neither of these features had been discovered when the students left."

"Opening the slab over the bull-pit required the block and tackle from the crypt above, and two men."

"Sometime today, after the discovery of the murder and a cursory glance from a local constable, someone infiltrated Melville's college rooms and created the scene we discovered just now."

I allowed myself a grand sigh. "I confess my confusion, Holmes. There is too much evidence and too many suspects, all of whom have vague but unconvincing motives."

"Motive is not sufficient to indicate a murderer in this case. We have heard of many people who had academic rivalries with Professor Melville. Others, including churchgoers like Steadfast, might have opposed his dig at St Edith's entirely. None of them were likely to be intimate enough to know exactly what Melville kept in his locked upper drawer."

"The murderer thought that something in Melville's desk might point to him."

"Feasible, although there is another possibility too. Remember that the killing was only accomplished a little over twenty-four hours ago. Had it not been for our interference Melville's body may have lain undiscovered for a significant amount of time. There would have been opportunity to extract incriminating or useful data from Melville's study some other way."

I racked my brains for detail, to try and understand the tangled skein that was always so very clear to my companion. "Who is Leonard? You mentioned him as you examined Melville's tobacco box."

"Leonard is the subscriptor whose name is engraved on the inner lid. 'With affection and gratitude from Leonard.' As for who he is, did you not read names upon the Professor's photographs? There is a recent one of his student Leonard Appledore."

"That was a rather expensive gift from a student to his tutor," I opined. "A bribe?"

"More likely an affectionate token, Watson. Our Professor is a classicist. He may well follow the Greek paradigm of teacher and pupil relationships."

"I say."

"Our society is somewhat less tolerant of such things than the Athenians. We place such relationships beyond the law. A quiet venue such as the Convent House Hotel would be a convenient place for Melville to rendezvous with Appledore without scandal or opprobrium."

My mind raced ahead. "If Melville remained in London on Saturday night to secretly meet with Appledore… it was Appledore alone who claimed to have purchased his tutor's ticket… Appledore said he stayed in Town with family… If Appledore then summoned the Professor to a secret meeting at St Edith's…"

Holmes held up his hands to caution me. "I do not say what you conjecture did not happen; I only say that because it *could* have it does not mean that it *did*. The Convent House Hotel will help us fill in the blanks. Indeed, if the Professor paid for his room for several nights then his things may still be in situ for us to see."

"He would have had with him his current cheque book."

"More importantly, Watson, his academic notes. Where are his researches into the Mithraeum? Not likely in his chambers at College when he would have needed them at St Edith's. So where? Either at the Convent House or with his killer."

The train speeded us through the gathering darkness towards revelation.

❀❀❀

The desk clerk at the Convent House Hotel quickly folded under interrogation by Mr Sherlock Holmes. A register was produced that recorded one night's stay for an L.J. Melville. The clerk had not been on duty beyond 8pm on Saturday and could not say whether the guest had received a young visitor after that. Pressed, he agreed that the same guest had stayed there on occasion before and had sometimes met with young men whom he greeted affectionately and retreated with to his room for private discussion. It was clear that Melville was not the only gentleman to stay at the Convent House who kept such habits.

The clerk recalled that a piece of mail had been hand-delivered to the desk early on Sunday morning, since it was he who had handed the letter over as Melville checked out at noon. He could not remember anything remarkable about the envelope, which was plain, brown, and common. Melville had not opened the letter before vacating the building.

The Professor had left the hotel with a small suitcase and a bundle of books. Where were they now?

"The letter was probably what led him back to St Edith's," I surmised.

"A distinct possibility," Holmes agreed. "However, tracing Melville's movements up to noon on the day of his death has suggested another intriguing question. The keys."

"Keys? What of them… oh! You mean, how did Melville gain entrance to the church and to the crypt? The archaeologists were lent a set of keys for access, but the Professor had handed them to Appledore to open up for the students on Monday morning. So how did Melville gain entry on Sunday night? Unless it was Appledore who murdered him, then removed the keys from his person?"

"All of the students have had access to the keys since the dig began. Any of them could have procured a duplicate copy from a wax mould. What is significant is that, assuming the Professor had indeed handed off his keys to Appledore, he still went to St Edith's *expecting to be let in*."

I nodded agreement. "Then what now?" I wondered. The trail, if not grown cold, had at least grown complicated.

"We have questions for young Appledore," the great detective replied. He glanced at his pocketwatch. "It is growing late but matters are urgent. Let us disturb him at his family's Highgate address and discover what happened since Sunday lunchtime."

❁❁❁

Appledore was not at home. He had received a telegram a mere ten minutes earlier and had hastened away. He had taken the missive with him.

Holmes received the news gravely and with surprising urgency. He dragged me back into the waiting growler and gave the cabbie the address of St Edith's. "And hurry man. Don't spare the whip! A life depends upon it!"

We climbed into the carriage and had scarcely taken our seats before the driver lurched his vehicle on with commendable haste.

I was alarmed by my friend's urgency. "What is it Holmes? What has provoked such haste?"

"Don't you see, Watson? The telegram was the last clue. On Sunday, Melville went to St Edith's to meet a blackmailer who threatened to expose the Professor's irregular relationship with at least one of his protégés. Such revelation would have ended the academic's career and probably seen him in gaol. Today Appledore has been lured to that same spot, presumably by the same blackmail. He has been summoned there to be questioned and then to be silenced."

I wished we had brought our firearms "Why would the murderer return to the Mithraeum? If Appledore must be silenced, anywhere might do. What possible reason is there to go back to the scene of his crime?"

"Because the killer has not yet achieved his ends, Watson. Luring the Professor to the church secretly did not yield the result our felon hoped for."

"Was the Professor's death not the whole plot, then?"

"If I am correct then Melville's murder was a cold-blooded practicality to eliminate a man who would otherwise have objected to the murderer's intentions."

"Your reasoning?"

"There are many puzzles about that site. There is old malice there. If one seeks to fathom the secrets of a mystery cult, who better to involve than a detective?"

"Professor Melville called you in."

"Professor Melville was convinced to call me in. Remember what Appledore told us when we first met: 'It seemed like a good idea when the suggestion was made.' Made by whom?"

"Why would the murderer want Sherlock Holmes on his trail?"

"Because the murderer was not yet set on murder," my friend suggested. "In the two days that passed between our invitation to examine the Mithraeum chamber and our discovery of the late Professor much had changed. His meeting with the Professor evidently did not go as planned. Perhaps Melville was not as susceptible to blackmail as he had expected. Or maybe the Professor and his notes did not offer the answers the killer sought."

"I still don't see why the murderer must return. He presumably absconded with the box that lay at Wizot's feet."

"And it did not yield him what he hoped," Holmes surmised. "You see why, of course?"

"Not entirely."

"Then I shall beg your patience a short while longer, Watson. There is still much to unravel about this chain of events. I must reflect." Sherlock Holmes pressed his index fingers to the bridge of his nose and closed his eyes.

Our Clarence hastened on.[17]

❁❁❁

The bells had tolled eleven by the time we reached the old gothic church in its deserted back-street. A heavy rain did nothing to wash that soot-blackened frontage. St Edith's lay dark and silent.

Holmes produced a lock-picking tool and made short work of the massive old tumblers on the iron-studded vestry door. "We must move carefully, Watson," he cautioned me as we found candles. "If the murderer has not yet finished his work we must not startle him to it."

We padded silently across the sanctuary to the west tower stairs that descended to the crypt. The vastly quiet of the deserted church was unsettling to me. The undercroft door was also sealed; it likewise succumbed to Holmes' tool-roll.

The sense of oppressive menace intensified under the low crypt ceiling arches. Piles of digging soil loomed on either side. Old church furniture, long since discarded for ecclesiastical use, cast fantastic shadows by our flickering candles.

I found a workman's pick and took it with me.

Our light betrayed us. "Come down to the Mithraeum," called the murderer. "One at a time, with your hands on the ladder where I can see them. I have a sword to Appledore's throat. I have no hesitation about ending him."

I recognised the voice.

"Of course it is Levizad," Holmes told me as if were evident all along. "Ignore the French prefix and you see at once his family interest is in the site."

"Wizot!" I realised. "The wizard!"

"Come down now!" the killer demanded.

---

17 Named after Prince William, Duke of Clarence and St Andrews, King William IV in later life, the "Clarence" was a four-wheeled enclosed carriage, popular in the 1840s amongst the upper classes as a personal vehicle. These coaches had both forward and backwards-facing seats and could accommodate up to six passengers. The windows were all at the front end of the compartment, allowing for private travel in the rear. Many were later sold as hackney carriages and became a common form of taxi in Queen Victoria's reign. They were nicknamed Growlers because of the noise they made travelling over street-cobbles. Lord Brougham's lighter two-passenger carriage was the other popular choice for public transport.

"We must move carefully, Watson."

"I am coming," Holmes called back, gesturing for me to snuff my candle and remain hidden. He found the hole bored through the Mithraeum's roof and descended down the ladder.

"And your inseparable colleague Dr Watson," Levizad insisted. "Do you take me for a fool? Come down now!"

It had been worth the attempt. I laid aside my pickaxe and followed Holmes down into the sunken chamber. The trickle of Fleet-water washed over my boots as I climbed to the floor.

Levizad stood by the stone chair where his ancestor's skeleton sat in a dead man's judgement. Appledore knelt before his fellow scholar, gagged and with bound hands. The sword that had presumably ended Edward Wizot and had certainly killed Professor Melville was pressed to the captive's throat.

"How did you know we were coming?" I asked Levizad.

"Ask your clever friend," the murderer challenged.

"You bribed the clerk at the Convent House," Holmes replied. "First to say nothing of your own visit to check that the Professor had left nothing behind that might incriminate you, but also to send word by telegram if any other came asking. The Post Office wire service moves swifter than a cab. In the thirty minutes it took us to reach Appledore's home, a telegram had delivered the clerk's warning to you and you had dispatched your wire summons to bring Appledore here. Did you tell him to bring money? He came expecting to pay off a blackmailer, not to face an assassin."

Levizad smiled dangerously. "Very good. I can see I was right to trap you, Sherlock Holmes."

"You knew if you brought Appledore here that Holmes would deduce where he had gone and follow," I accused.

"Of course. I wanted to check that the Professor had not shared with his pet some scrap of knowledge about this place that he had not passed on to the rest of his students or recorded in his notes. It seems as though he did not, but we shall shortly know for certain. If Appledore really is as ignorant as he seems I will have to rely upon the ingenuity of the talented problem-solver who has tracked me thus far."

"So he *hasn't* yet found what he was looking for," I breathed to Holmes.

My friend gestured to the tied Appledore. "Levizad, I am unlikely to comply with your demands if you intend to murder your hostage in any case when we are done. Release that poor fellow and we shall see what can be done to solve your historical enigma."

The murderer chuckled grimly. "I have no wish to be overpowered by you and your lapdog, Holmes. However, I do have a solution." He gestured to the bull-pit where the invading stream washed away. The block and tackle were again in place to lift the slab. "Open that up. You and Dr Watson climb down. Once you are safely there and cannot leap on me I will allow Appledore to descend too. Then you or he will tell me what I need to know."

I did not relish being pressed with two other men into that tight deep shaft; but Holmes gestured me forward and between us we winched up the cover. Holmes was the first to splash down into the two feet of rank water that covered the base of the well.

I followed reluctantly. "What is to keep him from killing us while we are pinned down in this hole?" I murmured to Holmes.

Appledore crashed atop us. Levizad had hurled him down. We steadied the captive student and released his bonds.

"He is mad!" Appledore insisted, peering up at the man who now watched us from the chamber above. "He was the one who killed the Professor!"

"We'd got that already, old chap," I advised the panicked student. "Steady now. Let us deal with this."

Levizad sneered down at us. "Deal? Yes, we'll deal. You are dealing for your lives."

"Is that what you told Melville before you ran him through with that Roman blade?" Holmes challenged. "You forced him to meet you here last night with anonymous threats to expose his homosexual proclivities. You either had some evidence about his relationship with Appledore or else more direct experience of his behaviour. Was that the material you removed from his College desk? You feared that a search might eventually expose some correspondence, or a token of affection similar to the tobacco-box that Appledore gifted? Or did you require some more tangible proof of Appledore's affections to compel his attendance here tonight?"

"I ask the questions here, detective!" Levizad insisted. "There are things I want to know — must know."

"You fight against the decay of history," Holmes told him, almost pityingly. "Remembrance of this place must have been passed down the Wizot line, I suppose. A family legend, half-forgotten, long-neglected. Yet enough to inspire you to seek whether such a place really existed. Hence your visit to the National Archive and your subsequent convincing of Professor Melville to undertake an excavation here."

"You are correct. How many generations have passed since Crown and church robbed our lineage of its fortune? Since petty-minded superstitious fools murdered our great forebear Edward Wizot at the moment of his coming glory? That our lands and goods were declared intestate and seized by a greedy monarch? But they were not intestate, and all his treasure was not lost!"

"You hoped that the hidden compartment in the throne Wizot installed in his conjurer's den might contain some long-hidden will," Holmes understood. "Some dusty document that would offer you a legal foothold to reclaim some part of the inheritance that was taken from your family. You'd be unlikely to gain title to this ecclesiastical donation, but Wizot undoubtedly had other estates which you hoped to prove yours by ancient deed."

If the detective's easy understanding of his intentions dismayed Levizad he did not show it. "I should have realised about that casket," he spat. "As you said, Holmes, the decay of history." He gestured to the dirty stream that now sprinkled over those of us confined in the pit. "The same occasional floods that washed away the plaster covering up the hidden compartment rendered illegible the papers locked into the box. Anything of value there, all that Wizot had concealed from his persecutors, was destroyed by years and flooding."

"But your family tradition described more than that rusty box that you extracted after Melville's death, did it not?" Holmes pressed on. "Else you would not have convinced your Professor to call me in to explain your sealed-chamber mystery, would not have lured him here secretly to interrogate him and silence him after."

"Your deductions border on the supernatural," Levizad admitted. "Perhaps it is this place? It seemed right to end the Professor with this ancient sword, to let his blood spill into the pit where so much blood had gone before, to toss him into darkness as a sacrifice for my success." He pulled himself together. "If Melville told you anything, Appledore, now is the time to save your life. If you can fathom the secret, Holmes, your only chance is to tell me now."

"I don't know anything!" Appledore bleated, terrified. "Lev, I promise..."

"You have not yet presented to me the puzzle I am expected to solve, Mr Levizad," Holmes pointed out calmly. "What extraordinary datum drove you to such extreme obsession and the murder?"

"A riddle," the killer confessed. "In a manuscript letter, handed down in our family from the very time of Edward Wizot. '*In deepest darkness, holy light shall show the way to fortune restored.*' That is what the wizard told his daughter before greedy Catholic peasants dragged him to his death. Of course, she knew about the concealed place in the throne where the Gospel of Mithras was kept but she could not retrieve it. When Wizot was executed the Mithraeum was sealed, covered over. Eventually it was buried under this wretched church. But she wrote there was also another compartment somewhere here where Wizot concealed even greater treasures still. There, perhaps, is the last will and testament that will restore our family's stolen fortune; secrets and artefacts that eluded Bloody Mary's pious hypocrites."

"That is all?" I demanded of Levizod. "A simple riddle brought you to murder?" If I had brought my service revolver I would have ended the fellow then and there.

Holmes' laugh surprised me. "Why, your answer to that is simple, Mr Levizod. It is the same answer as to how the man who bricked and plastered shut the entrance to this temple was able to depart. Is it not clear?"

"A secret passage!" I decided. "There must be!"

"Is there?" Levizad demanded. "We have all searched. Nothing in concealed. Only..." He looked over to the tauroctony frieze on the end wall. "Behind that?"

"No," Holmes scorned.

"Yes!" insisted the murderer. He snarled down at us. "Wait there," he mocked. Before any of us could say him no, he released the slab again to cover the pit, trapping us in absolute darkness in that confined space.

"No!" Appledore almost screamed. "Lev! *Lev!* Let us out!" And then, belatedly, he added, "Don't harm the bas relief!"

Noises of crunching stone and splintering plaster suggested that Levizad had less respect for the ancient Roman site than a student of history should have.

"What shall we do now, Holmes?" I asked, perplexed. "If you lift me up on your back I can try and put pressure on that slab, to lift it away, but..."

"Something that took two men with a tackle and chain to open?" Holmes asked sceptically. "No, Watson, that is not the solution."

"We must do something!" Appledore insisted.

There was an especially loud crash from above, and the sound of falling bricks. There was also a splash of heavy waters. The stream trickling into our shaft became a surge.

"He has broken into some other underground water channel," I realised. "The level here is rising appreciably."

"Nothing!" came Levizad's distracted howl from above. "There is nothing behind there! Only some unsuspected escape route of the covered river. No passage! No secret place!"

"Of course not," Holmes called up through the merest crack that remained to connect pit and chamber. "I already told you that. You are not thinking clearly, Mr Levizad. *How* did the mason exit this Mithraeum?"

"I don't know! Tell me!"

The water had reached our waists as Holmes replied. "Think of your scholarship, man! Mithras was a god of light, in a religion of light and darkness. Men were entombed down in this pit then released reborn into the light. Where did that light come from, in this subterranean temple?"

"A… a hole in the roof!" Appledore realised. "Of course! It makes sense. As morning came, light hit a shaft at the exact angle needed to illuminate the Mithraeum. In deepest darkness, holy light! And if there was a light-shaft in the roof, then that was how the last man escaped, before it too was plugged. We found no evidence of it because we dug in right over where it had all been. The brickwork around it collapsed across the floor, and we swept it away."

"Indeed," confirmed Holmes. "And tell me, Mr Levizad, where do you think that beam of sunlight fell? Where in this Mithraeum is the place of deepest darkness? What part has never been searched?"

"The base of the pit-shaft!" the murderer groaned. "It was already flooded when I forced Melville to help me reopen it. I never thought to fathom that murky depth!"

"A shame you have sealed us in here and provoked a flood that will cover forever the very things you sought. A pity that it takes two men to lift the slab and you are alone. You have undone yourself, Mr Levizad."

"And us," I objected. The water was now chest-deep.

"I can open the pit," Levizad insisted. "I must."

We heard him straining at the lifting chains. "He will not be able to do it," Appledore predicted. "We will die here."

"I think not," Holmes responded. He drew a box of Vestas and struck a light. "Remember that at the end of the postulant's ordeal there was illumination. Some cunning arrangement of mirrors, I would hazard, that channelled the sun's rays through the narrow crack where the flood now cataracts, and shone particularly on this spot… here."

Holmes' fingers traced one of the rimed bricks on the wall. He produced a pocket-knife and cleaned round the edges. "Yes, this is it, as I had hoped. The reborn Mithraic worshipper spotted this once-painted stone that had previously been obscured by darkness. He drew it out and – let us hope that the ancient counterbalance still works to lift the slab that pins us in here."

"Hold off a moment, Holmes," I advised. "Appledore, as the slab rises hoist me up from the pit so I can deal with Levizad while he struggles with his block and tackle."

Holmes nodded approval. He struck a fresh match — it occurred to me then that he must have held the packet out of the water with exactly this intention — and heaved out the loose brick.

There was a scraping of stone on stone. One edge of the pit lip shifted. The thick covering slab pivoted aside as its creators had designed it to do.

I leaped out, using Appledore's back as a springboard, and scrambled clear of the pit. Levizod lunged for the gladius he had discarded in his frantic attempts to raise the cover. I lunged for Levizod.

We dropped together onto the wet stone floor of the Mithraeum, struggling for life under the disfigured carved gaze of forgotten gods, washed in the effusion from the shattered taurobolium. The lantern went over, plunging us into absolute darkness.

Levizod's hands closed around my throat.

My hand closed around the hilt of the Roman sword.

I did not hesitate.

❊❊❊

We discovered afterwards that the murderer's body had tumbled back into the bull-pit from which Holmes and Appledore had just climbed. Levizod's blood was the last to feed that ghastly hole before the intruding waters covered it and claimed the forgotten temple at last.

If Wizot's secrets and treasure lay concealed at the bottom of that dank flooded shaft they were never recovered. Mithraeum, bull-pit and all, fell to the decay of time and were lost.

The buried god kept his mysteries to the last.

The History Detective

I.A. Watson considers Sherlock Holmes and the mysteries of time

Many of Sir Arthur Conan Doyle's stories depend upon some historic event having provoked present mayhem. Right from *A Study in Scarlet*, Holmes was required to delve into the past and discover how it had affected the present. Sometimes he has had to dig deep into history; "The Adventure of the Musgrave Ritual" in *The Memoirs of Sherlock Holmes* featured Holmes' own account of how the young detective uncovered the remnants of King Charles I's lost crown.

I was interested to turn in a story of that kind for *Sherlock Holmes: Consulting Detective* volume 8.

"Mysteries of the Buried God" is set in the early part of Holmes' career, in those days before any Mrs Watson or Professor Moriarty, when Holmes and Watson were still becoming acquainted with each others' habits and dispositions and no popular public account from the good doctor had yet brought Holmes to the glare of public attention. At that time Holmes was still establishing his reputation as a unique consultant, taking most cases from baffled experts rather than from desperate individuals.

It was in these years that Holmes began regular authorship of an eclectic range of monographs in a wide variety of professional publications. Around sixteen of these are mentioned in the Canon (experts differ on what to count), ranging from "Upon the Distinction Between the Ashes of the Various Tobaccos" and "Upon the Influence of a Trade Upon the Form of the Hand" to "Early English Charters" and "On Malingering." His "On the Polyphonic Motets of Lassus" was held to be definitive by experts in medieval music. He authored two essays "On the Variability of Human Ears".[1]

Much later Holmes would issue accounts of certain cases[2] and complete his definitive *The Whole Art of Detection*;[3] but it was during his lean

1 Sceptical readers may refer to "The Cardboard Box" in *The Memoirs of Sherlock Holmes* (British editions) or *His Last Bow* (American editions).

2 "The Blanched Soldier" and "The Lion's Main" from *The Case-Book of Sherlock Holmes* are the two included as Canon, the only stories therein that are not narrated by Watson and in which he does not appear at all, although he is mentioned in "The Blanched Soldier".

3 Of course this discounts his possibly-final publication, "Practical Handbook of Bee Culture, With Some Observations Upon the Segregation of the Queen".

first years after graduation, when he was slowly establishing his business in Montague Street and Baker Street, that Holmes seems to have spread his researches widest. Nor is there indication that the list compiled by assiduous Holmes readers from Canon references is in any way his whole bibliography. Enough to say that Holmes had a habit of latching on to some matter that attracted his attention, criminal-based or not, and a tendency to scholarship on the results of his investigations.

It seemed likely to me that this early-phase Holmes might have had brought before him a wider range of problems than the criminal investigations for which he later became best known. Why would he *not* be consulted on an archaeological enigma, a veritable Roman locked room mystery? And how could the puzzle-addicted detective fail to respond and test his skills against a mystery so outside his regular scope?

Hence Sherlock Holmes versus a mystery religion.

The worship of Mithras and the nature of Mithraeum were not well understood in Holmes' time (if they are now), and there are limits to how far fictional history can be bent in a Sherlock Holmes story. Less than a third of the sites now associated with the cult had then been discovered or identified, and Mithraism was largely understood as an astrological religion because of the influence of the scholar K.B. Stark who is referenced in footnote 7. It therefore seemed prudent to include a second more recent historical enigma, lest the tale be bogged down in scholarly interpretations of fragmented artefacts and opposed academic interpretations.

With a sixteenth century murder we can be on slightly more solid ground. London is built on older London, but also upon charters and ledgers, tax rolls and legal documents stretching back a thousand years and preserved as Watson describes by the Master of the Rolls in the Public Record Office.

King Henry VIII and his daughters Queen Mary and Queen Elizabeth were undoubtedly real, as was global circumnavigator and swashbuckling sailor Sir Francis Drake. Henry "dissolved" the monasteries, seizing their wealth and lands for the Crown at the time he established the Protestant Church of England to displace the Papally-ruled Catholic faith. His elder daughter reversed his changes, persecuting and martyring Anglican clerics so fiercely that she earned her epithet 'Bloody Mary'. Elizabeth shared her father's Protestant sentiments and swung the state back that way to the downfall of Catholic worshippers. Drake was considered a national hero in Elizabeth's younger days and was heaped with rewards and honours.

Edmund Wizot is fictional, a necessary addition to the historical record to account for the doings at the Fleet-side buried Mithraeum. He shares the characteristics of many merchants who were part of the rising middle-classes during the fourteenth and fifteenth century, a lot of whom purchased former ecclesiastical lands from the cash-strapped Crown to establish estates of their own. At a time when witchcraft was considered real and dangerous, when even members of the royalty might dabble in the dark arts, Wizot's reputation and appetite for the occult is not unlikely.

And as the footnotes attest, there was a real-life Mithraic temple close by that other great lost London river, the Walbrook, although the buried site's existence was unsuspected by the Victorians and not discovered until exposed by post-World War II clearances for modern office buildings.

As "The Mystery of the Buried God" unfolded on my computer screen it became evident that it was going to be about beliefs, procedures, permissions, disavowed customs, and the inevitable triumph of time over knowledge.

Holmes was and is the very avatar of the Victorian genius of cataloguing and indexing the world. His enquiries are always about discovering the truth, although he often disseminates it cautiously with a delicacy characteristic of his era's sensibilities. It intrigued me to take him away from his customary investigations of the criminal habits of felons preying on Victorian society and push him into darker hidden underground places, where long-lost currents still trickle beneath London's modern façade.

I hope his digression entertains and his solution satisfies.

IW
Yorkshire, England
December 2014.

❁❁❁

I.A. WATSON has so far contributed to each volume of *Sherlock Holmes, Consulting Detective*, for which he has received four shortlistings and one trophy for Best Pulp Short Story in the annual Pulp Factory industry awards. He has published ten novels and six novellas, most recently *Vinnie de Soth, Jobbing Occultist,* with *Labours of Hercules* and *Holmes and Houdini* coming next. A full list of his works is available at http://www.chillwater.org.uk/writing/iawatsonhome.htm

Sherlock Holmes

in

"Adventure of the Charwick Ghost"

By

Raymond Louis James Lovato

It was an early Wednesday morning on a warm September day and Holmes and I had just settled in the drawing room for our breakfast. As I read *The Times*, my companion began perusing several newspapers at lightning speed. It would take a normal man hours to read all the newspapers that he read in less than an hour. Any time that I would find myself in a position standing behind Holmes, I would glance down and marvel at the articles that he was reading. And weeks later I would be astonished when he dredged up a fact that was contained in one of the obscure articles that he had committed to memory.

We had barely touched our biscuits when Mrs. Hudson's familiar knock sounded on our door.

"I assume that you did not have an appointment set with Inspector Lestrade," she said. "But he is at the bottom of the stairs and is insistent and very anxious to see you."

"Well," Holmes said to her, "if Scotland Yard's finest is at our door before breakfast, he must have started his day quite early. Please send him in, Mrs. Hudson."

As Mrs. Hudson turned to leave the room, Lestrade came charging up the stairs, passing her on the landing. He quickly nodded to her, bowler hat in hand, and muttered a quick thank you as he entered the room.

As the Inspector stood there recovering his breath, Holmes lifted his cup. Holmes had a strange relationship with the Chief Inspector Lestrade. He needed to be connected to someone like the Inspector if he wanted to be a consultant for Scotland Yard. Indeed, Sherlock Holmes and I could hardly go around investigating and interrogating suspected criminals, much less turning them over to the police without some official sanction. There were even times when I had to pull my weapon on a wrong doer. However, Lestrade's propensity to do things by the book, in a slow, methodical, time-consuming manner, often tested Holmes's patience. Often times my friend would mutter, "Please keep up, Inspector."

Mrs. Hudson stood there arms akimbo at Lestrade's audacity.

Holmes smiled. "Now, what could make the good Inspector from Scotland Yard get up so early and march around a large estate except for a mystery involving murder?"

Lestrade was dumbfounded at the pronouncement.

"How on earth did you know that, Holmes?" His rodent-like face twitched slightly. "We've done our level best to keep Vice Admiral Harlington Wilbury Charwick's death a secret. I haven't said a word to you yet. Are you reading minds now?"

"Well, now that it is not a secret, why don't you sit down and tell us about it," Holmes motioned to a vacant chair. "Perhaps, Mrs. Hudson will be so kind as to get you some tea."

Our landlady flashed a forced smile and started down the stairs.

Lestrade heaved a weary sigh and looked at the floor. "Thank you. I have been up for several hours since we was notified by the Charwick staff about the murder and the strange circumstances surrounding it."

"Strange, Inspector?" I inquired as Holmes finished his tea "What exactly do you mean by that?"

Lestrade blinked three times before he answered, and then said, "Well, he was found dead inside his study."

"And what is so strange about that?" I finished my biscuit and wiped crumbs from my moustache. I thought I would give Lestrade an opening before Holmes became bored with the case at the offset. Nothing stopped a conversation quicker than the detective announcing that the direction of the exchange was boring him.

Lestrade pursed his lips. "Well, the door to the study…It was locked."

Holmes immediately perked up.

Lestrade continued.

"The staff couldn't find Vice Admiral Charwick when they showed up in the morning. They did a quick search of the house and the grounds; he was nowhere to be found. But the door to his study was locked and bolted from the inside." Lestrade began eying the biscuits on the silver tray that Mrs. Hudson held as she re-entered the room. His nose wriggled slightly, and he went on. "So they had a housekeeper go down to the road and flag down a boy and send him straight away for the constable who notified Scotland Yard."

"Really," Holmes set his cup down, crossed his legs under his blue silk dressing gown and steepled his hands under his chin. He fixed his sharp, piercing eyes on our visitor. I could tell that his interest had been piqued. "Go on, Inspector."

Lestrade accepted a cup of hot tea from Mrs. Hudson, thanked her warmly, but was clearly disappointed that the tray of warm biscuits was set down on the opposite side of the room. The Inspector returned to his tale.

"Tuesday night is when the vice admiral goes out to the Royal Navy Club. He gives his staff that night off. The butler was the last one to leave and said he saw Charwick going upstairs to his study with a book. The butler noted that the vice admiral was feeling under the weather. He checked all the locks on all the doors and windows and everything was secure." Lestrade paused again and eyed the biscuits. I was ready to hand over the platter when Holmes raised a finger and shook his head.

"This is not the time for distractions, Watson. Please proceed, Inspector."

Lestrade's nose wiggled. "Well, when the staff all came in around five this morning, they didn't find the vice admiral in his chambers. His bed had not been disturbed. After several attempts at knocking and shouting, they sent for a copper. When the constable got there they found that the study door was bolted from the inside. The constable then broke the handle from the outside to get into the study. They found the vice admiral dead in his overstuffed chair, which was toppled over on the floor. It was obvious that he had met with foul play. There was blood on the floor where the vice admiral's head had struck hard. They then sent for me."

"An excellent decision." Holmes uncrossed his legs. "You didn't disturb the room, did you, Inspector?"

"Of course not. We kept it untouched, just as you prefer, Holmes." Lestrade eyed the biscuits again. "But what is even stranger is that nothing was taken. The room was untouched according to the butler. So it doesn't appear to be a robbery."

"No sign of a break in at the manor, a room locked from the inside, and apparently nothing stolen. Correct?" my companion said quietly. "Tell me, Inspector, do you have any theories?"

"I figure that it was no accident, so it had to be an assassination. Or part of the Charwick supernatural occurrences." Lestrade replied. "But I have already been knicked by the police commissioner and then the Admiralty itself to find this killer and solve this case. They want it solved quickly. That's why I was hoping you would look into this as soon as possible."

Lestrade's eyes again drifted to the tray and I glanced toward Holmes, who nodded slightly.

"Would you care for a biscuit, Inspector?" I asked.

"Why, yes, I would." Lestrade said as he grabbed two of the muffins. "And, Holmes, please don't let the papers get a hold of this. I have already told the Charwick staff to keep quiet with all their whispers. They have started about the Charwick Ghost. I don't need the Admiralty ordering me to capture and cuff a phantom."

"The Charwick Ghost?" I asked incredulously. "When did an apparition become a suspect, Inspector?"

Lestrade was slathering butter onto the biscuit. "There's a long list of tales that points to the Charwick manor being haunted, Doctor."

"Inspector," Holmes interjected, "if you are going to solve this case quickly then I would suggest that you leave the ghost stories to Charles Dickens and concentrate on the facts of the case."

"But, Holmes, the staff swears to seeing strange lights and noises at night around the manor for years. And you can't ignore the facts about all the deaths of the Charwick's under very bizarre circumstances over the decades." Lestrade finally paused long enough to take a sip of his tea.

"Nonsense, Lestrade." Holmes looked away from the Inspector as if to further dismiss his allegations. "And as we know, the newspapers rarely get their facts straight."

"What are these supernatural stories?" I asked. "I'm not familiar with any Charwick ghost tales."

"Well," the Inspector was refreshed and ready to talk again, "it began with the vice admiral's grandfather, Sir Edgar Burlington Charwick. He was an official with the East India Company. He was very successful and he built Charwick manor and purchased all the woods surrounding it for miles. But the Charwick's had a run of bad fortune. Hard times, you know, when the East India Company dissolved. He had to sell most of the land off over the years. Sir Edgar's wife died suddenly back in the mid-fifties," Lestrade stopped to sip his tea. "Then one year to the date Sir Edgar was found hanging from a beam in the kitchen. They say he was walking around the manor grounds talking to his dead wife's spirit for months before."

Holmes quickly crossed and uncrossed his legs, straightening his dressing gown. I had the feeling that my friend was not in the mood for stories of apparitions while the trail of a murderer was growing colder.

"Oh heavens, Lestrade, the simple facts of the case are that the woman died of natural causes, the cholera outbreak I believe. And Sir Edgar was known as a melancholy man given to fits of grief. He could not take his fall in the social status. His suicide was inevitable."

Lestrade was smearing more butter on his second biscuit. "But how then do you explain the other mysterious deaths in the family? Vice Admiral Harlington Charwick's father, Admiral Pouncy Swearington Charwick drowned to death in his bathtub. A man who spent his entire life at sea dies in water on dry land. Then, one year later, Admiral Pouncy's wife falls into a fountain on the property and drowns herself. More water. It's obvious that house is cursed."

Holmes was anxiously pulling at the hem of his garment.

"My dear Inspector, Doctor Watson and I have chased ghosts before," he spoke in a clipped manner, "and every time the natural explanation was the true one. My recollection of the incidents was that Admiral Pouncy Charwick suffered from a disease common to seafaring men: a fondness for rum and brandy. There was no foul play or phantom involved in his death, just two empty bottles of rum in the corner on the floor next to his bathtub. And the admiral's wife started a treatment of laudanum after her husband's death. She was also very myopic, nearsighted, and on the rainy night that she was wondering around the grounds, she most likely fell into the fountain and hit her head. No pair of eye glasses were found at the fountain. They were later discovered on her dressing room table. Now may we get back to Vice Admiral Harlington's demise?"

"Well, Holmes," Lestrade said, placing half the buttered biscuit into his mouth, "I don't need no angry spirits popping up to muck up the investigation. They're holding my feet to the fire and you're the best detective we got, so?"

"Consulting detective," my companion corrected him. "Yes, we will dress and ride with you to the Charwick manor," he said as he took his last sip of his strong morning tea. "Shall we, Watson?"

In less than twenty minutes we were in Lestrade's carriage and headed to London's west end through West Minster, Hyde Park and Saint John's Wood. There was something I had been anxious to ask my companion since the Inspector had first appeared.

I leaned into his ear and quietly whispered, "Holmes, when the Inspector first arrived in our room, how did you know that it concerned an important murder at a large estate?"

Holmes allowed himself a slight smile. "That was relatively easy to deduce, old boy. It had to be of some importance by the way Lestrade impatiently rushed up the stairs anxious to start his tale of woe. I thought, if it was crucial, it might concern someone of wealth or social standing in the opulent estates surrounded by woods on London's west side. That was due to the fact that the west end of London had periods of spotty rain showers over the past two afternoons and the Inspector's boots and the bottom of his great coat were splattered with fresh mud. That made me hypothesize London's west end. My statement to him was very general and he, naturally, filled in the pertinent facts."

As I settled back into my seat, I shook my head and marveled at the powers of observation and deduction of my good friend. And chuckled as

I recalled the look on Lestrade's face when Holmes informed him of the reason for his visit before the Inspector could begin.

It took twenty-five minutes to reach the outskirts of London where large stretches of woods surrounded huge estates with only a ribbon of narrow drives stretching to the grand manors. It was unlike central London where people lived side by side, piled atop one another. Here there was a sense of privacy and entitlement, the grace and elegance and trappings of the well-to-do, where things moved at an old world pace.

At the end of the drive were two more police carriages and a bright blue and gold carriage with the crest of the Royal Navy.

"Just what we need, Watson," Holmes said to me as we stepped down from the carriage, "more interlopers traipsing through the manor. We will be lucky to find a corpse with all this help."

An officer held the front door open for us. To the right was a large parlor where several maids, a cook and the butler were being questioned by Lestrade's men. A few of the housekeepers were sobbing. The butler was going back and forth to the kitchen bringing trays of cookies and biscuits and tea to calm the staff's nerves. The policemen were generously imbibing of the repast.

"Next time, Inspector, you might want to remind your men that this is not a social gathering. And no one is accompanying the butler during his trips to the kitchen. Who knows what clues are being hidden or destroyed in there, out of their sight?"

Lestrade barked out orders to his men as Holmes and I ascended the stairs to the second floor study. Holmes moved slowly, first studying the plush carpeted hallway that was completely trampled flat with all the traffic it had borne. Yet there were no muddy footprints anywhere. He looked closely at the door handle and lock that had been smashed by the police to open the dead-bolt to the study. There was no key hole. Stepping inside the doorway, he paused and looked up and down, then left and right. He studied the transom above the door. The door could only be locked from the inside with a large dead-bolt. To the left of the door was an old club chair covered in purple velveteen. Above it slightly to the left was a painting of the Royal Naval Academy.

Crouching down on all fours in the doorway, Holmes turned his head sideways to study the thick carpet in the study.

"I see your officers have been all over this room," he said wearily.

"Indeed they have," Lestrade replied, taking that as a compliment. "We searched it thoroughly for clues."

"Yes, Inspector, and left the carpet looking like a herd of sheep have been shepherded over it."

Across the room, in front of an extinguished fireplace, was a wing-backed chair tipped on its side. Hanging over the puffy arm of the chair was the vice admiral's head and a pool of blood on the carpet. Holmes stood over the body looking down for a minute, then walked to the upright side of the seat, bent down and inspected the blood-stained back and arm of the chair. He returned to the side where the vice admiral's head lay on the carpet and knelt, raising the vice admiral's head slightly exposing the gash on its right side. Pulling his magnifying glass out of his coat pocket, he made a closer examination of the wound.

A loud voice intruded from the doorway. "What is that man doing?"

It belonged to a mustachioed naval captain.

"It's all right," Inspector Lestrade stepped forward quickly. "He's working with Scotland Yard. A consulting detective."

"I do not care if he is Chief Inspector George Clarke of Scotland Yard," the captain sputtered referring to one of London's the most famous chief detectives who had recently retired. "He will treat the vice admiral's corpse with the proper respect."

Holmes, as was his way, ignored the outburst. He called me over to the chair and asked me to hold the Vice Admiral's head up as he pulled tweezers from his inner coat pocket. Guiding his hand with the magnifying glass, he extricated a small sliver of wood from the head wound. He had me set the head down gently as he placed the sliver in an envelope that he withdrew from his pocket. This only further infuriated the captain.

"I say," the naval officer said. "What's he doing there?"

Holmes continued to ignore the man and walked over to the fireplace. Beginning on its left side, he moved slowly along the walls, bookcases, paintings, and large locked windows of the study. He crouched down low and then brought himself up to the full height of his lanky frame, all the time moving his arms and hands against the wall up and down like a frenzied spider, feeling every inch of the wood panels and touching every nook and cranny.

When he had completed a full circle of the room, he ended up at the immediate right of the fireplace feeling around the edges of a painting of a frigate. He gave it a hard tug, and then quit his strange dance.

"How much longer are you going to let this continue?" the captain demanded of Lestrade, who stood beside him.

Holmes walked up to the officer, stopping only inches from his mustache.

"It's all right, he's working with Scotland Yard. A consulting detective."

"Excuse me," Holmes said sternly.

The officer, startled by the lack of space between himself and my companion, quickly backed up. Holmes then stepped into the space previously held by the officer, spun on his heels to face the fireplace, and addressed Lestrade.

"Inspector, I can tell you that Vice Admiral Charwick was not killed by the chair being tipped over. Nor was the blow to the right side of his skull caused by his head hitting the floor. If the blow to his head was caused by the floor, then there is no possible way for there to be traces of blood on the back of the high-backed chair or on the left arm of his chair. The blood would have traveled outward on a rather straight line. It could not curve around a head to reach the other side of the armchair. The skull turned violently to the left when it was struck from behind on the right temple.

"Additionally, because the arm of the chair is so padded, the spot where his head might have hit the carpet would be much higher up on his skull. The gash is lower towards the temple. Too low to have been caused by striking the floor. There is a sharp indentation at the top of the crease in his scalp. A strange semi-circle, deeper than the rest of the groove. He could not have received that from hitting the floor. The chair was tipped over after the vice admiral was struck and killed." He paused and glanced over at the body.

"And, as to the reason that someone paid the vice admiral a visit last night," my friend then strode across the room to the right side of the fireplace. He placed his hands on the frame of the painting of the frigate and gave it a very hard pull. The painting swung back on old, creaking hinges revealing an antiquated wall safe that had been pried open near its keyhole. Holmes reached into and withdrew a Royal Naval receipt stub from the back of the safe. He leaned in a few inches from the spot where the door had been pried open. Reached in again, pulled out a long, thin wooden sliver just like the one he had found on the body. He shook his head slightly as he removed the envelope from his pocket and deposited the sliver inside with the first one.

"I would speculate that the vice admiral kept his pension hidden here."

"Amazing, Holmes. I don't know how we missed that," Lestrade said giving his officers a withering look which meant that they were all in for a severe tongue lashing when they returned to Scotland Yard. "But how did they get into the locked study?"

"I'm still working on that, Inspector."

"May we remove the Vice Admiral's body now, Inspector?" the captain asked, with some exasperation.

Lestrade shot a quick glance over to Holmes who gently nodded his head.

"You can have your boys come up and take the deceased away now, Captain," the Inspector said. "The rest of you boys," he said sternly to his bobbies, "check this room again."

"I would like to see the hallway outside the study," Holmes said. "I believe you said the window lock was broken at the end of the hall."

Lestrade, the naval captain and I followed Holmes to the study door. There Holmes paused once again, looking intently at both sides of the door frame, touching the hinges on the inside of the jamb. He looked at the legs of the club chair next to the door. His head shook slowly from side to side. Then we all gathered at the tall window leading to the small stone balcony. The naval captain began impatiently tapping his foot. The aged latch was broken open. Holmes leaned in close and observed the handle, which was a rusty, simple hook style. There was no key lock on the window exit to the balcony.

Holmes stepped out onto the balcony, the only such abutment on the manor's west side. He observed that the stone was still damp in places from yesterday's rain and lack of direct sunlight on that side of the house. He suddenly bent down and picked up a discolored piece of straw amid the few leaves on the balcony floor.

"Does Charwick manor have a byre or stable?" he asked.

"No, Mr. Holmes. It does not," the officer answered haughtily. "The vice admiral was a sailor, not a cavalry man."

Holmes continued to ignore the man's sarcastic tone and moved over to the edge of the balcony and peered down. "No marks from a ladder, Inspector?"

Lestrade shook his head.

"Was there anything down below that could be used to gain access to this balcony?"

"Nothing. And I had my men inspect all around the manor for any sign of anyone gaining entry to the house. No ladder marks. No broken windows or locks except this one. No muddy footprints inside of any doorway or window or on any carpet or floor." Lestrade replied in an assured tone.

"Well, from here, the plethora of imprints down below," Holmes said, "the Royal Navy Military Band could have been prancing around. Come, Watson, it is time to interview the staff."

Holmes brushed past the navy man and proceeded downstairs to the parlor where the staff sat silently except for a few occasional sobs. Holmes grabbed an empty chair and indicated that I do the same. My old wound was beginning to throb because of the dampness of the old manor and forest's humidity and welcomed the chance to sit. I was never far removed from memories of my military campaign in Afghanistan.

Holmes directed that a chair be brought over and placed directly in front of us. He asked Lestrade to kindly send over the butler. Lestrade fetched the houseman, knowing that with the new information that Holmes had uncovered that the interrogation would reveal more facts than his men may have uncovered. The naval officer hovered over us to the right. Holmes watched as the tall, gaunt, balding servant walked stiffly over to us and sat down.

"This is Mister Jefferies, the butler here at Charwick." Turning to the servant, Lestrade wagged his finger and said, "You had better tell Mr. Holmes the truth. You hear me."

"There, there, Inspector," Holmes chided. "No need for truculence." He smiled at the butler. "How long have you been in the service of the Charwick's, Mister Jeffries?"

"About forty years now, sir."

"Did you serve in the military or do you work around horses?"

Now, I have sat through a hundred interrogations by my good friend, but this line of questioning confounded me. I knew that Holmes did not waste time or words, but before the detective could continue, the naval captain interrupted.

"What in God's name do horses have to do with this? I told you that there are no stables on this estate."

Holmes sprang to his feet, spun quickly to face the captain and raised himself up to his full height. There was a look of total disdain and a tinge of anger in his voice.

"Sir, you will kindly leave my sight immediately so I can get about solving this murder without your inane and dim-witted remarks. You are delaying one of the most important steps of an investigation, the questioning of witnesses, while their recollections are still fresh. There can be no flow to the narrative if you keep blundering in with useless comments and inconsequential observations."

The captain's jaw clenched tightly and his fists balled up.

"Perhaps you should help oversee the removal of the Vice Admiral's body by your men, captain," I offered, stepping in as a peace maker. The two men stared at each other, neither wanting to be the first to blink. But Holmes' stare grew more intense by the second. I could see the muscles in the officer's face begin to sag. Without saying a word, the naval man turned and stomped off to the stairway and disappeared upstairs.

Holmes pulled on the front piece of his suit and sat back down in front of the butler.

"Sorry. Where were we? Yes, military and horses."

"I was never in the military, sir. But I was a stable boy when I was a young'un."

"Yes, that is where your left leg was injured?" Holmes said pointing to the man's left foot. "You could not join the Service and improve your station in life because of your injury. That caused you to then apprentice with the serving staff?"

Mister Jeffries was astonished. "Why, yes. That's exactly what happened. A work horse fell on me and broke me ankle in several places and it just never healed right. I took up being a servant and butlering after that for three years with the Wickershams. Then I came to the Charwicks and have been here for nigh on forty years." Jeffries brought his knees closer together and leaned forward. "And I tell you, sir, I have seen a whole bunch of misery dealt to this family over the long years. First with Mister Charwick of the East India Company and then his wife, Mrs. Annabelle Christina. Then Admiral Pouncy Charwick and his beloved wife Elizabeth. Now the Vice Admiral Harlington Charwick, himself." The butler shook his head sadly. "He was a committed bachelor, but a right nice master."

"Do you have any theories as to his death?" Holmes asked.

The butler glanced around quickly, then leaned forward and spoke in a hushed voice. "Sir, I do believe it was the work of the Charwick ghost. This house has long been haunted. It was the ghost who passed through the locked door to kill the Admiral."

"Yes, quite," Holmes smiled. "Where do you live, Mister Jeffries?"

"I live in the West End, on Potter Lane off of Winchester Square."

"And do you walk from your house to get to Charwick Manor?"

"Yes, sir. Ain't no other way. Takes me about an hour with my leg and all."

"Is there any other way into the study? A hidden passage behind the walls."

"No, sir, it was like a sanctuary to the Admiral. He took his brandy, his book and told me that he felt secure locked in. The last time I saw him was when he was going up the stairs. He told me to lock up and have a pleasant night."

"And did you?"

"Yes, sir. It was a good night with the missus. Until I came back here early in the morning and could not find him."

"I meant did you secure the premises."

"Why, of course, sir. I always lock up and secure the doors and windows and check twice before I leave."

"Did you check every door?"

"Yes, sir."

"And did you check the window by the balcony at the end of the hall by the study?"

"Yes, I always check all the windows. Even on the second floor. You can't be too careful, you know."

"Obviously," Holmes stroked his chin. "Tell me, did you serve the vice admiral eggs every morning for his breakfast?"

"Why, yes, sir. Poached eggs was his favorite." I could see the quizzical look on the butler's face at the last question. But even I could see the egg stain on the left cuff of the butler's shirt. Still, I wondered why Holmes was pursuing this line of questioning.

"And where is the hen house?" my friend continued to rub his chin awaiting the answer.

"Well, we ain't got one, sir. He liked the eggs, but could not stand the feathers blowing around the estate. The feathers made him sneeze, so years ago he gave the chicken coop to Mrs. Postelwhite, the cook." The butler paused, turned stiffly in his chair, and pointed to a sobbing, short, plump woman being comforted on the sofa by a housekeeper. "She brings the eggs here every morning to make breakfast."

"One last question. By any chance, does she carry the eggs in a straw basket?" Holmes leaned into the butler as if this was going to the most important answer that the man would give.

"No, sir. She carries them in a small burlap sack. Each of the eggs is wrapped in cheesecloth."

Holmes placed both his hands on his knees and abruptly stood up. He extended his hand to shake the butler's hand.

"Thank you, Mr. Jeffries. You have been most helpful."

The butler tried to stand as quickly as possible. It was probably the early morning dampness that had a grip on his old bones. A feeling I was not unfamiliar with. I glanced across the room as the naval boys were taking the Vice Admiral's body on a stretcher out the front door.

Holmes was standing close to me. "Looks like Lestrade lost the jurisdictional battle," he said. "Watson, if you don't mind, could you ask the

Chief Inspector to look up the financial situation of the wait staff here. I would appreciate any unusual circumstances passed on to us. Otherwise, I am fairly certain that no one in this room could have murdered the vice admiral. But we should see if any of them had a reason to have someone else do it for them."

"Certainly," I replied. "Any theories about the locked door?"

"In due time, Watson. In due time. I am going outside to look around the grounds and the manor. I will meet you out front. Can you see if Lestrade will have a carriage take us back to Baker Street?"

Shortly I joined my friend as he walked the edges of the Charwick Manor. He concentrated most of his time on the steeply-sloped ground directly underneath the second story balcony and in the flower bed underneath it. The same balcony with the broken latch on the window to the second story hallway outside the study. That seemed perfectly natural as reason dictated that the opened window on the second floor balcony appeared to be the only logical way of access to the manor. It was difficult sorting out the muddy impressions from the thorough investigation by the Scotland Yard, but no indentations or grooves from any type of ladder were visible.

"Watson," Holmes said, "this ground slopes steeply away from the building by approximately fifteen-feet from the manor at the first floor into a steep drainage ditch that runs along the entire west side of the building. With the estate's fourteen foot ceiling on the first floor, a ladder would have to be at least forty-feet long to reach the second floor balcony from that angle. Setting a ladder in a wet ditch is hard enough, but a ladder like that would surely snap in its center under the weight of an ordinary man. And transporting it along the roads and carrying it through the woods at night would be a remarkable feat."

"Quite," I agreed.

"I found no ladder indentations in the soft ground," Holmes continued. "I checked the outer wall of the manor. It is very old, crumbling stone and mortar. Worn almost sheer by the elements from its age and the west-facing location. Its precipitous face allows absolutely no place for a foot hold or the ability to scale the outer wall and reach the balcony."

He paused, "But I did find two more pieces of discolored straw in the geraniums besides the wall."

"So," I said, placing my hands in my pockets for warmth while in the shade, "there appears to be no way to reach the balcony, if that was the way in. And we cannot begin to explain how someone can pass through a door that was dead bolted from the inside, murder the vice admiral, and leave the study with the door still bolted." I chuckled. "Perhaps it was an apparition."

A thin smile crossed the lips of my friend. "Watson, I am not yet ready to change my title to consulting ghost hunter."

❁❁❁

Thursday morning could not come soon enough for my friend. I was awakened at six o'clock to the sound of Holmes playing Bach's Sonata Number One in G Minor, an early morning favorite I was getting used to hearing over the years. I threw on my robe and went down the stairs and retrieved the bundle of newspapers from the stoop and brought them up to our drawing room. My companion immediately put his violin down and seemed more intent on scanning the news of the day. His excited state was noticed and commented on by Mrs. Hudson when she brought the tea and scones up for our breakfast. Holmes, as was his way when locked into case, did not eat anything, nor was he very talkative. Rather, he wrapped himself tightly in a contemplative state. I kept to myself and read more slowly, waiting for Holmes to announce our next move.

That next move didn't come from him, but rather from a constable sent over from Lestrade who inquired as to whether or not we would like to sit in with the Chief Inspector when he questioned a new person of interest in the Charwick case; one Mr. Charles Weldon Charwick, the nephew of Vice Admiral Charwick and the probable heir to the Charwick estate.

Holmes replied that we would be happy to assist. We retired to our rooms to dress for the day and met at the bottom of the stairs twenty minutes later. After I whistled twice to get a hansom cab, we rode to Scotland Yard. It was a quiet ride as Holmes was still deep in thought. I mumbled a few observations about the early morning sun feeling good and the cloudless skies above sending portents of a fair day. Holmes reply was courteous as what I had just said was really not germane to our case.

After arriving at Scotland Yard we did not go immediately to Lestrade's office. Instead, I followed Holmes to the sergeant's desk. We were quite familiar with Sergeant Moppet due to our past dealings with the Yard. After exchanging quick pleasantries, Holmes asked the sergeant if he could see the daily record of police activity for the past few months for London's far west districts and the area around the large estates near Charwick manor. Moppet was only too glad to accommodate Holmes' request. He knew that the detective was quite generous to any police staff who had aided him once a case was successfully completed. He led us past the Criminal Investigation Department down to a room full of files at the opposite end of the building. There Holmes quickly began to scan all of the police reports for the past six months involving that particular district.

Approximately fifteen minutes later, my friend thanked the sergeant and we left for Lestrade's office. Two floors up and down the hall to the left we entered a small office in the older part of the building. It looked like it had just gone through the Irish Nationalist Fenian Dynamite Campaign of May, 1884 when the yard was bombed late at night. Its disorganization, clutter, and collections of stacks of paper would afford my friend days worth of clues on which to use his powers of observation in describing Chief Inspector Lestrade. But Holmes was far past that stage in his relationship with the Inspector. Now, my friend seemed anxious to meet this new person involved in the case.

We joined Lestrade in his tiny office. There were three empty chairs around the disheveled desk in the room's center which was dimly lit from the thin rays of morning sunlight dribbling in through the long, narrow window. Sitting across from the Inspector was a stout man with no chin, or several chins, depending how you looked at it. His skin was pale, framed by stringy hair combed from one side of his head over to the other, neither covering nor concealing his baldness. He had on a well-worn frock coat. His left hand supported his right elbow which supported his right hand that clutched a lilac-drenched, violet handkerchief. He continually dabbed it underneath his nose.

"Sorry for our tardiness, Inspector" I apologized for our lateness as I knew that Holmes would not.

Lestrade nodded.

"This here is Mr. Charles Weldon Charwick, the nephew of the late Vice Admiral Harlington Charwick, and only living relative," Lestrade said, pointing to the man sitting across from him.

"Pleased to meet you," I said.

"It's my pleasure, undoubtedly," Charles said, waving his handkerchief under his bulbous nose.

"He contacted my office early this morning," Lestrade said. "He was wondering about the disposition of Vice Admiral Charwick's estate. I informed him that the law firm handling the estate is waiting for the outcome of our investigation before having a reading of the will." Lestrade then shifted in his worn leather chair, pulling himself up to his full height.

"I was going to call Mr. Charwick in for a few questions because his name came up when I spoke with the housekeeping staff on Wednesday."

Charwick dabbed at his nose again.

"It seems,"Lestrade continued, "that his relationship with his late uncle was not on the best of terms and his reputation with the staff was not exactly immaculate. The servants told me that Charles here would come around every so often to visit his uncle, mostly to ask for money. The discussions were often very loud and heated. I was told that many a time Charles was caught snooping around the manor. Additionally, items were reported missing after some of his visits." Lestrade held up his small note pad as if to verify his accusations.

"Those ungrateful churls," Charles said. "When the manor's mine, I'll sack them all." Color rushed to his cheeks and he trembled slightly. "I never took anything from my beloved uncle. The truth be told, he was growing so feeble he often complained about things moving mysteriously from one room to another, or being out of place or disappearing. It was either the work of his *trusted* servants, or the Charwick Ghost, most assuredly."

"Oh, not the ghost again," Lestrade wiped his forehead with the back of his hand.

"Mr. Charwick," Holmes had an air of exasperation in his voice, "the only thing growing more feeble is your story. It's painfully obvious that all you are interested in is any possible inheritance from your late uncle's estate."

"Balderdash," Charwick exclaimed. "I cared very deeply for my uncle."

Holmes frowned. "You care very deeply about certain things, but I seriously doubt your late uncle was one of them."

"How dare you?"

Holmes held up his index finger to silence the man.

"Sir, your overcoat is threadbare, and the cuffs of your trousers and shirt are frayed. You are wearing a striped shirt, a style usually associated with a con man or a loafer. Serious businessmen wear white shirts. Your shoes are caked with clay from the horse paddocks and stalls like the ones from The Turf, a race course with which Watson and I have had some acquaintance." Holmes suddenly stood up to tower over the rotund fellow. "A copy of the *Pink 'Un*, the racing sheet printed on pink paper by *The Sporting Times*, is visible in your front coat pocket, leading to the obvious conclusion that you are in currently in debt to numerous bookmakers of unsavory character at the race track."

Charwick's face seemed to pale visibly.

Holmes continued. "Your affectation of sniffing your perfume-drenched handkerchief is most likely due to inhaling the smell of the stables where you linger, most likely attempting to obtain possibly tips about the upcoming races. Your pale complexion is due to staying out of the sun, huddled by the horse stalls while at the race track or sitting in the enclosed stands."

Charwick crushed the handkerchief in his hand.

"And," Holmes concluded, "as the Chief Inspector so aptly pointed out, your appearance at your uncle's estate seems to coincide with your times of financial distress and continued poor choices in horses."

Lestrade jumped up. "Admit it. You killed your uncle, didn't you?"

Charwick looked as if he were going to faint.

Holmes held up his finger again, this time addressing Lestrade. "While he had a definite motive, Inspector, his poor physical condition eliminates him from direct suspicion. He could hardly carry a ladder, much less climb one. And if he had enlisted any accomplices in a plan to rob your uncle, they would have taken all the stolen property and pension money for themselves rather than turn it over to him. People of that criminal ilk would have most certainly killed you, poor Charles, to eliminate any witnesses." Holmes regarded the sniveling man with a look of contempt. "No, he wouldn't be sitting here in his pathetic attempt to get you, Inspector, to close the case to facilitate the reading of the will."

"I...I... I protest, vigorously," Charles blabbered. "It had to be the Charwick ghost. And I'm still due whatever share of my uncle's estate that he left to me. That is a lawful fact."

We sat in silence, all of us staring at one another for several seconds.

"I will notify you when the last will is to be read, Mr. Charwick," Lestrade said. He flipped his tiny book open. "But perhaps you will be so kind as to answer some questions about your finances and your whereabouts on the night of your uncle's murder." Lestrade wetted the tip of his nubby pencil with his tongue.

"Well, Chief Inspector," Holmes said, "you seem to have this well in hand. I will let you get on with your business. Come, Watson, we have work to do."

❁❁❁

After a light lunch back at Baker Street, which Holmes barely touched, we engaged a Clarence cab for the rest of the day to take us around. Before settling in the solid carriage, Holmes instructed the driver to make haste for Hyde Park then up to Edgeware Road, the major road leading to the Charwick manor. But it was not the Charwick estate that my friend planned to visit, but rather to scour the woods around the large estates in that area. Once we arrived in the vicinity of the Charwick estate, Holmes tapped on the carriage roof and the driver reined in his horse. The detective hopped out, climbed whatever embankment was alongside the road, looked around using his small, collapsible telescope, and then come back to the carriage. Another tap set the driver moving forward again. This was repeated many times over. Gradually, Thursday was coming to a close. The sun was beginning its descent in the western sky when Holmes scampered back to the road, told the driver to wait right there for as long as it took for us to return, and bade me to follow him into the woods. I was glad that I had decided to bring my service revolver along as the daylight slipped away.

Now, climbing small mounds and slopes was not what I had imagined our trip out to the Charwick manor would include. The tangled tree roots, scattered rocks hidden underneath the fallen leaves, made the trip hazardous, to say the least. I was glad that I had my silver-tipped walking stick with me. My friend moved like a Welsh hare ahead of me. The only way that I kept up with him was due to the intermittent stops he made to get his bearings. I began to wonder if he was wandering aimlessly in the woods, or if he was following some unseen sign. I hoped we would soon reach our destination.

Then, over a rise ahead, I saw a wisp of smoke rising up. An encampment came into view on the lip of the next knoll. There were various colorful wagons with canvas tents stretched off of their sides, which formed a circle around the campfire. A string of mules were tied between two trees. A cauldron hung over a small crackling fire. It was a camp of gypsies.

As I wondered how we were going to approach them, Holmes simply called out, "Hello there. We are wanderers, like you, and would ask to share your camp fire for a spell."

Our sudden appearance set all sorts of events in motion. Women grabbed their children and headed for their wagons. Two gypsies quickly drew their long, thin knives and took a defensive position by the mules. Two nomads closest to the fire stepped forward, taking command of the situation after our unexpected incursion.

"We have the right to be on this land." the shortest Romany descendant called out. "The master of these woods gave us his permission to stay here. If you are the police, then go away."

"I assure you that we are not the police," Holmes said calmly. He walked slowly towards the short man with a scraggly black beard and red bandana around his head. "As I said, we are travelers too. We are seeking the truth. I am Sherlock Holmes and this is Dr. John Watson."

The gypsy eyed us suspiciously. "What do you want?"

"Is there someone in your camp who communes with the spirits?" Holmes smiled. "I wish to engage that service, and will pay a fair price."

At the mention of money the gypsy's face lit up. "How much will you pay?"

"First, tell your fellow wanderers by the mules to put their knives away." Holmes kept moving slowly toward the man. "Watson, would you be so kind as to join us down here by the fire."

The gypsy boss shouted orders in Romany to the men by the mules. They sheathed their knives and walked over to the flames. He called out in their native tongue once again. One of the men strolled over to an old wagon that was once brightly colored, but was now covered with chipped paint. Some of the ancient mystic symbols still remained as our eyes grew better accustomed to the approaching twilight. The male gypsy nomad stood by the closed wagon door.

"Ah, very well." Holmes said. "And what is my fortune going to cost me?"

"A shilling," the leader answered.

"A shilling," the detective replied with some indignation in his voice. "I would expect some of the stew that you are cooking in your cauldron to be included with that price."

Here we were surrounded at sunset in the woods by a band of cut-throat gypsies and it seemed that Holmes was going to start bargaining about the cost of nonsensical babble from a fake gypsy fortune teller. I patted my hand against my coat pocket just for the reassuring feel of my revolver. A shilling would buy a hot beef pie and two pints of ale at any inn and was an exorbitant amount to pay for gypsy parlor tricks. But from where Holmes and I stood with the nomads by the fire, they could easily draw their knives and rush us before I could free my pistol from my pocket.

"If you do not like a shilling, then, perhaps, I should raise it to two shillings," the gypsy boss said, flashing a smile that contained one gold tooth right in the middle of his grin.

"Is there someone in your camp who communes with the spirits?"

"I will tell you what I propose," Holmes said, returning his smile. "I will pay you a shilling now, and if your fortune teller is a speaker of truth and can commune with the spirits, then I will give you my last shilling when I leave the wagon." Holmes slowly reached into the left front pocket of his gray wool Coburn great coat and withdrew exactly two shillings. He held them up so that the flames danced across the shiny silver metal of each coin. "But only if your fortune teller is a true soothsayer, connected to the spirit world. Then I will give you these and my eternal thanks."

I began to slide my hand up towards the top of the pocket of my coat. Would our nomads use the cover of impending night to slay the two of us just for two shillings and whatever else they think that we might have in our wallets? How trustworthy were this band of thieves? Were we actually going to enter that wagon?

The gypsy licked his lips, deep in thought about the proposition. Or perhaps he was thinking about how to kill us once we entered the wagon.

The gypsy glared at Holmes.

"Come now, man," Holmes intoned. "The truth is slipping away along with the sunlight. Make up your mind quickly."

"All right," our host agreed. He took a few steps toward Holmes and extended his palm. Holmes put the shilling in the man's hand and then put the remaining silver coin in his outer coat pocket.

"Come, Watson. Our fortune awaits us. It will be a little tight in that wagon but I believe we can all fit."

"Quite." I gingerly approached the fire, careful to note exactly where the remaining gypsies took up positions around me. My left hand tightly gripped my walking stick. My right had a firm grip on the handle of my revolver. I followed my friend as he climbed the three rickety steps behind the wagon, pushed open the old door, and we entered into the dimly lit core.

The interior of the wagon was slightly wider than the bed that stretched across its front portion. It was lit by a lantern hung from the center rafter. The candle in the lantern was only a few inches tall. A curtain of beads was strung across, affording a modicum of privacy from the door to the sleeping area. Clothes and cooking utensils were strewn about. In front of the bed, sitting on a wooden stool, was an old gypsy woman clothed in layers of slightly faded, once gaily-colored, cloth. Her cragged face and long nose poked out from underneath a babushka. From where I stood I could make out several gold rings dangling from pierced ear lobes.

"I am Magdalya," she motioned to a spare stool in front of her. "I am told that you come seeking the truth."

"Yes," Holmes replied. "I have been seeking the truth my entire life. In fact, I was hoping that we could trade truths."

"Trade truths? What can an Englishman tell me about truth?"

"Watson, if you will. Please have a seat and be very still while Magdalya and I commune with the spirits." Holmes pushed a stool over to me to allow me to rest my weary bones. Holmes sat cross-legged on the floor, in a seemingly subservient position in front of the gypsy woman. I have seen him do that before allowing the other person to assume that they had the position of power in the conversation.

"Magdalya, fortune has smiled on your people as of late," Holmes began. "The woods have offered up many rabbits to feed your troupe. It was wise of you to move to this spot in the woods several weeks ago. The only unfortunate incident that has happened of late was the accident with the mule. But your fellow Romany tribesman will recover in time from his injured arm. But you must get the axle fixed on your wagon before you travel again. I would not want any harm to come to someone such as yourself in a wagon accident."

I could see the eyes of the old woman narrow as she studied my friend.

"Lastly, if we are to speak the truth to one another, there can be no more lies, such as your band receiving permission to camp out in these woods. No such permission was given, nor have you seen or talked to the land owner."

The old woman's eyes flickered with a trace of fear. "You intend to see us evicted?"

Holmes shook his head. "The land is open and free. You are here because you are here."

In the dim, flickering candle light I could make out the astonished look on the old crone's face, even with my attention being evenly divided between the door behind me and my friends' discourse. I wondered how much of Holmes's speech was correct, and how much was pure conjecture.

Magdalya exclaimed an oath in Romany which I could not understand. Then she spoke in English. "How is it you know all these things? The plentiful game ... the accident with the mule … the broken axle. It is as if you have been among us the past month. Are you one of the spirit people who have been prowling the night?" She quickly made the sign of the cross.

"I am no spirit, but they interest me. I would like you to tell me all that you know about them. Please reveal all that you know about what goes on in the night. Anything that you have witnessed the past month while camping in these woods. My fortune is tied up with the happenings in these woods."

"I can do that," she said, as she arranged several sticks of incense in a bowl in front of her. "Strange things began happening about one full moon ago. We were camped down the road in another woods. We could hear small bands of people coming in the night. Always in the dead of night. Moving up and down the long lanes that lead to the great estates.

"Mario saw them twice, keeping to the edge of the forest and just off the main road." She extended a crooked finger that seemed to point several directions at once. "He said their dress was strange," she then wagged her bent finger at the detective. "Not like Englishmen. And when the wind carried their whispers to his ears, it was a strange tongue, similar to Romany, but different."

"Did you see this band of strange men again after that night, Magdalya?" Holmes asked. The candle light flickered queerly inside the wagon, giving the fortune tellers' story an even more portentous tone.

"No, we were run off that campsite the next night by the police. But the ghost men came back, a few nights ago. It was little Fredrico, not obeying his mother, but being out looking at night for more rabbits long after dark. He came running back into camp with a look of terror on his face. Like the devil himself was chasing him. He said he was hidden along an old path to the house down the road ..." Her deformed digit pointed east.

"And that would be the path to the old house and the woods that the police told you to move away from, correct?" he interjected.

"Yes, the woods by that house." She recoiled slightly at the knowledge the strange man in front of her displayed. "Fredrico said he saw tiny men, wood fairies no taller than him. Then there was a giant, so tall he blocked the moon. Then he saw the small wagon being pulled by ghost horses."

"Ghost horses," I exclaimed, forgetting that my role was to not interrupt. Holmes quickly turned his head and gave me a sharp glance.

"What did he say about the ghost horses?"he continued in his most soothing tone.

"He said they looked like horses, but not normal horses. He could see only parts of them at a time. One moment they were black as the Devil's eyes, then the next as white a ghost from the grave. A white apparition that was half in our world and half in the spirit world. He said it was like they were there, but then not there in the same moment. After they had passed, he ran back to our camp as fast as he could. He did not stop crying for a long time."

"And you are sure, Magdalya, that this happened two nights ago?"

"The night before last. The entire tribe was on watch to see if any of the creatures would return. Fredrico is a good lad. He does not lie or tell tales." She quickly made the sign of the cross again.

"Magdalya," my friend said standing up slowly from the floor, "you are one of the best mediums I have ever encountered. The gods of fortune smile on you." He reached into an inside pocket of his suit and withdrew four shillings. "This is for you to fix your axle on your wagon. All I ask is that you please keep it between us until long after my friend and I have left your camp. I have not heard or read of any malicious acts or personal injury attributed to your tribe, and feel that I can trust you. Money makes men do odd things. I shall pay your leader the agreed upon price for your excellent services and be on our way. I would hope that our paths cross again someday."

The old woman nodded graciously as Holmes placed the four shillings in her outstretched hands. There seemed to be a moment of understanding between them. I turned to open the wagon door, now slightly anxious as to what would greet us on the outside, and stepped cautiously down the few steps into the evening darkness. We were surrounded by the gypsies, some with their hands concealed behind their backs. My hand slipped back into my pocket to grip my pistol.

Then, behind us in the wagon's doorway, Magdalya appeared. "He is truly blessed," she intoned. "He may walk in peace."

The group shifted to make a clear path from the wagon to the fire and out of the camp. Holmes walked directly over to the gypsy chief and dropped one shilling in the man's outstretched hand. His golden grin flashed in the night.

"Come, Watson, we have many miles to walk until we set up camp." I knew that was strictly for my benefit, but I somehow sensed that Holmes was not worried about our gypsy companions now that the fortune teller had placed us under her protection.

It was eerily dark in the woods, save for a half moon that was slowly rising in the east. I don't know how my friend found the main road, as all I could make out was knolls and gullies that I navigated with much difficulty. We came out of the woods about sixty meters from where the carriage stood waiting. Holmes whistled to the driver who stirred his horse and came to pick us up. Once inside the safety and warmth of the Clarence cab's cabin, I had several questions to ask my friend.

"I suppose it is silly, but did we come all the way out here to speak with gypsies?"

Holmes nodded. "A necessary step."

"How the devil did you know we would find any?"

"Elementary, Watson. While going through the police reports at Scotland Yard for this district, I came upon a report of the constables forcibly evicting a band of gypsies from the Charwick estate woods about six weeks ago. Naturally I assumed that they would stay in the vicinity to take advantage of hunting small game in the fall. We were lucky to find them right next door camped on the Edmond's estate. If anyone saw anything in the woods, it would be our gypsy companions."

"But did you expect them to see giants and fairies and ghost horses?" I said calming down from the excitement of our encounter.

"There will be a logical explanation to what the lad said he saw, my good fellow. We are still gathering facts."

"Facts?" I asked incredulously. "Gypsies are an unsavory and superstitious lot. They are notorious liars. Are ghost horses' facts?"

"In due time. In due time," came his reply.

"Might I ask how you came up with all your 'truths' that you dazzled the fortune teller with?" I shuffled my weight to get a better view of my companion in the gloom.

"Of course, Watson. I told her that they were wise to move to better grounds six weeks ago. That was easily surmised due to the aforementioned police report. I said that fortune was smiling on them because the stew they were cooking had a strong, meaty smell. It was not watered down. I saw nine fresh rabbit pelts hanging from a string next to one of the tents. Hunting has obviously been good. One of their mules on the string continually was favoring its left hind leg and could not yet bear its full weight. The gypsy handler's accident was ascertained by observing one of the armed guards holding his knife on us in his right hand but keeping his left hand clutched around his right forearm. He was either kicked or stepped on by the injured mule and needed to support his injured arm."

"My word, Holmes. As a physician I should have noticed that. And rabbits and mules. I never thought of observing the animals in the camp to determine facts about the inhabitants."

"It was simple to tell Magdalya about the bad axle on her wagon due to the wagon wheel marks left in the soft, muddy ground. The trail to where she was parked was not straight but rather a wobbly set of tracks. Every two feet the indentation in the ground was deeper than the next foot was, signifying that the weight was not evenly distributed on its axle."

"Remarkable," I applauded. "And the lack of permission to be staying there?"

"The Edmonds are out of the country, Watson, on their annual sojourn to Australia to escape our winter season. Again, a police report from two months ago showed a request from Lord Edmond to have a constable periodically check the manor. Since Lord Edmond's has been gone eight weeks and the gypsies were evicted from Charwick's woods six weeks ago, I knew right away that the gypsy boss was lying. They never received permission to camp there."

"You never cease to amaze me, Holmes," I chuckled. "Spotting things in a dark camp and drawing from police reports to win over the old crone. I dare say you had her convinced that you were as much of a fortune teller as she claimed to be."

"Watson, how do you know that I am not a soothsayer?" That familiar grin spread across my friend's thin lips. "Today we have unearthed more questions than answers. I would suggest that tomorrow we begin to put solutions to these riddles."

❁❁❁

As I awoke Friday morning, I was startled to hear Holmes talking to someone as I rounded the corner to our sitting room for breakfast. The gentleman's back was to me, but the large, rounded shape was unmistakable as was the booming tone even when Mycroft Holmes was speaking softly. I hadn't heard him come in, but as Holmes often said, he most assuredly has a key to every door in London.

"Well," Holmes said impatiently to his brother, "go away. I do not have time for you now. The answer to whatever you are going to ask me is 'no.'"

"Well that's typical," Mycroft retorted. "The question was do you have any leads on the death of Vice Admiral Charwick?"

I forgot how exhilarating the dance was between Holmes and his older brother.

"Good morning, Doctor Watson." Mycroft acknowleded me with a nod of his large head.

"If people keep bursting in here early in the morning, we might as well open a guest house," my friend snarled, snapping his newspaper in half at arm's length. "Don't you have a government to overthrow somewhere, Mycroft?"

"You know I have a special interest in the Admiralty in my official position." Mycroft looked down to check the time on his pocket watch. "I have a meeting at Whitehall in one hour. They are very concerned about losing one of their most revered, retired vice admirals to such a savage death. I haven't got time to waste."

"Yet you excel in wasting mine," Holmes replied barely looking up from his paper.

"The case, my dear brother. What about the case? You are consulting on it," Mycroft stated in his all-knowing tone. "Does that mean you intend to solve it and apprehend the killer or sit around playing with your fiddle? Now it's in all the papers. The ineffectiveness of our society to protect our admiralty. Bold headlines in the liberal press about Vice Admiral Charwick's death saying that we cannot even safeguard Britain's greatest heroes."

Holmes rolled his eyes. "Obviously, the Vice Admiral's rather undistinguished career has been substantially enhanced by the press as well."

"Whatever," Mycroft sighed. "That is of less importance than the vulgar penny press, which has been circulating the ridiculous story about the Charwick curse." He paused and shook his head. "Scandalous headlines and macabre ghoulish narratives. Ancient banes and the ghastly ghosts of Charwick Manor. My dear brother, if you can't find the actual killer, surely you can hunt down and capture a ghost. Whitehall does not fancy the newspapers spreading reports across the country and all over Europe about the Admiralty having its men assassinated by apparitions. Makes us look weak."

"I thought you controlled all the newspapers in London, Mycroft."

"Don't be daft, Sherlock. I only control half of them. So what can I share with Whitehall?"

Sherlock Holmes folded the newspaper violently on his lap." I am sure that I know more about the case than Scotland Yard does. And Scotland Yard knows more about the case than the Royal Naval investigators. So that means that they know the least about the case. Those Naval-trained incompetents can no sooner solve this case than they can juggle."

"You are so right, Sherlock. Jugglers and ghosts." Mycroft shifted his considerable weight. "The papers are turning this into a circus. And what are you going to do about it?"

Holmes looked pensive for a moment, and his voice lowered dramatically. "A circus. Or maybe acrobats or tumblers."

He began to methodically scan the *Daily News* in his hands, his head bobbing up and down each column and then turning the pages in rapid succession. "Quickly, Watson get me yesterday's *Morning Post.*"

As he looked up, he seemed surprised to see Mycroft still sitting there.

"What are you still doing here? Can't you see that I have a task at hand? Now, please show yourself out the same way you came in so I might get on with my work."

"I'll expect to hear from you soon, brother," Mycroft said, getting in the last word as he lifted his substantial bulk from the chair. "Good day, Doctor Watson," he nodded to me as he left the room.

I was sure the purpose of Mycroft's visit was to prod his younger sibling. The rivalry between the two of them was only overshadowed by the secret respect and esteem they held for one another. I suspected that Holmes was quick to brusquely dismiss his brother partially because he did not have any idea who the murderer was, or how he had gotten in and out of the locked room. But judging by the renewed fervor with which my companion was now tearing through the newspapers, I surmised that something had piqued his interest. Holmes discarded the *Daily Chronicle* and quickly opened the *Morning Post*.

"Yes," he said underneath his breath, "I saw it over the past several weeks. Two columns wide, four inches deep, yet hardly worth my notice." He continued to rifle through the pages until, "Ah, yes, there it is. The Maximus Backstrom Traveling Circus of Wonderment. Their advertisement says that they have visited several large cities and towns before their arrival here in London. This circus has been here for over four weeks. They have just one engagement left Saturday night."

Holmes mumbled quickly through the advertisement. "'Maximus Backstrom A Circus of Wonderment for the Better Accommodation of Ladies and Gentlemen. Thursday and Saturday only. Unparallel Horsemanship, Trained Dogs, Tumblers, Acrobats, Exotic Animals, Camels, Ostriches, Zebras...'"

He dropped the rest of the newspaper on the floor, adding to the pile in front of him, and moved swiftly to his writing desk holding the half folded page with the circus advertisement. He grabbed a pencil and pushed several pieces of paper off the desk until he found a blank sheet. He rapidly began to write names and dates.

"Watson, dear fellow, as I am still in my dressing gown and you are already dressed, might I trouble you for a shilling?"

"Certainly," I replied. Our finances were so intermingled that we might as well have been an old, married couple. "Here you go," I tossed him the coin.

Holmes addressed an envelope to Lestrade, placed the letter in it and sealed it. "It is for the messenger to assure that this gets where I intend with all haste."

I was slightly stunned. "But a messenger service only costs a sixpence. I always thought you a frugal man," I said with a jovial hint in my voice.

"I am going down to the street to flag down one of my Irregulars and entrust this letter to him."

"A shilling. For a letter delivery. To one of those street urchins. You know how I dislike it when you involve those wretched, little pickpockets, Holmes."

"And why is that, my good man?"

"They are most unsavory characters. How can you trust them so implicitly? There is no telling what a street waif will do with that amount of money."

"Watson, you would rather I send for a messenger service and pay him to deliver my urgent missive in his own sweet time. And if I were to pay a messenger two six pence to expedite my request where do you think he will go? Directly to Scotland Yard, or stop off at the nearest pub and buy himself a pint or two? Surely you must suspect that almost every messenger reads every letter that is entrusted to him, no matter what their service claims. And if he has read the letter and stopped off at a pub, drunken men have a nasty habit of talking, do they not?"

"Well, I do suppose..."

"On the other hand," he continued, "my Irregulars mostly know only the basics of the Queen's English. They have little interest in the contents of the letter. And even if they would disobey me, open the missive, and read it, they would have no one with whom to share its content with except the other street urchins. Our business is in good hands, I assure you."

Holmes had moved over to the fireplace and picked up his cherry-wood pipe. From the mantle he fondled his Persian slipper filled with shag tobacco and bounced it in his hand. Clenching the pipe between his teeth he made his way to the landing. "By the way, Watson, on Saturday night we are going to the circus. We shan't want to miss their last performance. Tell Inspector Lestrade that he should join us."

This last line left me somewhat mystified.

Holmes went downstairs and out to the street. When he returned, he began to search the drawing room for what he liked to refer to as "tools of his trade."

After he had gathered up various items and placed them in a leather case, he turned to me. "I shall get dressed and be with you shortly. We will need a cab for one last trip to Charwick manor."

The rest of the morning was spent at the Charwick manor where my friend carefully measured the exact length of the steep angle from the ditch up to the small stone balcony. He used a ball of twine, carefully knotted to designate every yard. Then he went up to the balcony and dropped the ball of twine down to me as I stood in the geraniums directly against the estate's sheer outer wall. Tossing his end of the string down to me, he asked me to count out the length from his end to mine.

Later, inside the study, he stood for ten minutes staring at the door, the velveteen club chair to its right and the portrait of the Royal Naval Academy that hung above the chair. Of course, in their usual military precision, the naval attendants had reset the large, over-stuffed wing-backed chair where the murder took place to its upright position after retrieving the vice admiral's body.

Upon returning to Baker Street, we ate a light lunch. Holmes barely touched his as he could not wait to finish and then move over to his make-up table in the corner of the room. Even after all these years, it was astounding how he could change his hawk-like nose into a bulbous, red snout. A nasty jagged scar ran like one of London's back alleys from his left eye down to his chin. Heavy, coarse eyebrows sprouted like weeds above both eyes. A painful-looking mouth appliance was inserted to change the shape of his lips and jaw and give him crooked, yellow teeth. Finally, a dirty brown wig of long, ratty hair was applied. He was done with this complete transformation in less than thirty minutes. He then went to a second small closet where he kept his costumes and disguises and chose a tattered tweed vest, pants and a short, well-worn town coat with two deep front pockets and a torn left breast pocket.

"Going out, are we?" I asked when he was finished.

"Not 'we,' Watson." He opened his desk drawer and withdrew his small pistol, putting it in the pocket of his coat. "This is a solitary assignment."

"Just where are you going, man, that you need a gun? Should I join you?"

"Thank you for the offer. But you would not quite fit in with the den of thieves with whom I wish to make inquiries. Old Scar Face Teddy here has a reputation amongst the London underworld."

"But what do you hope to accomplish?"

"Elimination of possibilities, Watson. Remember our credo: Eliminate the impossible, and whatever remains, no matter how implausible, must be the truth."

He shoved both hands into each pocket and pulled forth a handful of pence from one and tupence and six pence from the other. I knew that a few sterling were safe on the inside of his vest pocket. It was a trick that

Holmes had taught me years ago for when you want to show your wealth to a potential mark. You can choose how much you wish them to think you have by emptying whatever pocket is most apropos, as he did back at the gypsy camp.

After watching him go out, I got my medical bag and made the rounds to several patients I'd been neglecting of late. When I returned, it was evening and I heard my friend shuffling around our drawing room. He had most of his make-up off and was applying cream to his face.

"And how went the hunt?"

"Both good and bad," he replied. "Bad in the fact that I did not stumble upon the Charwick medals being sold on the black market, which would have solved the case right there and then. This means that the medals are likely still with the murderer waiting to be melted down. Good that none of the regular sources seems to know who pulled off the heist, which indicates it was not one of our local cut throats. It also means since nothing else was stolen but money and the copper and silver medals, the culprit does not know whom to approach in London. Thus, we are not looking for a home grown thief, Watson.

"Also very good in that I now know who has the three sterling silver monogrammed tea sets that were stolen from the German Embassy last month. Remind me to alert Mycroft. We may help avert an international incident and improve relations between our two nations. Who knows, it might prevent a future war."

Holmes put on his purple dressing gown, went over to his favorite chair by the window and reached down for his violin and bow. He began with "The Volga Boatman," a clear sign that the detective was now deep in thought about the case. I closed the door quietly behind me and left for my bed chamber. Tomorrow held the promise of new discoveries.

❊❊❊

Saturday morning began as all of our mornings did. But Holmes didn't eat, as was his custom when he was preoccupied with a case. It gave him more time to read all of the London morning papers plus several of yesterday's papers from France and Germany. Holmes seemed anxious as he tore through the *Morning Post*; almost as if he needed justification for getting out of bed that early in the morning. Finally he paused, folded the newspaper vertically and then horizontally to stare at what he had been searching for. He dropped that page to the floor and then went back to perusing the news of the day and sipping his tea.

Later, after Mrs. Hudson had cleared away the breakfast tray, my friend immediately sank into his favorite chair by the window, placed his elbow on the arm rest, and his chin in his right hand. I knew that he would be in deep thought for hours, not aware or requiring my presence. So I excused myself under my breath, went back to my room and retrieved my medical bag. I had to make a few more of the rounds to my homebound patients.

I returned that afternoon and heard my friend rummaging around in his quarters getting prepared for our night at the circus. I must admit that I could come up with no plausible reason that we would be spending our evening in northwest London at such an event. Traveling circuses have become all the rage for an evening's entertainment, but we were in the middle of a murder investigation.

Holmes came out of his room wearing his gray wool Coburn great coat with its black collar and attached cowl. He was prepared for the slight September chill in the night air.

"Let me change into my black wool frock coat for warmth," I said as I always liked the way the large silver buttons on the front and sleeve gave it a military look. Plus its large front flap pockets were perfect for my service revolver.

Lestrade pulled up in front of 221b Baker Street almost exactly at five pm. We joined him in the first carriage which was followed by three other police carriages holding four coppers each.

"Inspector," Holmes greeted our Scotland Yard host. "Your men have been instructed to stop and wait a half mile from the circus and not join us until the performance has ended, correct?"

"Yes. And I must be crazy to let you talk me into this ridiculous scheme. Assigning twelve officers to sit in the woods up the road from a circus while we're inside watching it." Lestrade's voice was a mixture of agitation and trepidation. "I had a personal visit yesterday afternoon from the Assistant Secretary of State for Home Affairs from the Home Office. His lordship wanted to know why the case has not been solved and why no one was in custody for a murder 'most heinous' ... his exact words."

"Did you tell him you were pursuing the Charwick Ghost?" Holmes flashed one of his crooked smiles.

"You might think this is funny, Mr. Sherlock Holmes, but if something isn't done soon my next assignment will be guarding the docks down in the east end." Lestrade looked like a petulant child. He removed a folder from his coat pocket and handed it across the coach to Holmes.

"And here is something else I don't understand. Why I'm wasting my precious time sending telegrams to other cities' police departments asking about burglaries in their jurisdictions? There's only one crime that I am concerned about, and that's Vice Admiral Charwick's death last Tuesday night."

Holmes tore into the file, shuffling telegrams to put them in the proper order. Then he reached into the breast pocket of his great coat and withdrew a folded two-column piece of the morning newspaper which he unfolded and placed next to the telegrams. He had to hold the folder close to his face to read the small print in the shifting light.

Seeing the detective's face shielded from him, Lestrade knew that Holmes had not heard a word the man had said. The chief Inspector was not to be ignored. "Why the bloody hell are we going to a circus?"

"Everything will become clear shortly, Inspector." He went back to his comparisons. "Including the explanation of the Charwick Ghost."

I chimed in. "As reluctant as I am to admit that I might possibly believe in spirits and apparitions, I have to state that I have seen things in my lifetime that defy rational description. Things on the battlefield. Things on the operating table. Places in this world that send unexplained shivers down a man's spine for no apparent reason. It seems that the more we explore the darkest regions of the globe and the more we find out about the world's strange religions, the same strong belief in the afterlife and spirits of the dead seems to be an unavoidable part of the human condition. Perhaps ghosts are part of our human condition also."

"Nonsense, Watson. There is a logical explanation for everything. Things can happen by coincidence or chance that makes it seem as if they were influenced by supernatural happenstance. We're dealing with a very human killer or killers here."

"I only hope we catch him soon," Lestrade said. "I don't want to be the one who has to go to the Admiralty and say I arrested a ghost for the vice admiral's murder." The Inspector was calmer now and quite pleased with himself for his little jest. It was greeted with total silence. "Anyhow, I'm pegging that foppish nephew Charles as the murderer. Or at least the brains behind it all."

"Hardly, Inspector," my friend said, "that man doesn't have the sense to come in out of the rain."

Lestrade leaned forward. "See here now. After I interrogated him, he admitted he had over eighty pounds in gambling debts. They beat him badly a year ago as an incentive to make faster payments. He must have lifted a few items from his uncle's estate, because he said he got his debt down to thirty pounds, before he managed to lose more and bring it back up to around eighty again. Stealing all that pension money from his uncle would settle his current debt, and if he is mentioned in the vice admiral's will, he will have gained more money to lose in the future. And for all the times that he was over at the manor, he could have stolen the house keys."

"My dear fellow," Holmes began, "if he'd stolen the keys, why would he need to pry open the second floor balcony window from the outside? And how did he get into a locked study to force open the vice admiral's safe?"

"Perhaps he had help."

Holmes shook his head. "If the wastrel nephew had accomplices, then, as I stated before, he would have not left that room alive. You may be able to prosecute him for petty theft from his past visits to his uncle's home, but not for murder."

Holmes handed the file back to Lestrade. "Keep this close to your heart. I suspect that we shall be needing it before the night is through."

"Then it must be the gypsies," I offered as our carriage clattered along.

"Gypsies," Lestrade yelled as if I had just told him that Father Christmas was also a suspect. "What gypsies?"

"Thank you, Watson." the detective said wryly. "Inspector, we came across a band of vagabonds next to the woods. They had been camping and hunting on Vice Admiral Charwick's property for some time before he had them forcibly removed by the district constables a few weeks ago."

"Gypsies," Lestrade was practically sputtering, "And they held a grudge and probably came back and robbed and murdered him? You're just telling me now? That's fine kettle of fish. You're supposed to help me solve this case."

"Which is what I am doing now."

"Oh," I could not resist adding, "did we mention that during our séance with the gypsy fortune teller she told us about strange lights, giants and ghost horses in the Charwick woods?"

"Where are these gypsies," the Inspector demanded, not finding any humor in the situation. "We must arrest them immediately before they uproot and disappear."

"Lestrade," Holmes voice was calming as if speaking to a distraught child. "Let me assure you that they had nothing to do with the Charwick murder."

The Inspector's lower lip protruded, as if he'd sucked a sour lemon.

"Fear not, Inspector," Holmes soothed. "Rest assured that tonight we'll put the case to rest."

For the remainder of the trip, the detective sat in silence while I filled

"Keep this close to your heart. I suspect that we shall be needing it..."

Lestrade in on our visit to the vagabond encampment. The Inspector, of course, questioned the veracity of the tale, with its strange phantoms and ghost horses.

A short time later we pulled up to a large clearing in a field with a huge canvas tent surrounded by kerosene lanterns. All of the carriages, wagons, and buggies were parked behind the tent and everyone walked around to the opposite side of the big top. There a small boardwalk about five-feet wide and thirty-feet long funneled the crowd to the entrance where the tiny box office sat. The first sign of the circus to greet us was the sound of a band playing. It was only a few instruments, but its cacophonous attempts at setting a circus mood were well-intentioned.

There were three featured acts on the raised platform, each with their own bizarrely painted canvas banners behind them. The first was a lady of enormous girth and size. Her legs resembled the stumps of an African elephant. She sat on three stools which were swallowed up by her overhanging pantaloons. *Zelda, the Fat Lady,* read the words behind her, barely visible because of her size. The second performer was a huge, barrel-chested man with dark curly hair and beard wearing one piece long underwear with a leopard-skin costume over it. He wore a matching thick leather belt and sandals. His muscles bulged as he flexed mightily for the passersby. The gaudily-painted banner behind him proclaimed *Korko the Mighty—The World's Strongest Man.* The illustration showed him lifting a heavy barbell over his head. Lastly was *Bersei the Contortionist*, performing on the final stage. The small fellow was folding himself up like a pretzel, his legs behind his head, his arms coming out from behind his thighs and then tucked under his ankles. It was almost too painful to observe the human torso being bent into such positions.

We queued up in the line that funneled everyone to the ticket booth. Since the column was moving slowly, Holmes announced," Watson, would you care to accompany me on a short walk. Inspector, would you mind to stay in line and secure our tickets? Get tickets for the red painted seats nearest the ring. I am sure that Scotland Yard can afford them."

I could almost see the steam rising off Lestrade's bowler hat at the detective's request, as he clearly thought this entire evening was a colossal waste of time and man power. Holmes stepped out of the line and I followed, quickly tipping my hat to the Inspector out of courtesy. We made our way back past the fat lady's stage and I followed my friend behind the set of stages. The light was cut in half from the kerosene lamps in the shadows. Holmes was as nimble as a cat, picking his way behind the ropes and planks that supported the sets of stages. I carefully shuffled my way using my walking stick to tap the ground in front of me, following him as closely as possible. I was glad that Holmes allowed me to bring my service revolver. Sneaking around behind the scenes at a circus, surrounded by scurrilous circus folks, already put us in a dangerous situation.

When he reached the actual circus tent he stopped and knelt, inspecting the wooden stakes that held the thick ropes keeping the big tent taunt and secure. He scooped up dirt and hay that lay scattered around the outer tent area.

"Let's rejoin the Inspector," he said wiping his hands clean and standing up. "The show is about to begin."

We pushed through the queue to rejoin Lestrade who was waiting at the main entrance of the tent. "Did you want me to get you some peanuts also?" the Inspector asked sarcastically as he handed us our tickets.

"A capital suggestion," Holmes replied. "They may come in handy."

The inside of the large canvas tent was like a poor man's cathedral. A vaulted ceiling supported by a huge circular pole. It had a solemn half-lit atmosphere with unexpected smells. It was a strikingly beautiful scene despite the flickering darkness. Its vestibule was a circular arena seating made of wooden planks, painted red for the most expensive, closest seats and white-washed for the cheaper seats. There was an almost unworldly lighting thrown out by the dozens of kerosene lanterns hanging off the other support poles. The main stage was an arena encircled by bales of hay arranged in an oval pattern to form a large center.

Holmes made his way to the gallery of red seats close to the ring. I tried to get as comfortable as possible on the wooden plank while the Inspector just slumped forward in his seat. Holmes sat erect, perfect posture, his deep set eyes observing every aspect of the scene.

Soon the tent filled up and everyone was being treated to the opening strains of the circus band playing a joyous march. I had not noticed that the small band was sequestered in the bottom row seats opposite the main entrance partially hidden by the shadows. That told me that some of the acts would be entering and exiting from there and not clogging up the main entrance all the time.

The ring master came prancing in, high-stepping like a Prussian military drill team leader wearing the traditional black top hat, red, double-breasted jacket and carried a huge megaphone.

"Ladies and Gentlemen," he proclaimed. "Welcome to the Maximus Backstrom Traveling Circus of Wonderment."

With that, the grand march began with the performers entering from the secondary entrance through the ring door curtains and paraded three times around the center. First were three large white poodles, dressed in ballerina costumes, walking on their hind legs.

Holmes leaned over to my ear and said, "Dog acts or buffers are all the rage in circuses now."

I was amazed at his knowledge of the circus, as it had been several years since I had frequented even a penny gaff cheap circus. I admired the dancing poodles as they completed their three rotations. Next came the jugglers, keeping wooden pins spinning in the air like whirling dervishes. I was surprised to see a unicyclist come wobbling in over the uneven ground. He was at least five feet off the ground, see-sawing back and forth and spinning from side to side to keep his balance.

He was followed by the huge strongman and a horde of acrobats doing cartwheels, tossing one performer to the other high in the air, and doing backward handspring flic flacs. One was spinning a large hoop with a stick making it seem to defy gravity. Then the strange contortionist appeared.

He had his legs folded behind his shoulders and was walking only on his hands. Lastly came the comic tramps in bright leotards and flouncy outfits, with painted noses, and skull wigs with patches of absurdly colored hair.

Then from the far side of the tent entered a camel, a rather shabby looking ostrich, and two magnificent horses with their riders standing astride their mount's backs. I looked closer and saw that these were not regular horses, but rather a pair of African zebras, an animal not often seen outside the London Zoo.

As the last of the animals circled the ring and made their exit, the tent-men began lowering the kerosene lanterns. Only the center ring was well-lit. The drums of the circus band began to pound out what passed for a jungle rhythm. The crowd strained to adjust to the loss of luminescence as the ring master raised his megaphone.

"We are proud to have in our possession one of the most horrific, perilous, vile beasts that God himself ever created. He once ruled over hundreds of miles of fierce jungle terrain in the heart of the Dark Continent, Africa."

Fierce growls emanated from the far entrance. I leaned forward on my cane and could observe a huge megaphone mounted on a small wagon just inside the entrance. But it was the first time that I noticed that the opening had now been covered by twigs, branches, and vines forming a canopy of sorts. The bellowing became louder.

"Ladies and gentlemen, without further ado, I present to you, Gigantor."

In the flickering darkness, a hairy creature came galloping out of the entrance. From my seat I could make out the matted hair, short stubby hind legs, rounded belly, bare black circles on its chest, and elongated forearms.

The crowd screamed as one at the tableau unfolding before them. It appeared to be a huge ape. The gorilla was accompanied by a roustabout who was virtually chasing the wild beast from behind trying vainly to hold onto the leather leash around its neck. The primate stopped once it got a ways into the ring and raised itself up, flailing its arms wildly over its head and pounding its chest with savage fury. This caused the crowd to scream even louder. Each ferocious beat of its chest was accompanied by the beat of the big bass drum.

The ape then bolted towards the front row where we were seated. My first instinct, as I recoiled, was to slip my hand into my pocket and secure my service revolver. I glanced over at Inspector Lestrade who was fumbling with his right hand inside his coat pocket trying to draw his police pistol. Holmes calmly reached down, grabbed both of our wrists in his surprisingly strong grip, and shook his head. He sat unmoved as everyone else around us shrieked in terror and began to scramble backwards up the bleachers to preserve their lives.

The gorilla stopped in front of us and gave out a muffled howl that was quickly drowned out by the loud screaming and pounding drums echoing around the tent. Then the creature spun, flinging the roustabout to the ground and raced unimpeded towards the opposite side of the ring. The crowd on the far side screamed bloody murder as the beast approached them.

When it reached the center of the ring it suddenly stopped. Around the big top several tent men were slowly raising the lights, bringing the interior back to where it was originally lit. When the lights were on full, the roustabout stepped up to the creature and unfastened the plaster head piece with the frozen snarl revealing a sweat-soaked performer underneath.

The tent filled with applause and cheering.

As I applauded, I looked over to my companion and saw that he was not clapping. "Didn't you enjoy that, Holmes?"

"Sorry, old boy. Why any sane person would pay money to sit on a bench, have the lights dimmed, only to be scared half out of their wits is beyond me. Besides, it was obviously a ruse from the beginning."

Suddenly the jungle rhythm began again in the background.

"Do not despair, fair ladies and good gentlemen," the ring master said as the applause died. "We do have a real ape here tonight." The drums grew stronger. "He was brought to us by a British big-game hunter on a great and dangerous safari." The drums now grew to a steady crescendo.

I believe that the clarity of vision and the pounding savage drum beat increased the crowd's anticipation.

"Ladies and gentlemen, may I present ..." he paused for dramatic effect. Every eye was on the shrouded canopy entrance. The air was pierced with menacing roars echoing through the huge megaphone. Several ladies and children began screaming. The cacophony of drums, fierce howls and screams now all blended together. "Gargantua the Great," the ring master bellowed.

Suddenly from the far end of the ring, a clown came running out in green tights with red stripes and yellow polka dots. One could hardly see the thin leash he held. On the end of the strap was a small spider monkey wearing a tiny top hat racing alongside him on its hind legs.

As one, the audience gave an audible sigh of relief and burst into applause. When the clown reached the center ring, the tiny monkey jumped up and grabbed the ring master's coat tails. It climbed his red coat and stood on his shoulder. Then the monkey grabbed the master of ceremonies top hat and threw it down to the ground. The audience was beside itself with laughter.

Lestrade leaned over to me and shouted over the ovation, "Now that's what I call entertainment."

The crowd settled back in and the show began. Every circus had an exquisite equestrian act, and Maximus Backstrom Traveling Circus of Wonderment did not disappoint. All during the acts, my friend sat rigid, following each movement, taking in every motion. Then he leaned forward slightly when the strongman came out. He was a mountain of a man, burly and bulky who must have weighed at least thirty stone. Holmes watched intently as Korko bent an iron bar around his bulging shoulders. Then the strongman gripped the bar in his two hands and straightened it.

"It'd take three pair of duffies to hold that big lout," Lestrade said.

"I'm sure you could restrain him with your voice of authority, Inspector," Holmes replied.

I saw that Holmes sat slightly back when the comic tramps entered next. They seemed beneath his notice. The clowns were followed by the troupe of Albanian acrobats. Most of them were approximately five-foot tall, thin but with incredible balance and strength. After throwing each other through the air, somersaulting, and landing on each other's shoulders, they ended with a human pyramid formed with three bodies as a base, then two acrobats. Finally they flung the last performer sky high only to have him land perfectly on top of the pyramid. It was a tremendous feat of dexterity.

I was not as impressed with the contortionist. And I could see the Chief Inspector actually turn his head away as the performer twisted himself into shapes that should cause the human torso to shatter and break. But my medical training allowed me to understand how certain joints in exceptional people could be flexible enough and allow for the slippage to contort oneself into seemingly impossible positions.

The ring master announced the grand finale, the return of the parade of exotic animals joined by the clowns to end the evening on a high note.

"Thank you, one and all, for blessing us with your company," the ring master said. "I hope that you appreciated the wonderments you witnessed here tonight and will tell all your friends about us the next time we visit London. I wish you all a good evening."

The crowd gave the performers a standing ovation and slowly began to drift towards the exit.

"I would suggest that you send your undercover man stationed outside the front entrance to summon your force now, Inspector," Holmes said. "They should arrive by the time the audience has left and we will have the tent and its performers to ourselves."

"Eh?" Lestrade said. "But what does any of this have to do with the Charwick murder?"

"All shall be revealed shortly."

Within ten minutes the tent had emptied out except for Lestrade, Holmes and myself. The circus folk were gathered by the front entrance, puzzled by the sudden arrival of several police wagons. If there was one thing that Chief Inspector Lestrade was good at, it was taking charge of a scene. He put all the performers in the center of the ring and had his men encircle them.

"I'm Inspector Lestrade of Scotland Yard," he said, using the megaphone he'd taken from the ringmaster. "And this here is Mr. Sherlock Holmes. We've got a few questions to ask you."

"What's this about," the ring master protested. "We got all the permits and paid all the proper fees. Tonight's our last performance in London. We have to break down the tent and move on to Hertford."

"Well, we shan't be long," Holmes said. "I'm glad that you've already started packing. Searching through clutter is such a long, messy process."

"This is outrageous," the ringmaster said.

"This better be good, Holmes," Lestrade said as he walked past the detective.

"Let me explain it this way," Holmes began. "We had a murder most foul a few nights ago. A naval man was killed during the robbery of his home. The main suspect was purported to be a ghost who can pass through walls and locked doors."

The group of circus people remained silent.

"We eliminated household staff, forthwith," Holmes continued. "As we did with the wayward nephew and a band of gypsies." He paused to glance at Lestrade, "So now who has all the skills to perpetrate this impossible crime? There was no visible forced entry into the house except for the broken latch on an inaccessible second story balcony window. There was no way into the bolted study. No footprints or muddy tracks were found on any carpet. A safe was torn from the wall." The detective turned and began to stroll in front of the assembled troupe.

"I did find a small piece of discolored straw on the balcony and two more pieces down below it on a steep incline. Since the vice admiral has no barn or coup on his manor, these things were completely out of place and must have been brought to the manor. I must admit that I was stumped for a time."

Holmes paused again and looked around at the tent.

"It was then that I recalled seeing the advertisement for your circus in the newspaper." The detective stopped in front of the ring master. "Reading about your amazing performers and their acts set off a scenario in my mind. What could be a possible solution? All the observations that I had made at the crime scene, that were disjointed, now fell into place. The ground below the balcony was too high and too steep for any ladder." Holmes now walked slowly down to face the acrobats. "But you don't need a ladder, if you could form a human pyramid to reach the second story balcony. It was on the balcony where I found two pieces of straw, obviously dislodged from the perpetrator's clothing. It matched the other piece when he removed his shoes after he punched in the old latch on the window. His silk slippers kept the carpet clean. But one other piece of straw was most likely brushed from a pant leg. Once he gained entry to the house, he walked downstairs and let his accomplices in, who also changed their footwear, leaving their muddy shoes on the outside entrance."

"But how did they know when to hit the house, Holmes?" Lestrade asked.

"They have been in London for four weeks, which," Holmes turned back to the ring master, "was plenty of time to search out and spy on the rich homes in the west end that would be easy targets. The acrobats and the strongman…the fairies and a giant creeping through the woods late at night, as the gypsy boy observed. Through their clandestine reconnoitering, they knew that Vice Admiral Charwick's manor would be empty Tuesday night because they observed he always gave his staff the night off when he attended the Royal Navy Club. Unfortunately for the vice admiral, he stayed home that evening." Holmes turned to the ring master. "I am glad, sir, that in your public notice you featured your prize zebra and the names of your star performers which gave me a clue to their nationalities. After talking to the gypsies in the woods, they told me about hearing a strange tongue similar to theirs. It was the Albanian acrobats on their scouting mission of west end manors." He gestured toward the exit.

"And the ghost horses drawing the wagon…the ones that disappeared ... was nothing more than the black and white stripes of the zebras, shining in the moonlight."

The small acrobats began to shuffle their feet and anxiously look around.

"Don't nobody think about making any funny moves," Lestrade warned. "My bulls will beat you down if you try anything stupid." All of the coppers present had their billy clubs in their hands.

Holmes walked to the end of the group where he stood in front of Bersei, the contortionist. Holmes towered over the skinny, five-foot performer, so he bent slightly at the waist.

"And you, you are the Charwick Ghost," he announced. "I am sure that you were all instructed to only steal certain items that could be easily fenced at your next stop. Simple items such as money or medals. Where else would they be stored but in the study? But you found the study locked. From the inside. Not a problem for someone nimble enough to slip through the transom, which was the only other way into the study. You were probably hoisted up by the strongman."

The acrobat's furtive glances toward the ground were enough to confirm Holmes's statement.

"But what you didn't expect to see was the vice admiral sleeping in his chair. Now, silence was part of your entrance. You could not simply drop to the floor. So you managed to contort your body so that you hung off the bottom of the transom and swung yourself to your right, hooking the top of the velveteen club chair next to the door to lower yourself down quietly. But your weight and force moved the chair from its original position. The legs of the chair were not in the same carpet indentations that they usually were. Its indentations in the carpet were slightly off. That is also why the painting of the Royal Naval Academy is askew. You brushed it either on your way in or on your way out. It was the only picture in the manor that was off kilter. Once safely inside, you quietly unbolted the door for your fellows."

Holmes walked to the center of the group and stopped in front of the strongman, who towered over the detective and was twice his bulk. Holmes raised himself up to his full height. "I'm sure that you thought the blow to the head would merely render him unconscious. The mallet you brought seemed too heavy-handed to use on the old vice admiral. So you chose to hit him with the wooden stake for prying open any safe or strongbox that you might find. That's where those slivers in his temple came from. You also used it to break into the wall safe, leaving several more splinters." Holmes gestured over his shoulder. "The wood is identical to those tent stakes."

Holmes sighed, and then made a shrugging gesture. "I would hope that you did not intentionally try to kill the vice admiral, but murder is murder. You are responsible. After you hit him so hard, you then realized that you had killed him so you decided to tip his chair over to make it look like an accident."

The huge man cocked his right arm and flung a round house punch at the detective. But Holmes was quicker. He dropped down into a crouching position in an instant.

"Watson. Cane!" he shouted.

Without hesitation, I flipped my walking stick forward. It flew forward horizontally. Holmes caught it about one quarter of the way down. Like a viper, he drew the cane back and then lashed out, smashing the silver tip into the strongman's knee. The giant grunted in pain and dropped to the ground like a tree felled in the forest.

An officer rushed over and clapped a pair of handcuffs on the writhing giant.

"Suddenly realizing that you now had a murder on your hands, you needed a new plan," Holmes said, righting himself and brushing off his coat. "You decided to confound the authorities by making it a locked door mystery. After the safe was cleared out, everyone left and the contortionist bolted the study door from the inside leaving the same way that he entered: up through the transom, leaving the club chair slightly turned and the picture twisted. One of the acrobats then locked your compatriots out after they left by the front door with their plunder. He then returned to the balcony and climbed down the human pyramid." Holmes turned to Lestrade. "Inspector, I'm sure that you'll find the proceeds, most particularly the admiral's medals, within these circus wagons."

Lestrade dispatched two of his men to begin the search.

"I believe as well," Holmes said, "that you have a folder in your pocket with pertinent information that you might like to share now."

"Eh?" Lestrade asked.

Holmes patted the Inspector's coat pocket.

"Acting on a hunch, Inspector Lestrade sent several telegrams to the authorities in areas in which the circus has played in for the past few months. As he suspected, every one of them reported that one to three estates in their district had been burglarized in unusual and bizarre manners."

Lestrade's face twitched and he puffed out his chest. "All in a day's work." The chief Inspector turned to Holmes and said under his breath, "That's all these telegrams, right?"

"Very well done, Inspector," Holmes smiled. "Scotland Yard has come through once again."

As if on cue, two of the constables who had been searching the wagons approached Lestrade with a box containing the medals of Admiral Pouncy Charwick and Vice Admiral Harington Charwick.

"And here's my proof," the Chief Inspector said tilting the open box to the crestfallen circus troupe.

With that, Holmes stepped back and opened his clenched right fist, and dropped a handful of discolored straw.

The End

The Story Behind The Story

Now that I had said 'yes' to Ron Fortier, what case would be worthy of the great sleuth? A dozen plots, since there are only a dozen plots available to writers, raced through my head. So, in my usual insanity I chose the hardest one—a locked room murder. The first three weeks were spent trying to figure out how it was done and immersing myself in research: actual Victorian newspapers; hansom and clarence cabs; barns and byres; shillings and tupence; the history of Scotland Yard; the roads to the affluent estates that were nestled in the woods west of London, and real Victorian era circuses.

Then a solution hit me to the locked room. I swear it came late at night and it was Holmes who whispered it in my ear. I was ready to start.

If I was going to be allowed to visit the decade of the world's greatest consulting detective, then I wanted to experience as much of it as I could. The comradeship between Holmes and Watson, clever dialogue between the detective and Lestrade, the duel of wits between Mycroft and his younger brother, Holmes venturing out in disguise, the Baker Street Irregulars, and the violin.

Like every good mystery, there are red herrings: the butler, the nephew, the gypsies, and the Charwick Ghost. In writing the story, I chose to have Holmes eliminate them as they came up. He dismissed possible guilty parties which continuously left himself with no murder suspects. There were very few disjointed clues and no large picture presenting itself. This case must have weighed heavily on the great detective's mind.

But, as only Sherlock Holmes can do, he takes his one small physical clue and works it until the very end.

Thank you to Susan for allowing me a few months to indulge myself in a fantastic world. To Michael A. Black for ideas, edits, encouragement, and a lifetime of friendship. To Carl Wayne Ensminger, the true 21st century Sherlock Holmes. To Ron Fortier, editor of Airship 27 Productions, for keeping the flame alive. And to Sherlock Holmes, who shall live forever.

❁❁❁

Raymond Louis James Lovato loves writing pulp fiction with his lifelong friend author Michael A. Black. Ray also enjoys traveling the world with his lovely wife, Susan. Years ago, on a five-hour flight to Sint Maartin, he was inspired to draft an homage to Doc Savage, the Man of Bronze. After presenting the first chapter as a serial birthday gift to his best friend, the Adventures of Doc Atlas was born. Black wrote the first Doc Atlas novel, A MELODY OF VENGEANCE, as a tribute to the Pulp Age of Heroes.

For information and Doc's complete history visit doc-atlas@aol.com.

Since then, Doc Atlas has appeared in the Lovato and Black co-authored novel THE INCREDIBLE ADVENTURES OF DOC ATLAS. You can also find Doc in short stories like *The Green Death* in the TALES FROM THE PULP SIDE anthology and *His Masters Voice* in the TALES OF MASKS & MAYHEM V. 4 anthology. Together they have stepped outside the time period but adhered to pulp sensibilities with their recent *Stretched to the Limit*, a super hero satire, in the WITH GREAT POWER anthology, and an E-Book, DARK HAVEN, about a secret military facility for failed monstrous experiments.

The highlight of last year for Raymond Lovato came when Michael mentioned Lovato's name to Ron Fortier, the foremost author in keeping the spirit of pulp fiction alive. Raymond has been a fan and admirer of Ron Fortier for decades. The e-mail inviting him to submit a Sherlock Holmes story is framed in his casita. Of all the things that he has ever undertaken, Lovato states the preceding story was written with the most apprehension and offered the most reward.

Sherlock Holmes

in

"The Adventure of the Vampire's Vengeance"

By

Aaron Smith

"One of the most frightening facts I have learned in my years in this profession is that the mind is such a fragile thing that a single book, if read at a time in one's life when one is most vulnerable, can completely distort a human being's understanding of reality."

Those words were spoken to me by Sherlock Holmes at some point during the series of events I am about to relate. Of all the cases on which I worked with Holmes over our many years together, this was surely one of the darkest and bloodiest, so much so that my hands tremble a bit even now, many years after the fact, as I write this narrative. Browsing my notes from the time may, I fear, give me nightmares, and there are few things in this world that have the power to burden my mind even in sleep.

While the rather lengthy quote from Holmes may give some indication of the essence of the affair, a perhaps more powerful indication of its character may be found in a much shorter quote, repeated several times at the beginning of the case by a certain Scotland Yard man who normally wore a cool, even callous demeanor that seemed to shield him from being deeply affected by the horrible crimes he encountered in his work. Such defenses were of no use on this grim occasion, and I can still recall the chilling tone in the voice of Inspector Tobias Gregson as he said, "It's a nasty business."

❋❋❋

In the summer of 1899, Sherlock Holmes and I had just concluded a rather dull case involving the theft of a very old and valuable piece of Japanese sculpture. It was solved quickly and with little difficulty, the sort of case I prefer to leave in my notes rather than risk boring my readers with its full details. Still, a successfully finished case is a thing to celebrate and I looked forward to a few days off once the sculpture had been recovered and returned to its rightful owner. However, such a lull between investigations was not to be.

A pounding on the door of 221B Baker Street woke me. It was still dark. I quickly lit a lamp and glanced at the nearest clock, which told me that it was a quarter past five in the morning. I rushed to don my robe and slippers, feeling sorry for poor Mrs. Hudson, who would surely be awakened by the noise if I did not reach the door quickly. I shot out of the flat I shared with Sherlock Holmes, raced down the stairs, and flung the door open. I was prepared to viciously scold whoever dared make such a clamor.

I stopped short of shouting when I saw that it was Inspector Gregson at the door. I would still have put him in his place had it not been for the look on his face. Gregson, normally calm no matter the situation, wore a grim mask of shock, like a man who had just learned of the death of a close friend or been through some other sort of traumatic experience.

"Gregson, what is it?" I asked.

"It's a nasty business, Dr. Watson," he said with trembling lips, "a nasty business. I'm … I'm truly sorry to intrude at such an early hour, but I … I need to see Holmes at once."

"Come in," I said, feeling truly sorry for the inspector. Despite his frequent callousness, Tobias Gregson was a good man, a detective who Holmes considered the best Scotland Yard had to offer (which could have been construed as either a compliment to Gregson or an insult to the Yard, depending on how one chose to interpret Holmes' tone). Now, seeing him in such a state, I was honestly concerned.

Gregson followed me up the stairs. As we ascended, I listened for any sign that we might have roused Mrs. Hudson, but heard nothing and was grateful for such. When we had entered the drawing room and I had shut the door, Gregson stood there, swaying slightly back and forth, clearly in shock over whatever matter had brought him to seek Holmes long before daybreak.

"Sit down, Inspector!" I barked at him, eager to get to the core of the problem. He sunk into the closest chair, mouth moving as if he were struggling to summon words.

I poured him a brandy, shoved the glass into his hand.

"Drink," I ordered him, "whether you're on duty or not!"

Gregson took a long sip, swallowed. I watched some of the color reappear on his too-pale face. He began to look like himself again.

"Forgive me, Doctor," Gregson said. "Had Lestrade or any of my other colleagues seen me in such a state, I'd have never heard the end of it."

"Think no more of it," I assured him. "There must be a code of confidentiality between a man and his physician, and I, having just administered a remedy to you, was, for a moment at least, your doctor. Now tell me, Inspector, what has brought you here in such haste?"

"Murder," said Gregson, and in such a way that it chilled me, for I could hear in his voice and see in his expression that it was no common homicide that had occurred. "It is murder of the most grotesque sort," he continued, "the kind of crime that sent my mind spinning into a dance of horror and confusion. I couldn't think clearly. And I was the least affected by the scene. One young constable ran screaming from the room, the sergeant became physically ill, and the widow... oh the poor woman, to have to see her husband like that!"

I held up a hand in front of Gregson's face. Letting him go on and on about the horror he had seen without his relating the actual details would do neither of us any good. Yet, I knew all I needed to know. The mention of murder indicated that Gregson's unexpected visit was for a reason worthy of interrupting Sherlock Holmes' sleep.

I opened the door to Holmes' room, called his name.

"Holmes."

I could see his silhouette in the bit of light entering through the half-open curtains.

"Holmes," I repeated.

The detective did not stir.

"Holmes!" I shouted.

The tall, slim figure sat straight up in bed, as quick as if he had been awake all along. "What is it, Watson?"

I stepped a bit closer, explained in a quiet, even voice.

"Gregson is here, Holmes, and he is terribly upset about a murder."

"What sort of murder?"

"I have thus far been unable to coax any real information from him, Holmes. Gregson is shaken to a degree I've never seen before. He is not himself, though his condition has improved somewhat since his abrupt arrival."

"I will be with you presently," Holmes said, as he cast aside his blankets.

I turned to go back to our visitor.

I found Gregson still sitting there, but looking much better. Seeing that he had finished his brandy, I was about to offer him another when Sherlock Holmes rushed past me, having dressed faster than I thought humanly possible, and muttered, "Get dressed, Watson, for I suspect we shall soon be departing Baker Street," and then tearing open the door and, immediately accomplishing what I had hoped to avoid, shouting down the stairs, "Mrs. Hudson! Coffee for three! Our minds are in dire need of rejuvenation! Make it quick and make it strong!" He slammed the door shut, turned to us, and said, "Tell us what has happened, Gregson, straight and without the dramatics I hope you've already purged from your system."

Gregson's expression cleared, the trembling of his lips ceased, he looked more alert and aware of his surroundings than he had been since his arrival. He seemed to be reassured by Holmes' firm, confident presence. When he began to speak, he sounded like a steady, competent detective stating the facts.

"The victim was a solicitor named John Harper, aged thirty-two years, married, with no children. His wife, Elizabeth, discovered the body shortly after four o'clock this morning. She had gone to bed rather early while her husband was still in his study, which was down the hall from their bedroom. He had promised to join her when he'd finished recording some figures from a contract he'd been hired to oversee. When Mrs. Harper woke to find the other half of the bed still unoccupied, she rose and walked down the hall to see if her husband had fallen asleep at his desk.

"When she entered the room, she found her husband dead. She went into hysterics at the sight and her screams woke the neighbors, who summoned the police. I arrived on the scene at half past four."

"What was the method by which Harper was killed?" Holmes asked.

"From the short look I got at him before I could gaze no more upon the horror of it all and came to fetch you, Holmes," Gregson continued, "it appeared that Mr. Harper had been felled by a blow to the head. Once he was unconscious and prone on the floor, a wooden spigot with a sharp end was thrust into his neck, causing the blood to flow out at a rapid pace. He must have bled to death very quickly indeed. The corpse was pale, as if all life's fluid had left the body, and on the floor were wide puddles of red."

"Did you see," Holmes asked, "any signs that might tell you who had been there or how they had gained access to the residence?"

"The office window was open," Gregson said, "so I assume the murderer entered easily, as the room is on the ground floor. But I could detect, in my horror and haste, no clue as to the identity of whoever committed this terrible deed. I am, I admit, quite ashamed of the effect I allowed this incident to have on me."

At that moment, Mrs. Hudson entered with a pot of coffee. The poor woman looked disheveled and half asleep.

"What has you gentlemen up at such an ungodly hour?" she asked as she set the cups down and poured the steaming liquid.

"A most ungodly crime, Mrs. Hudson," Holmes said.

"A nasty business," Gregson repeated his earlier description as he took his coffee from our landlady, "the details of which I would never explain while a woman is present."

"And I'm sure I'd thank you for that, Inspector," Mrs. Hudson said. "Some of the circumstances Mr. Holmes and Dr. Watson attend to are fit to give anyone bad dreams!"

With that remark, Mrs. Hudson left us.

"Drink quickly," Holmes barked, "for we must be on our way to the home of the late Mr. Harper. I trust you left orders for the scene to not be disturbed, Gregson."

"That I did," Gregson answered. "My mind may have been a bit addled, but not sufficiently to forget proper procedures."

Holmes turned toward me. "Watson, I already suggested you prepare yourself for an excursion!"

I glanced down, realized I was still in my robe, having been so caught up in Gregson's description of the murder that I'd forgotten to go and dress. I put down my cup and rushed to don my clothes.

❀❀❀

Dawn was beginning to break as we arrived at the Harper residence, a modest flat with rosebushes on either side of the front door. A stout sergeant stood watch, ignoring the neighbors who had gathered close by to crane their necks and stare wide-eyed at the place of the tragedy.

"Has anyone been inside, Sgt. Thorne?" Gregson asked.

"No, sir," Thorne answered. "As per your orders, not a soul has gone in since you left. And all the others have since come out. I sent Constable Wright home for the day. The poor lad was shakin' like a leaf. And I had the poor widow taken to hospital."

"You did well, Thorne. Good man! Now kindly let us in. Follow me, Holmes, Dr. Watson."

We followed Inspector Gregson in and down a corridor, the floor of which was marked in several places by bloody footprints, both large prints left by, I supposed, policemen's boots, and smaller prints in which could be seen the outlines of bare toes, and those I presumed to have been put there by Mrs. Harper as she ran frantically about, screaming after having made her shocking discovery.

We soon entered John Harper's study, which was larger than what I had expected. The scene inside was so ghastly that I found it unsurprising that even an experienced investigator like Tobias Gregson had been sent spiraling into a state of shock. Had I not been a physician and so used to sights of death or severe injury, and had not Holmes been a man practiced at exercising great control over his emotions and reactions, I doubt we would have been able to stand it for more than a moment. But time and experience had hardened our hearts in some ways, and so we began to look the room over thoroughly and without sentiment.

Holmes was first to enter, with me close behind. Gregson waited in the doorway, looking in, but seemed hesitant to cross the threshold. Holmes walked about the room, careful to avoid stepping in the blood. That was not an easy task, as there was quite a lot of it pooled here and there, splattered on the lower shelves of several bookcases, and trailing both toward the door and in the direction of the open window.

After spending a few moments wandering, closely examining the window, sticking his head out the window for a moment, checking the floor, and, especially, the body, Holmes stopped and turned to me.

"While it is obvious that our murderer," Holmes said, "entered and exited by way of the window, he or she has left no signs from which to begin pinpointing an identity. This was a careful though brutal criminal. This killing was planned, as is shown by the weapon used and the gruesome way in which the victim was dispatched. Watson, you may approach the dead man and apply your medical knowledge."

I did as Holmes suggested, following his example and trying to avoid the bloodied areas of the floor as much as possible. I knelt beside the body.

John Harper, I noticed, had been a handsome man in life, but he was now a pale corpse stretched across the floor beside his desk. A toppled chair rested a few feet away. Harper was still dressed in his pants, shirt, and shoes. His jacket lay nearby, apparently having been hung on the back of the chair while the young solicitor worked.

Harper was on his back, eyes wide open, face a mask of shock and pain. On the top of his head, I could see a gash where Gregson guessed a blow with a hard object had knocked the victim senseless. I agreed with the inspector's theory. The skin had been split open and the skull may even have been fractured, though I could not be certain of that from my vantage point.

I then turned my attention to Harper's neck. Gregson had described it accurately before our arrival, but I was still not prepared for the brutal strangeness of what I found. A spigot had been inserted, piercing the jugular vein. The sharp end was still embedded in the neck, and traces of blood still wet the spout on the opposite end. Judging by the position of the spigot and the effect I assumed it would have had, it was my opinion that Harper's bleeding had been rapid and irreversible. I must admit I shuddered slightly at the thought. Realizing what such a death would have been like, I hoped the blow to his head had been sufficient to put him beyond the reach of full consciousness of what was happening to him. There are times when lack of awareness can be a merciful thing.

"The impact to the head came first," I said, though I was sure Holmes had already decided as much. "The spigot and its bloodletting was the ultimate cause of death and occurred when Harper was already in the position in which we now see him."

"Yes, Watson," Holmes replied. "Now what else do your physician eyes tell you?"

I stared at the body a moment longer and saw no other injuries, so was unsure what Holmes meant to imply. Thinking that a change of angle might offer me a glimpse of something else, I stood. I gazed down at Harper but still did not notice anything new. Frustrated, and wishing Holmes would simply tell me instead of making me play a guessing game, I turned in a circle, looking down at the floor, seeing the light of the room's lamps reflect in the pools of red liquid, noticing the spots where small droplets of crimson had stained the wall and the spines of books.

It was after considering the carnage that I saw what Holmes meant. I also knew why he had not just plainly stated it. He was unsure and wanted to see if I would come to the same conclusion independently of his influence. My realization chilled me to the core.

"Now I understand, Holmes!" I shouted. "There is not enough blood in this room!"

"I thought not," Holmes said. "Then you confirm this conjecture?"

"I do," I said. "The body of a man of Harper's age and size would normally contain approximately five liters of blood. While this room has been gruesomely decorated with the stuff, I do not see nearly enough to account for the full volume I would expect. But what has become of the rest of it?"

"That, Watson, explains why the tap was used to bleed Mr. Harper. Whoever committed this act desired to drain the man's blood and take it away from here."

"But what kind of ..."

"Let us not speculate wildly, Watson," Holmes said sternly. Then, with a smile that might have been considered, under the circumstances, obscene by one who did not understand Holmes' personality, the consulting detective turned to the inspector and said, "Thank you, Gregson, for summoning us. This is a most fascinating crime."

Holmes' happiness...if one can call it that, considering the horrific circumstances…was short-lived. A loud shouting from outside broke the relative quiet of the dead man's office.

"What do you mean he's got that meddling Holmes in there? Move aside, Sergeant! Gregson, get out here immediately and bring those two unauthorized interlopers with you!"

"Rawles," Holmes muttered with dislike.

Gregson turned and started down the hallway. Holmes followed Gregson, and I walked behind Holmes. As we exited through the front door of the Harper home, we found Superintendent Ernest Rawles impatiently tapping his cane on the stones of the short pathway to the street. Sergeant Thorne stood behind him, apologetically shaking his head.

Rawles, Gregson's superior on the police force, disapproved of Holmes' and my involvement in any case that involved Scotland Yard. He scoffed at Holmes' methods and seemed to resent the fact that Holmes was a publicly known figure whose notoriety often overshadowed any attention given to the men who served in an official police capacity. On one hand, I could sympathize with Rawles' stance on the matter, for Gregson, Lestrade, and the other men of Scotland Yard certainly deserved credit for their hard work. But Rawles' personality was another matter. Loud and opinionated, there had been occasions on which he seemed to go to great lengths to keep Holmes and me from assisting the inspectors, often delaying or even preventing a case from reaching a satisfactory conclusion. I was not surprised that a murder such as this one, sure to attract the attention of the press and public, was sufficient bait to rouse Rawles from his bed so early in the day.

"Sir," Gregson said as he approached the superintendent.

"Why was I not summoned?" Rawles roared. His ruddy cheeks flared like the jowls of a bulldog, his large stomach bouncing as he scolded poor Gregson.

"I wished to complete my initial examination of the scene first, sir."

"Yet you had time to bring this charlatan here," Rawles said, lifting his cane to point it at Holmes like an accusing finger.

"I'm sorry, sir," Gregson said, "but this already appears to be a most unusual case and I thought …"

"No, Inspector, you did not think!" Rawles stormed past Gregson, cast a look of hatred at Holmes, and hurried into the Harper house, striking the ground with his cane at each step, as he often did to emphasize his presence.

When Rawles was out of sight, Sherlock Holmes let out a hearty laugh.

"What is so amusing?" Gregson asked.

Holmes raised his hand, three fingers pointing up while his thumb held down the little finger. He began to count, backwards, lowering a finger with each number, "Three … two … one …and …"

"By God's beard!" a holler came from within the house. An instant later, Superintendent Rawles, carrying his cane, his face pale and perspiring, looking like a very deflated and shaken version of himself, returned to us. He leaned against a lamp post, struggling to catch his breath.

I heard Gregson cough to camouflage a chuckle. Holmes said nothing, but grinned at the trembling superintendent.

"Sergeant Thorne!" Rawles cried out when he had recovered sufficiently from the shock of the murder scene.

"Yes, sir," Thorne answered.

"Have that room cleared immediately. The body must be taken to the morgue for examination."

Holmes tried to interrupt. "Superintendent Rawles, if you will allow me to have another …"

"Holmes," Rawles' voice blasted across the air, "I'll have you in cuffs if you try to interfere! Take your pet sawbones and vacate the area at this instant!"

Holmes closed his eyes, breathed in and out once, then opened them, nodded at Rawles, and began walking away. I followed. As we left, I glanced back to see Rawles smiling as if he had just achieved victory over a dreaded foe. I, however, understood what had truly just occurred. Holmes had taken that moment, that single breath, to paint what he had seen in the office of John Harper permanently onto the vast canvas of his mind. He would have no more need of going into that room or examining the method in which the unfortunate solicitor had met his demise, for the information was now as ingrained in the mind of the detective as a numeral chiseled into a marble column in the ruins of a Roman temple. Holmes could revisit the scene as often as he wished until he had made sense of the mystery we now faced. Harper's death had Holmes' full attention now, and I knew that nothing Rawles said or did would keep my friend from the hunt.

❊❊❊

With the morning sun now shining overhead, Holmes and I walked back to Baker Street. It was a long journey, but Holmes was, I could see, deep in thought, so I simply walked beside him, hesitant to interrupt. After we had walked for twenty minutes, Holmes spoke, not excitedly, but calmly, evenly.

"There was nothing more to be found in that room, Watson. Our killer left no clumsy clues, no certain signs of identity. We have two obvious options as to what must be done next."

"Interview either the widow or Harper's colleagues," I guessed.

"Very good, Watson, yes, we must determine if there are any obvious enemies who would wish to dispose of the young attorney."

"But surely this is a personal matter," I said. "If this were some professional grudge, wouldn't an enemy simply have hired someone to shoot Harper or beat him in a way that looks like violent robbery?"

"That is probable," Holmes said, "but we must be sure to eliminate the most mundane possibilities before we focus on the stranger aspects of the case."

"With the foremost strange aspect being the missing blood, of course," I said, still disturbed by the idea. "But won't Rawles already have men questioning Harper's associates and wife?"

"No," said Holmes, "but Gregson will. Rawles has forgotten…if he ever truly knew at all…how to proceed with a proper investigation. He is all wind and thunder now. Rawles will talk to the press and reassure the public that the Yard is doing all it can to keep them safe and catch the killer, while he happily takes credit for any true progress made by Gregson, or by us."

"Do you think," I asked, "Gregson will still welcome our involvement, or has he been dissuaded by Rawles' wrath?"

"Gregson is competent as far as his kind go," Holmes opined, "but this is a case that, I suspect, will carry us down dark and deadly roads the likes of which Scotland Yard training does little to prepare a man for. Gregson will be glad to have us with him on this chase."

❁❁❁

"I hope you're both ready for a proper breakfast," said Mrs. Hudson, with a slightly angry edge to her words, as Holmes and I arrived back at our flat. "Scurrying about before dawn without an ounce of food in you is an unhealthy way to live."

"I hope you're both ready for a proper breakfast."

I eagerly devoured my meal, while Holmes just barely sipped his tea and stared scornfully at his eggs. His attention was focused on the case, and he had no desire to devote energy, physical or mental, to anything he considered as trivial as food.

After breakfast, Holmes went to his usual chair, lit his pipe, and sat with his eyes closed. I knew better than to try to engage him in conversation when he was in such a state of contemplation. I took to another chair and halfheartedly tried to read the day's paper, but my thoughts kept drifting back to the horrors we had seen at the home of the Harpers.

Shortly past noon, Mrs. Hudson announced the arrival of Inspector Gregson. The news broke Holmes' meditation and we gladly welcomed our associate, hoping he would have something of substance to tell us.

Gregson settled into his chair, taking out a cigarette. He looked tired.

"What have you to tell us, Gregson?" Holmes asked.

"Some," the inspector said, "though not as much as I'd hoped. This is a nasty business."

"Yes, that has already been established," Holmes muttered impatiently. "Get on with what new details you've brought."

"Well, Holmes," Gregson said, "Superintendent Rawles' favorite surgeon was brought in to examine the body of John Harper and he decided exactly what you and Dr. Watson had already decided: that Harper was first struck on the head from behind, then, after he'd fallen from his chair, that awful spout was stabbed into his neck to let all his blood come pouring out."

"And what were his thoughts on the amount of blood on the floor and walls?" Holmes asked.

"No thoughts," Gregson said. "Rawles, more worried, as usual, about appearances than procedure, had the gore mopped away immediately, so even if the doctor had bothered to come and look, he'd have seen nothing but a freshly cleaned office with perhaps a speck or two the poor constables assigned to the job had missed."

"Most unfortunate," said Holmes, "but that does give us insight into the case that Rawles does not possess, unless, of course, you told him of our theory of missing blood, Gregson."

"He'll not hear a word of it from me, I assure you," the inspector said. "There are quite a few choice words I'd like to tell that pompous blowhard, but I don't wish to lose my badge! So I'll have to settle for solving the case myself and letting him chew on that fact, and if you and Watson are of any help in that task, I'll welcome the aid."

"Yes," Holmes said with a nod, "your dislike of the superintendent is most obvious. Was there anything else you wished to tell us?"

"Two things," Gregson answered. "First, we've determined the weapon used to knock Harper from his chair."

"The heavy candlestick that was left on the floor ten inches from Harper's shoulder," Holmes said, as if it was the most well known fact in the world.

"You knew?" Gregson asked angrily.

"Immediately," said Holmes, "but it meant nothing to the case. It was soaking in a pool of blood, which would have made any substance left on it by the hand of the killer indistinguishable. So, that leaves only one fact to be learned from the candlestick, which can be determined by its position in relation to the body, which is where we must assume the murderer dropped it after striking Harper's head."

"And what fact is that?" Gregson asked.

"That the dealer of the blow was right-handed," Holmes revealed. "And since the majority of the people in the world favor the right hand, such information is essentially useless to us."

"I see," Gregson sighed.

"And the second piece of information you alluded to?" Holmes requested.

"I've been to hospital to see the victim's widow," Gregson told us.

"And how is she?" I asked, thinking of the terrible tragedy the young woman faced and the horror and grief she must have felt upon discovering what had become of her husband.

"Under sedation, I'm afraid," Gregson said. "The doctor in charge of her care said it was the only way to stop her hysterical screaming. We'll get no information from her today."

"And what of John Harper's business associates?" Holmes asked. "Did Harper work for a large or small firm?"

"He had been employed for the past six years by a Mr. Forks of Percy Street, in a small firm that deals mostly in real estate and other such contract matters. Inspector Lestrade visited Forks while I was at the hospital."

"And what was the result of the interview?" Holmes asked. He was growing impatient, I could tell.

"Another dead end," Gregson admitted. "Forks could think of no enemies Harper might have made during his work there, at least none who hated him sufficiently to commit murder."

"Then morning has surrendered to afternoon and we have accomplished nothing today!" Holmes said as he slammed his fist on the arm of his chair before reaching for a match to light his pipe again.

"We'll catch whoever did this, Holmes," Gregson said. "With our brains and our experience combined, the murderer will be punished eventually for this nasty business."

"Eventually," Holmes said, "may not be good enough. Killings by bullet, knife, beating, poison, or other common methods can often be the work of a person inclined to eliminate another from this world for one of many reasons. Many of those who kill in such ways would never consider doing such a thing again. But the mind of one who would insert a spigot into the vein of the victim and then depart the scene of the crime with a substantial amount of the deceased's blood in their possession is a very abnormal mind indeed. We cannot, we must not, rule out the possibility that this murderer will strike again. We can afford no patience, Gregson, no leisurely pace to this investigation. We must leap over all obstacles, our own lack of progress and the interference of Superintendent Rawles included. This killer must be caught quickly before more blood is spilled and the people of London panic as they have not done since the dark days of the summer of eleven years ago, when the women of Whitechapel walked in fear. This is urgent, Inspector. Do not forget that."

To hear Sherlock Holmes make such a prediction filled me with dread. It would not be long before his theory was proven correct.

❁❁❁

Inspector Gregson visited us frequently over the next three days, mostly to tell us how little of any use to the case had been discovered.

Superintendent Rawles, to our surprise, used some sense and was selective in what he told the journalists of London. The Times reported the murder of John Harper, but did not include the more lurid details, such as the use of the spigot to drain his blood. This was fortunate, as it did not cause the public uproar that would have occurred had such horror been made known.

Sherlock Holmes spent much of the time in deep thought, occasionally getting up from his chair to grab one book or another from the shelf, search through its pages as if seeking some vital piece of information, and then toss it aside like rubbish only to return to his pipe and his contemplation.

On the fourth day following the crime, Gregson arrived in mid-morning, this time politely declining Mrs. Hudson's offer of tea, which indicated to me that he finally had something new to tell us.

"I was informed an hour ago," Gregson said, "that it has been decided to allow the cloud of sedation Mrs. Harper has been placed under to disperse naturally. She was not given any drugs this morning and should be quite lucid by now. I requested that her doctor inform me first when he chose to take that course of action, but it will not be long before Superintendent Rawles finds out as well."

"Then we have no time to waste!" Holmes shouted, displaying more enthusiasm than I had seen from him in days. He jumped up from his chair, grabbed his coat and hat, and called, "Come, Watson, and you too, Gregson!"

A short time later, we arrived at Charing Cross Hospital. Gregson, already familiar with the layout, led us in.

Our first stop was the office of Mrs. Harper's physician, Dr. Jacob Stewart. He greeted us warmly and invited us to sit.

"I have heard much about your work, Mr. Holmes," Stewart said. He was about thirty-five years of age, a thin man with short brown hair that bore a slight reddish tint. He had a habit of holding his spectacles by the stem and twirling them as he spoke. "Your profession sounds quite fascinating."

"It has its rewarding moments," Holmes said, "but I'm afraid this is not the time to discuss such matters. I am far more concerned with our present case than any past successes. What is the condition of your patient?"

"I've decided to cease her heavy sedation," Stewart answered. "When she woke today, we did not administer the drugs we had given her on her previous days here. Hence, she has become fully aware of her surroundings and, difficult as it may be for her, of the circumstances that brought her here."

"And how has she responded to this newfound clarity of perception?" Holmes asked.

"She is quiet, saddened, still in a bit of shock," Stewart explained, "which is understandable considering that the state she was in until today most likely makes her discovery of her husband's body seem more recent than it does to you and I."

"May I see her?" Holmes asked.

"Yes," Stewart agreed. "For a short time, though if she shows any notable distress I shall have to insist the interview be terminated at once."

"Holmes," I offered, "perhaps I should be the one to ..."

"No, Watson," Holmes said as he raised a hand to request my silence. "I realize I am often abrupt, but you have also seen me at my gentlest, and my bedside manner can, when the need arises, rival that of any man of your profession."

"Yes, Holmes," I agreed. I had seen many times how Holmes could shift his way of speaking to and acting toward a person depending upon the needs of the case. He would do no harm to Mrs. Harper. It had merely been my instincts as a physician that had made me think of the patient's comfort first, and the mystery of her husband's death second.

Holmes was led into Mrs. Harper's room, while Dr. Stewart accompanied Gregson and me into the next room. Stewart slid open a small panel in the wall that would allow us to hear the conversation without distracting Holmes or the grief stricken young woman. The panel, Stewart explained, was often used to monitor patients who had to be observed constantly while still being allowed a chance to rest in solitude.

"Mrs. Harper, how do you feel?" we heard Holmes ask.

There was silence for a moment before Holmes spoke again.

"Mrs. Harper? May I call you Elizabeth?"

"Who are you?" a soft female voice said. "Another doctor, or a policeman, perhaps, and I don't care what you call me."

"Then Elizabeth it is. To answer your question, my name is Sherlock Holmes. I am not a doctor, nor am I a policeman. I am a detective, though not affiliated with Scotland Yard, except for the fact that I assist them from time to time. My interest here is not to improve my standing with the police or to gain the approval of the public or the press. My only goal is to discover who committed the terrible crime against your husband so that they may face justice."

"My poor John ..."

"I ask you again, Elizabeth, how do you feel?"

"Why does it matter? John is dead."

"It matters very much. Let me explain why. For the past few days, you have been feeling, I have been told, quite confused. You have slept many hours. This is because of the medication you were given. Now you are awake and understand what has happened. I imagine your feelings now are primarily of shock and grief. Am I correct?"

"Of course they are! How else could I possibly feel? My John is dead. He's dead, dead, dead!"

"If I may dare say so, Elizabeth, there is another feeling you should be experiencing today. Were I in your place, it is most certainly what I would feel. Your husband, your John, whom you pledged to be faithful to and spend your life with, did not die of an illness. He was not killed in an unfortunate accident. He did not die at war fighting for the good of his country. Had he perished in any of those ways, your quiet grieving would be understandable. But he did not die in any of those ways, did he, Elizabeth?"

"N … no …"

"You saw how he died."

"Someone … someone … the blood on the floor, on the wall, under my feet … the blood …"

Hearing Elizabeth Harper's voice hesitating and stuttering, then droning out words like she was in some sort of trance, alarmed me greatly. Dr. Stewart reacted in much the same way.

"He's going to send her into a breakdown!" Stewart said. "This has to stop."

I almost let the doctor rush in and interrupt, but my trust in Holmes stopped me. I grabbed Stewart firmly by the arm and held him back.

"Give him a moment more," I said. "Please."

"That is correct," I heard Holmes say. "Someone did this. A person crept into your home and murdered your husband. John is gone, not because of some chance tragedy or some disease that is only an act of nature at its most dangerous. A person entered your home and took John away from you, and the deed was done in a terrible way. I know you understand this."

"Yes," Mrs. Harper said.

"And how do you feel now, Elizabeth?"

"Angry."

"That is as it should be. Doctors and ministers and others who think they are doing the right thing will tell you acceptance is the first step to surpassing grief, or they will say it is divine to forgive or suggest some other gentle path to healing from a grievous wound of the emotions. They are wrong, Elizabeth. If you truly wish this pain to leave your heart, then the person who did this to John must be found and punished."

"Yes. Can you find him, Mr. Holmes?"

"I promise you I will do everything in my power to find him … or her. I must not assume anything, as I have not yet determined if the one we seek is a man or a woman. Do you have any reason to believe it was a man, Elizabeth?"

"No, I assumed because they had to be stronger than John …"

"That is not necessarily so. Your husband was struck from behind, so he had no chance to defend himself."

"I see."

"Tell me, Elizabeth, what do you recall of that night? I know it is painful to think of, but I must have your help if we are to succeed in this quest."

"I remember telling the inspectors everything that happened, or did I dream that? It's hard to be sure."

"You did provide them with an account."

"I told them how I woke to find John had not yet come to bed. I got up to see if perhaps he'd fallen asleep while staring at all those papers he was always carrying around in his case. I worried about him exhausting himself, you see. I walked down the hall, entered his study, and found him ... like that. I knew right away he was dead. And I felt the blood on the floor under my feet. I screamed, I ran. The neighbors came to see what the matter was. I think I fainted then, and regained consciousness a short time later, for just long enough to speak with the police. I was vaguely aware of being taken from my home and brought here. I was given an injection and everything was quite foggy until today, until I saw the doctor earlier, and then you, Mr. Holmes."

"And that is all you remember? Are you certain?"

"Yes. I'm sorry. I wish I could be of more help."

"You have done wonderfully, Elizabeth. If you recall any other details of that night, will you tell Dr. Stewart so he may summon me back here to talk with you again?"

"Of course I will."

"Thank you. Now, before I go, I must ask you one more question. Can you think of anyone who could have hated your husband enough to want to harm him?"

"No, Mr. Holmes, I cannot. John was a wonderful man. His family and friends adored him, and, as far as I know, he was honest and courteous in his business dealings even when immersed in a case that taxed his patience. I find it difficult to imagine anybody wanting to...to do such things to him. Oh!"

"Are you all right, Elizabeth?"

"I'm sorry, Mr. Holmes. Yes, I'll be well again in time. I just ... I just saw, in my mind, all the blood, John's blood. But I will recover from this. That is what John would want."

"Yes, he would. I am sure of that."

"Thank you, Mr. Holmes."

"It is I who should be thanking you, Elizabeth. Goodbye."

With that farewell, Holmes exited Mrs. Harper's room. Dr. Stewart rushed past him to check on his patient.

"That was most extraordinary, Holmes," I said. "You managed to bring the poor girl out of her shock and into the waking world once again."

"I simply did what had to be done, Watson. She was of no use to us in her stupor."

"Was she of any use out of it?"Gregson asked. "It didn't sound like she told us anything we didn't know."

"Not in words, perhaps," Holmes said, "but in her way of speaking and in the expressions of her face, which you, of course, could not see. Mrs. Harper was truly shocked by the death of her husband. Everything she said to me is the truth, at least as far as she is able to perceive the truth."

"So you have eliminated her name from the list of potential suspects," I guessed.

"Exactly, Watson, and I have also learned that the murder was not due to any conflict in John Harper's life that his wife knew of. Also, perhaps most importantly, I have earned her trust, which may be of use to us as we proceed."

At that moment, Dr. Stewart returned to us.

"How is she?" I asked.

"More alert than at any time since her arrival," Stewart said. He turned to Holmes. "Your methods seemed harsh, Mr. Holmes, but they have done the patient no harm, and perhaps even done her some good. Yesterday, I was afraid I'd have to have her transferred to the Holloway Sanatorium. But now she seems to have gone from the edge of a complete nervous breakdown to being just a grieving and quite angry—as is natural, of course—young woman."

"I hope you are right, Doctor," Holmes said. "Please keep us apprised if there are any changes to Elizabeth's condition."

"I certainly shall," said Dr. Stewart as he saw us out.

❊❊❊

Holmes and I parted ways with Gregson and took a cab back to Baker Street.

"What do we do next, Holmes?" I asked. "While I'm glad for Mrs. Harper's improved condition, we still have no leads as to the identity of her husband's murderer."

"We must focus, Watson," Holmes said, "on the most unusual aspect of the mystery, the detail that sets it apart from other crimes."

"The taking of some of Harper's blood," I said.

"Indeed," Holmes confirmed. "And to do so, we must overcome an obstacle. The attitude of Superintendent Rawles will prevent us from gaining the full cooperation of Scotland Yard. Gregson is willing to work with us, of course, but he must proceed with caution lest he anger Rawles and be removed from the case. In order to investigate the matter of the missing blood, we must act on our own."

"How will we do that?" I asked.

"I must become my enemy," Holmes said, and he closed his eyes for the remainder of our ride.

❋❋❋

I spent much of the afternoon and evening away from our flat. When Holmes and I returned from the hospital, Mrs. Hudson informed me that an acquaintance from my army days had called and left an invitation for me to join him for supper. With Holmes insisting that he would not require my assistance for at least several hours, I went to meet my old friend. It was an enjoyable time, with food, drinks, and reminiscences of the good moments that occur even during war.

It had grown dark by the time I returned to Baker Street. I greeted Mrs. Hudson, who was dusting the frames of the pictures hanging in the hall.

"I believe Mr. Holmes has company," the landlady said, "for I heard a voice that was not his. Yet, I admitted no one through the front door, so I cannot imagine how he got in. There's always a mystery with you two gentlemen living under my roof!"

I went upstairs, expecting to find that Gregson had come to us with some news. I was much surprised when I opened the door to find, instead of Gregson, Superintendent Rawles sitting in Holmes' favorite chair and smoking a cigarette.

"Good evening, Doctor Watson," Rawles said.

"What brings you here, Superintendent?" I asked, trying to be polite, despite my dislike of the man. "Where is Holmes?"

Then I understood. I stared for a moment and saw the truth. Rawles nose was a bit too long, his cheeks slightly redder than on the other occasions I had seen him. His fingers were not the thick appendages of a fat man, but the slender instruments of one who is equally adept with a violin or a test tube.

"Outstanding work, Holmes," I shouted, admiring, once again, the near-perfection of disguise that had always been one of Sherlock Holmes' most impressive skills.

"Thank you, Watson," Holmes said, his voice returning to normal. "It is not as difficult as it may seem. The superintendent's most noticeable features are those that are exaggerated beyond what one sees on most men: his girth, the ruddiness of his face, these mutton chops...which are beginning to itch...and, to complete the change, the man's voice, which had even you fooled for a moment."

"Yes, and it confused poor Mrs. Hudson as well," I said.

"Then I have succeeded," Holmes said, extinguishing his cigarette in a tea saucer, a habit that often irritated our landlady. He rose from the chair and straightened his coat.

"How did you acquire those large clothes in so short a time?" I asked.

"I've had them stored here for several years," Holmes answered. "There was an occasion when I had to impersonate my brother Mycroft."

"I see, and the badge?"

"It is a souvenir from yet another past case. It does not match the one worn by the real Rawles, of course, but will the constable or sergeant on duty late into the night inspect it closely when a superintendent appears and demands admittance to the records room?"

"I suppose not. So you intend to visit Scotland Yard disguised as Rawles to look at records? What if the real Rawles is there?"

"He left the Yard an hour ago. Have you forgotten my network of street urchins, Watson?"

"Of course I haven't. The Irregulars prove useful yet again!"

"Indeed," Holmes said, clapping his hands once in satisfaction. "I will return, I expect, in the early hours of the morning."

"What exactly are you searching for among the files?"

"I will know that, Watson, when I find it!"

Holmes picked up a cane and left the room, slamming the door behind him. I watched from the window as he marched down Baker Street, his large false belly bouncing in front of him, his entire body appearing shorter and fatter due to the padding and an expert adjustment of posture.

❁❁❁

Upon waking in the morning, I left my room to find bits of the disguise strewn about the place. Superintendent Rawles' coat lay on the floor by the door, his badge on the table, and his whiskers on a chair. Holmes, having returned to his slim appearance by shedding the padding, stood staring out the window, a trail of smoke leaving his pipe and rising toward the ceiling.

"Good morning, Holmes," I said. "Did you have a successful hunt?"

"Minimal success, if any at all," he replied. "I must have searched a thousand unsolved cases from the past year. Scotland Yard's percentage of concluding their investigations is truly atrocious! Reading the files quickly while looking for a certain significant word did not lead me to as much information as I had hoped."

"And the word was?"

"Blood, of course; I was looking for any unusual crimes in which blood played a key part, other than it being spilled in the usual ways during murder or mayhem."

"And you found nothing?"

"There was only a series of minor incidents that may be worth looking into."

"What sort of incidents?"

"Purloined pigs' blood," Holmes said, and I almost laughed at the alliterative absurdity of the phrase.

"And you suspect a connection between that and the killing of John Harper?" I asked.

"I suspect nothing as yet, Watson. I am merely investigating all avenues, chasing the wild goose, you might say, as this case has been an utter folly so far!"

"I understand. So what is this about pigs' blood, then?"

"A farmer called Bradbury, who lives in Shepherd's Bush, reported three separate occasions, weeks ago, on which he had just slaughtered a pig and discovered, a short time later, that someone had run off with the bucket he used to catch the animal's blood after the slitting of the throat. Several constables were assigned to investigate, but the matter was not deemed important enough to merit the attention of an officer of inspector's rank."

"Were any suspects named?"

"The report was lacking any thorough detail. It was an amateurish investigation, treated, it seems, more as a joke than a true case of crime."

"Do you intend to look into it?"

"I was hoping, Watson, perhaps you might …"

I looked out the window. It was a beautiful summer morning, with the sun having chased any gray from the sky. I decided the fresh air of Shepherd's Bush, a mostly undeveloped region on the outskirts of London, sounded like a welcome change of atmosphere.

"I would be glad to make the excursion, Holmes," I said. "As soon as I fetch my hat, I shall be off."

❖❖❖

Shepherd's Bush, a large, sparsely populated area, boasted many small farms. I found the one I wanted with little difficulty. It was not much more than a small shack for sleeping, next to which stood a barn of slightly bigger size, outside which was a pen of pigs surrounded by a fence that was badly in need of repair.

Ignatius Bradbury, the farmer, immediately insisted I do away with formalities and call him, "Iggy." He was a scrawny man, with unkempt hair and few teeth remaining in his mouth. He looked about fifty, but his way of speaking told me he was younger and had aged prematurely due to a hard life.

"So you're a copper, then?" he asked.

"No," I said. Though I thought I had already explained myself sufficiently, it seemed I would have to try again. "I work for a man named Sherlock Holmes. Perhaps you've heard of him."

Iggy shook his head as he scratched his unshaven chin.

"Mr. Holmes is a detective," I said.

"So he's a copper."

"No, he is not a police inspector. He is what might be referred to as a consulting detective."

"Is that like a copper?"

"Mr. Holmes would very much like to find out who stole the pigs' blood from your barn!"

"But he's not a copper?"

"No, he most certainly is not."

"Then he's tryin' to get me to pay fer him catchin' the damn thief. Now I get your meaning. Well I ain't fallin' fer no concentratin' detective tryin' to take money from me, whether he's a copper or no copper. You need to get off my land!"

"Mr. Bradbury! Will you please shut your mouth for a moment and listen to me? I do not want your money; Sherlock Holmes does not want your money! Nobody is going to charge you a single penny for this. I simply wish to talk about what happened with the blood of your pigs! Can you understand a word I'm saying, man?"

"You just want to talk? Why didn't you say that to begin with?"

"I did."

"What'd you say yer name was again?"

"Dr. John Watson."

"All right, Dr. Winston, why don't we sit and talk?"

"It's Watson …" I began to correct him, but decided to disregard his latest mistake lest I worsen what had already been a trying conversation. We

"So you're a copper, then?"

sat upon two tree stumps that jutted up from the ground a short distance from the pigs. Iggy pulled a blade of grass from the ground and chewed it while we talked.

"Can you tell me about the incidents of the stolen blood, Iggy?"

"There ain't much to tell, Doc. When I kill a pig...because I carve 'em up and sell the meat, it's how I make my livin'...I pick one of 'em from the pen and carry 'im into the barn. Then I tie it up and hang it from the beam that hangs over my head. I put a bucket under the pig to catch 'is blood and I take my knife and cut 'is throat. When e's dead, I take 'im down and put 'im on the table fer cuttin'."

"Do you begin carving the meat immediately?"

"No, I come out here and have me a smoke before I start, a little rest after the tyin' and killin' parta the job."

"So you leave the bucket of blood unwatched."

"Yes, Doc, that's what I do."

"And how many pigs do you think you've slaughtered in that barn?"

"Maybe a hundred, maybe a thousand; I don't keep a tally."

"How do you normally dispose of the blood?"

"I take the bucket and walk to those trees over there and spill it on the ground. Pig blood ain't much use unless it's in the pig, Doc."

"So on the three occasions you reported to the police, you killed the pig, took the carcass down, placed it on the table, and went outside for your smoke?"

"That I did, and when I went back to work, my bucket was gone! I wouldn't 'a cared about the blood bein' took, you see, but a bucket costs money and I ain't got a lot to spare."

"I understand, Iggy. Now do you recall seeing or hearing anything unusual around the times the buckets and their contents were stolen?"

Iggy scratched his head, spit out the blade of grass, bent forward to select a new blade, inserted it into his mouth, scratched his head again, and finally answered my question.

"Now that I think about it, Doc...and it's been a good long while since the blood got taken...there was whistling!"

"You heard whistling? Was anyone around?"

"Not that I could see, but somebody musta been if they was whistlin'!"

"Were they whistling a specific tune, Iggy? Did you recognize it?"

"I know nothin' about music, Doc, except that it sounds good when I hear it."

"That's all right, Iggy. I suppose we're finished here, then. Thank you for your time."

"Are you goin' to catch the bucket thief now, Doc, you and Mr. Hums?"

"I wish it were that simple, my friend, but only time will tell how successful the hunt will be. I shall let you know if I learn anything of the bucket thief."

I stood and began to walk away, eager to escape the smell of the pigs and the man who tended to them.

"Go get 'em, Dr. Winston!" Ignatius Bradbury shouted behind me.

❋❋❋

"And that was all I was able to get from him, Holmes," I explained upon my return to Baker Street.

"I did not expect much more," Holmes said. "A poor farmer asked to recall details of events that occurred weeks ago was a lead I had little hope in, although the whistling is interesting."

"What does it tell you?"

"It seems the thief's actions contradict each other. Why would one who wishes to commit theft, which entails not attracting notice, announce his presence by whistling? Had this Bradbury been a man of greater intelligence or alertness, he would have looked around upon hearing a tune carried on the air. Whoever took the buckets of blood possesses at least one of three qualities: overconfidence, foolishness, or insanity."

"But we still have no evidence that connects the theft of the pigs' blood to the murder of John Harper. I have a feeling, Holmes, that I wasted my day traveling to converse with an idiot."

"Did you not enjoy the clear country air, Watson, and the lovely scenery that begins to spring into view when one leaves the thickest parts of London?"

"Indeed I did, Holmes, until the stench of pigs filled my nostrils."

"No day is perfect," Holmes said, "and perhaps the hours were indeed wasted, but we will not know for certain until this case is concluded. Thank you for taking the journey."

"You are welcome, Holmes, as always," I said. "And what progress have you made here today?" I knew the answer, though. While Holmes had undoubtedly been deep in thought during my absence, he had not left the flat. This is could tell by the facts that he had not changed clothes…he still wore the large pants that had been part of his Superintendent Rawles disguise…and his violin case was open.

❋❋❋

A week passed and no progress was made in the case. Gregson's investigation went on, but he discovered nothing new. The life of John Harper seemed to have been a clean one, with no enemies, no acquaintances with motive to kill him. Superintendent Rawles continued to tell the press that all possible avenues were being explored, but the general reaction from journalists, who were quite correct, was that Rawles' statements were full of empty promises and little substance.

Mrs. Harper, I was glad to hear, had been released from Charing Cross Hospital in time to attend her husband's funeral, which had been delayed while the body had been in the possession of Scotland Yard.

Sherlock Holmes and I both thought often of the brutal killing and the stolen blood, though we did manage to occupy ourselves with other matters. I had several patients to attend to and Holmes found another case, this one involving blackmail among the Catholic clergy, which he solved in short order without requiring my assistance.

It began to seem as if the murder of John Harper would soon fall in with the rest of the many crimes Scotland Yard had been unable to solve. This was frustrating for me, and I can only imagine how Holmes, considering the seriousness with which he approached his work, felt at the time.

It was early in the evening when we received a pair of visitors. Mrs. Hudson announced that a man and woman had arrived asking for Holmes and me. I was delighted when, after Holmes gave her permission to see them in, she led Elizabeth Harper and Dr. Jacob Stewart in.

"Do sit down," I said. "Mrs. Hudson, if you would be so kind as to bring us some tea."

"Of course, Doctor," the landlady said, shuffling off to the kitchen.

"How do you feel, Elizabeth?" Holmes asked, turning from the window to face our guests.

"Physically, I am well, Mr. Holmes," Mrs. Harper answered, "but I am filled with grief … and anger too, as I know you understand."

"Indeed," Holmes said. "And I must ask, is there any particular reason you have come to visit us tonight?"

"I just wished to thank you for …"

"You must tell him, Elizabeth," Dr. Stewart interrupted.

"No, Doctor. You were correct when we discussed the matter earlier. I was only imagining things. All I have faced these past days is having an effect on my mood. That is all."

"You are not certain of that and neither am I," Stewart insisted. "It would be best if we left that judgment to Mr. Holmes and Dr. Watson."

"It embarrasses me, Doctor Stewart!"

"Elizabeth, as your physician, I strongly suggest you relate the incident to our friends here."

Hearing this, I decided to intercede. "Mrs. Harper...Elizabeth, if I may call you by your first name...as Dr. Stewart's colleague, I must agree with him. Even if this incident of which you are so hesitant to speak was, as you said, just something you imagined it may very well be of help to you to simply talk about it. You are among friends, I assure you, and you have nothing to be embarrassed about."

Mrs. Harper forced a slight, shy smile to cross her face, and proceeded to tell her tale.

"It was at John's funeral. A great many people attended the ceremony. Various members of John's family; my relatives; the solicitors of John's firm and others associated with the business aspect of his life; as well as a multitude of others who have come in and out of our lives over the years, some of whom I knew, others I did not recognize. Dr. Stewart was also kind enough to be there. It was, of course, a somber occasion, but the weather was beautiful and the minister spoke well. When it was over, those who had come to pay their respects dispersed slowly from the cemetery until only three of us remained: me, Dr. Stewart...who was quite concerned about my reaction to the event, though I assured him again and again that I was quite all right, considering the circumstances...and my mother. I wanted a few moments alone at my husband's grave, though Mother refused to leave my side. I'm afraid I was rather rude to the poor doctor, as I recall saying, loudly, "Do you not have any other patients to attend to today? I am perfectly capable of grieving without having a breakdown, Dr. Stewart!

"And it was at that point in time that he left, and it was only Mother and I who kept watch over the grave for a while longer. And then, I thought I heard something odd. I turned around in a little circle to see if we were truly alone, and I could find nobody else near, just a field of gravestones and some trees here and there. I asked Mother if she heard anything, but she is quite aged and half deaf, so she only shook her head in denial and offered me a handkerchief, which I did not need, as I had long since run out of tears.

"I stood staring at the grave for several minutes longer, and I thought I heard the sound again, but I must have been, as Dr. Stewart suspected when I told him about it later, imagining things, for another look around convinced me that we were alone. Finally, we left the cemetery and returned to Mother's home, where I am staying temporarily until I can face returning to the flat I shared with John."

Sherlock Holmes stared at Mrs. Harper for a moment, as if expecting her to continue. When she did not, he asked, "What was the odd sound you thought you heard, Elizabeth? You did not include that detail in your story."

"It was only whistling, Mr. Holmes," she answered, "but, as I said, no one else was around, and, even if someone was, who would be rude enough to whistle in a cemetery, especially after a funeral had just taken place?"

"Was it a song," Holmes asked, "or merely a series of whistled chirps, such as one might use to summon a dog?"

"It was...if there was anything at all...a tune, a melody of some kind, I am quite sure."

"But you did not recognize it?"

"No," Mrs. Harper said, looking worried. "Are you implying that I was not imagining it, Mr. Holmes? Is there some importance to this whistling?"

"I am implying nothing at this time," Holmes said. "It is my job to gather and consider all the facts when one comes to tell me of something they find unusual. Is there any more to this story?"

"No," Mrs. Harper said. "That is all."

Holmes turned to our other guest. "Dr. Stewart," he said, "In your opinion, has your patient been eating properly since having to deal with her recent tragedy?"

"Certainly not," Stewart said. "The food at the hospital, while edible, is far from excellent, and I don't imagine the cooking of her frail, elderly mother is much better, no offense intended, as I'm sure she does the best she can for a woman of her advanced age."

"I see," Holmes said. "Then it is time she had a proper meal. Dr. Watson, I'm afraid I have some business to attend to involving another case, but I'm sure you wouldn't mind accompanying our guests to one of the local eateries."

I understood what Holmes was doing and agreed. "I would be delighted."

"Good," Holmes said. "I will, of course, pay for the meal, as it was my idea."

"Mr. Holmes, you don't have to ..." Mrs. Harper began to protest, but Holmes raised a hand to quiet her.

"Watson," Holmes said, beginning to walk toward his bedroom, "let me give you some money."

I followed Holmes into his room. He spoke quickly in a whisper.

"Surely, Watson, you see the danger Mrs. Harper is in!"

"Yes, the whistling at the cemetery, just as it was heard by Bradbury the pig farmer when the buckets of blood vanished. It seems the incidents truly are related."

"She must be guarded, but we do not want to alarm her unnecessarily."

"I agree. This dinner outing is, I assume, to give you sufficient time …"

"To speak with Gregson and arrange surveillance."

"How long do you need?"

"Two hours should suffice."

"Then you shall have three."

"Where will you take them?"

"Pagani's, I think. The atmosphere and eccentric characters may distract their minds from grimmer matters."

"Very well, one of Gregson's men will follow Mrs. Harper when she leaves the restaurant. That will save us from having to ask her mother's address and alerting the poor widow to her potentially deadly situation."

"I will do my best to give our guests an enjoyable evening, and I will be sure to keep them safe."

"Thank you, Watson."

❁❁❁

"No, I have never dined there before, but I must admit to curiosity. It has quite the reputation," Elizabeth Harper said as we rode to our destination.

Pagani's, located on Langham Place, was well known for its colorful assortment of customers. Members of London's widely varied community of artists, musicians, writers, and actors frequented the place, so it was not uncommon, on any given evening, to look to the next table and see a famous novelist or singer, poet or thespian.

I had dined there with Sherlock Holmes on several occasions, most notably the night when the great detective gave a demonstration which triggered a round of applause from our fellow patrons. Holmes showed how he could tell which instrument a musician was skilled with by examining the positions and types of calluses on their hands. His accuracy of observation had impressed everyone involved. I did not expect such excitement on this visit to Pagani's. I simply wanted a delicious meal for myself and my companions, along with, I hoped, conversation that did not revolve around the gruesome event that had permanently altered the life of Mrs. Harper.

Our time at the restaurant went well. The food was good and the conversation turned to theatre, literature, and music, probably due to the influence of our surroundings. When we had finished, three hours after we had left Baker Street, which is the time I had promised Holmes, I said my farewells to Mrs. Harper and Dr. Stewart and watched them depart together in a cab, Stewart having promised to see his patient home before he went back to his own house. As their carriage rolled down Langham Place, I saw another take up its trail. Recognizing the two men in the second carriage as Scotland Yard officers, though I did not recall their names, I knew Holmes' plan had been communicated properly to Gregson. I began to make my own way home.

❁❁❁

It was nearly midnight when I arrived at Baker Street. I entered carefully, hoping not to wake Mrs. Hudson with jingling keys or a clumsy footstep. I went upstairs as quietly as possible, entered our flat to find Holmes calmly smoking.

"I assume all went well," I said.

"Perfectly," Holmes answered between puffs of his pipe. "Gregson chose six trustworthy men, divided them into teams of two, and assigned them eight hour shifts during which the home of Mrs. Harper's mother will be watched constantly."

"Good," I said. "I will rest easier tonight knowing the poor woman is safe. She has been through enough this past week. Good night, Holmes."

I retired to my bed with a full stomach and reassured mind.

❁❁❁

"Watson! Wake up, Watson!"

I opened my eyes, blinked several times to focus my vision. My mind was as blurry as my sight and I had no clue as to what the time was. Sherlock Holmes stood at the foot of my bed shouting, and I saw that his face was paler than usual. He looked horrible, as though the weight of the entire world had suddenly descended for him to bear upon his shoulders.

I sat up. "Holmes, are you all right? What is it?"

"I have failed, Watson! I have made the most horrendous mistake of my career, and a good, innocent man has paid for it with his life."

"Damn it all, Holmes, just tell me what has happened!"

"Dr. Jacob Stewart is dead, murdered in his home in the very early hours of the morning, in a method similar to that used to slay John Harper. While I had the police watching Mrs. Harper, our blood-stealing predator stalked the doctor and ended his life in a most gruesome way. Gregson is here. Get out of bed and dress, Watson, and he'll take us to the scene."

❁❁❁

Gregson, Holmes, and I rode in a carriage driven by a young constable.

"Do you think he'd been following them all day, Holmes?" I asked.

"It would seem so, Watson," said Holmes. "Perhaps Mrs. Harper was the intended victim but the murderer changed his mind when he realized her mother's home was being watched. At that point, did he decide to follow Dr. Stewart instead? But, that begs the question of why, if he intended to slay both Harpers, did he not commit double murder on the night of John Harper's death?"

Gregson, who had said little during our ride, finally spoke up to issue a warning to us. "You realize there's a good chance Superintendent Rawles will be there, don't you Holmes? We can't avoid him forever, and now that this second killing has happened, it will be even harder to pursue our secret investigation."

"Inspector Gregson," Holmes said with anger, "two men are now dead. I have not yet examined the particulars of the second crime, but if your description is accurate, it is as much an abomination as the first. I will most certainly find whoever is responsible for these foul deeds. I will see them brought to justice and, if the court so decides, I will see them hang! No pompous, incompetent, slow-minded Scotland Yard superintendent, no matter how loud he barks or how he tries to block my path, will keep me from accomplishing this! I will deal with Rawles, and you will continue to assist me in every necessary way."

Gregson fell silent; Holmes continued to glare at him. I decided to quell the tension between the two by bringing the conversation back to the important subject, the crime that had been committed hours earlier.

"How were the police alerted to the death of Dr. Stewart?" I inquired.

"Stewart," Gregson explained, "was scheduled to be at the hospital early this morning to perform surgery. When he failed to appear at the appointed time, one of the orderlies was sent to his home. The door was unlocked, so the man went inside. He found the body and summoned the police."

"Were you the first to arrive, Gregson?"

"Were you the first to arrive, Gregson?" Holmes asked.

"No, an inspector named Caraway got there first. By the time I reached the place, a handful of constables were present and word was that Rawles had been roused and was en route. That's when I hurried to fetch you, Holmes."

"They have surely made a mess of it by now," Holmes said.

We arrived moments later. It was a handsome house, which indicated that Dr. Stewart had done well financially. Several constables stood watch in front of the house, keeping reporters and curious bystanders from approaching the door.

"Does the house have a rear entrance?" Holmes asked.

"Yes," Gregson answered.

"Watson, duck down so we are not seen," Holmes said, stooping so his head was concealed behind the carriage door. "Get out, Gregson, and then let us in through the back door."

"But why would you want to ...?" Gregson asked.

"I have a plan that may help us deal with Rawles," Holmes said. "But we must not allow the journalists to see that Watson and I are present."

Gregson disembarked from the carriage and waded through the sea of uniformed police shouting, "Out of the way, lads!"

The constable drove us further down the street and stopped. Holmes and I got out, scurried through the small yards that stood behind several of the neighboring homes, and found the back of Stewart's residence.

Gregson, who had rushed through the house, admitted us.

We passed through the door, which I then closed. We had not gone more than ten feet into the house, which had a large kitchen as its rear room, when the fat figure of Superintendent Rawles filled the next doorway.

"Leave this place immediately or I'll have you taken out by force!" Rawles growled, pointing a finger at Holmes. "And you, Gregson, have been allowing these men to interfere with this investigation. I'll see you reduced to constable's rank for this defiance!"

"Rawles," Sherlock Holmes said sharply and without hesitation, "shut your mouth for a moment and let me have my say!" Then, lowering his voice to a more even tone, "I assure you that what I am about to tell you will benefit you, and the reputation you so often seek to grow."

The expression on Rawles' face at that moment betrayed his internal conflict. His cheeks puffed out as if he was about to erupt into a volcanic tirade and launch another barrage of angry words at Holmes, but he pulled back on the reins of his fury, the mention of his reputation drawing interest. It was clear to me that Rawles, with the tremendous conceit and self interest that guided his actions, was about to hungrily snap his jaws on whatever bait Holmes was manipulatively laying for him.

"Make it quick, Holmes, before I call in my strongest men to drag you to your cell."

"I am going to tell you several things now, Rawles," Holmes said. "First, there is little doubt in my mind that the person who killed Dr. Jacob Stewart...and I say this based on Gregson's description of the crime, without yet having seen the body myself...is the same who murdered John Harper. Also, he, or she, for we have not yet determined the criminal's gender, is right-handed. There is also the matter of the habit of whistling, which this as yet unknown person seems unable to resist. And, Superintendent, did you know that this very same wretched scoundrel had, several weeks ago, been occasionally stealing the blood of pigs from a farmer in Shepherd's Bush? So you see, although I have not yet determined the identity of the murderer, I have learned several facts which may be of importance to this case, which is more, I dare say, than you have done with all the resources of Scotland Yard at your fingertips."

"Blast you, Holmes," Rawles said, "bragging will not ingratiate you to me."

"I am not bragging, Superintendent. I am offering my services to you."

"How dare you?"

"Did you notice how Watson and I made our entrance through the rear door of this house?"

"Of course I did. You are not the only man in the world who has two working eyes."

"And did you take that observation to the next logical step and wonder why we chose to enter by that route? A good detective would do that. Ernest Rawles, if he was still functioning as a detective should, would have done that."

"What do you mean by this insult, Holmes?"

"Let me confess to a crime you are as yet unaware of, Rawles. Do you know how I learned of the theft of the pig farmer's buckets of blood? I found out by entering the records room of Scotland Yard disguised as you."

"You ... I will see you in prison for that!"

"Patience, Rawles! Let me finish! While there, I also looked up the service record of a certain superintendent. Doing so, I learned that you were once an astute investigator, surely the equal of Gregson here or any of a number of other fine policemen. You solved many difficult cases and were decorated for bravery on several occasions. Your career began gloriously, and I find it unfortunate that you are now a loud, pompous, demanding supervisor whose skills have diminished as you have allowed laziness to become your primary characteristic. Within you, Superintendent, is a real detective, one who could, if you would put the effort in, play a vital role in the solving of the mystery which now confronts us. So, you see, I entered through the back door of this house so those gathered outside would not see Sherlock Holmes arriving. They will assume that this investigation and all its progress belong to Ernest Rawles. You will have the credit when this case is done. I am merely here to help. I do not care what the newspapers say about me. My only concern is that the murderer is brought to justice. Let us speak to each other as civilized men, as colleagues. Gregson, Watson, and I will do what we must to finish this matter, but we would rather do so with you than against you."

Rawles stared at Holmes for a moment, rubbed his chin, and spoke.

"You may view the room where the victim lies," he said. "You will tell me what you think. This investigation will remain under my control, and if you attempt any trickery or make any public statement regarding our progress, I will have you arrested."

"I agree to your terms, Superintendent," Holmes said. "Now if you will kindly lead me to the scene of the crime."

❖❖❖

There is a supreme difference between seeing a person first as a dead body and seeing a man you knew personally now reduced to a lifeless vessel. My first sight of the solicitor, John Harper, had been disturbing due to the gruesome way in which he had died, but it was nothing compared to what I felt as the corpse of Dr. Jacob Stewart came into view. I had known Stewart and liked him. He had been a colleague in the medical field, a man of sensitivity and intelligence, and a pleasant dinner companion. Had I known him for longer, I suspect we would have become friends. But now he was dead, lying still and ghostly pale on the floor of the largest room of his flat, the place where he had seen patients while not working his hours at the Charing Cross hospital. It was a private examining room, complete with equipment similar to that which I used in my practice. In fact, it was Stewart's own tools that had been used in the process of murdering him, a fact which made the terrible scene even harder to digest. A man's own livelihood used to end his time upon this earth; a terrible irony indeed!

Gregson, Rawles, and I stood back and watched as Sherlock Holmes did what it often seemed he had been born to do. Now unleashed from worrying about Rawles' interference in the case, Holmes shot straight into the room and went to work with his analysis.

Stewart's corpse rested on the examination table. A tube, the needle of which had been inserted in the right arm, extended from the body, its open end dangling above the floor. Under that end, a few stray drops of blood had landed to stain the thin carpet. But that was all the blood we could see. The rest...and it was all gone, as we could tell from the pallor of the dead man...had been spirited away from the house, an amount far greater than that which had vanished from the home of John Harper days before.

Holmes walked to the body, looked it over for a minute, and began to speak.

"Stewart may have died on this table as his blood was drained, but he was not initially attacked in this room. Note the bruising upon his face and the shallow cut below the left eye. The doctor fought his assailant and was punched several times in the face. Also, there are scuff marks upon the rug, left there, I do not doubt, by the heels of Stewart's shoes as he was dragged here from another room. The transfusion equipment used to empty the body of its blood was taken from the cabinet against the wall, as is demonstrated by the doors remaining open and the unoccupied space upon the third shelf.

"Following the scuff marks will lead us to the place where this assault began."

With that, Holmes rushed from the room. Gregson and I followed close behind, while Rawles, slowed by his girth, struggled to keep up with our pace.

Holmes led us into Stewart's bedroom. The blankets on the bed were undone, as if he had been about to undress and go to sleep when the intruder struck. The bedroom window was open, which reminded me of the window to John Harper's study.

"The murderer," Holmes said, "entered here, caught Stewart off guard, and the two fought. Stewart was unable to fend off the attack, which leads me to believe...and this is an important revelation...that the killer was a man of considerable size and strength, as the deceased doctor was not small or frail. Stewart, now bashed out of his senses, was then dragged down the hall to the room where he practiced the medicinal arts, thrown onto the table...yet more evidence of the criminal's strength...and the bloodletting apparatus was put to use."

"A clear enough picture," Superintendent Rawles said, "but we still have nothing to identify the man who did this, other than his gender and build!"

"Perhaps," Holmes said, "we do have something else. Look at this!"

Holmes bent over the small table that stood beside Stewart's bed. I walked closer to see what the detective had found. There was a small note-book and a pencil. On the page to which the book was open, something had been scribbled, quite hurriedly from the look of the writing.

"Holmes, is that musical notation?"

"It would appear so, Watson."

"But Dr. Stewart was not, as far as I know, musically inclined. Had he been, I suspect he would have mentioned so during our evening at Pagani's, when the subject turned to the arts."

"But, Watson, lack of expertise in a subject does not imply complete ignorance. I suspect the doctor had very good reason to quickly scrawl these signs. It was, indeed, a courageous act."

I began to understand, though Rawles did not, which led him to loudly bellow, "Explain!"

"Dr. Stewart," Holmes said, "knew that Mrs. Harper had heard whistling at the grave of her husband. Perhaps he had noticed my reaction to hearing about the whistling, though I did not tell him that the blood thief who had struck at the pig farm had also, apparently, whistled. I might surmise that Stewart was about to retire for the night when, through the open window, he heard whistling coming from outside. At that point, it was possible that it was only some neighbor walking by on a late stroll, but there was also the chance that the sound foreshadowed something more ominous. Thinking it would be useful for us to know the tune that was being whistled, the doctor grabbed the closest pencil and paper. He took down, to the best of his ability, a notation of the music. As he finished writing, his fears were confirmed and the man who would end his life entered through the window."

"But we can't be sure of this!" Rawles protested.

"We cannot be certain of anything," Holmes replied, "but we must start with something. May I take this notebook, Superintendent, and try to identify the song written here?"

"Very well, Holmes," Rawles said. "I hope you will not waste time doing so."

Holmes put the book in his pocket, and then proceeded to examine the path of the murderer again, this time in the order in which events actually took place, rather than following the backward path that had brought us to the bedroom. When he had finished, Holmes went outside, looked at the ground beneath the window, but could find nothing of use except some flattened grass. Had there been only dirt, footprints may have been visible, but that was not the case, so nothing was learned other than the fact that large shoes had crushed the brush, which reinforced what we now knew of the perpetrator's size.

❋❋❋

"Do you understand the musical notation?" I asked Holmes as we were driven away from the scene by the same constable who had brought us to Stewart's house.

"Not thoroughly," Holmes admitted. "My violin playing was learned mostly by listening to the music and observing the hand movements of others who possess skill with the instrument. I can read music to some extent, but would prefer to allow an expert to examine Stewart's scribbling."

"Do you have a particular candidate in mind?"

"No, but it shall be easy enough to find a roomful of them, though we will have to wait for this evening."

"What can we do until then?"

"The blood, Watson; the blood must be our primary subject of contemplation!"

"But why is this man … this lunatic … so obsessed with the acquisition of blood?"

"That is the question, Watson, on which we must concentrate our minds today. If we do not uncover the specifics of this murderer's mania quickly, more blood will be taken, and from whom I do not know. These deaths will continue until we stop this cycle of murder!"

"Should I assume we will require a greater abundance of reference material than we have at Baker Street?"

"Most certainly," Holmes said, and he turned his attention to our driver. "Constable, take us to the library at St. James's Square!"

❋❋❋

We spent the afternoon going through page after page of books on many subjects. Holmes had decided that although the murderer was insane, he was no idiot, as he had figured out how to use the transfusion tube at Dr. Stewart's home without spilling much blood, but the fact of the killer's intellect did not provide us with a clear picture of his motivation. Blood, other than in its interest to those who study medicine, biology, and the related sciences, is mentioned under many other topics as well. It has a place in religions around the world including, most obviously to the English, Christianity, and the Catholic belief in transubstantiation tells the faithful that wine is literally transformed into the blood of Christ as it is consumed. It is also supposed to have potent magical powers, according to some of the occult systems practiced by those interested in more esoteric ideas. There have even been reports of blood playing a part in certain unusual sexual practices. All these things gave us ideas as to the reason for the murderer's penchant for taking blood from the scene of his crimes, but we still did not have enough evidence to narrow the list down to a few possibilities.

Also, we did not know why John Harper had been a target or why the killer had chosen to slay Dr. Stewart next. We could see the escalation of the desire for blood, as the first instance that we knew of had been the theft of animal blood without killing taking place. The next event of which we had knowledge did involve murder and some of the blood of Harper had been taken from the solicitor's flat. The Stewart killing demonstrated that the urge had grown even more as this time almost the entire blood supply of the victim had been stolen, and that had been done with the utmost care, using equipment specifically designed for the purpose.

But, still, questions outnumbered answers. Why was more and more blood required? What did the murderer do with it? And why did he choose to kill John Harper and Jacob Stewart? There had to be a reason why he went from one victim to the next, as he had been present at Harper's funeral. Yet he had not attempted to take the life, or the blood, of Elizabeth Harper. These were not random murders. There had to be a pattern.

By the end of the afternoon, Holmes and I had learned much about many rather bizarre, and some quite disturbing, reasons one might find blood of interest, yet we still knew no more of this particular person than we had upon examining his latest crime.

We left the library bloated with facts but famished for theories.

❊❊❊

The dining room at Pagani's was full almost to capacity by nine in the evening. The conversation was a persistent hum, punctuated here and there by the rising volume of sudden debates between customers about the quality of a play or the merits of one novelist when compared to another. It was the sort of conversation one expects to hear at an establishment frequented by artistic types, which is precisely why Holmes insisted we dine there. It was the second visit in as many days for me, though Holmes had not been there in some time.

We ate first, or, perhaps I should say, I ate as Holmes ignored his food and concentrated his attention on the others in the restaurant. He watched and listened and I knew he was categorizing the men and women around us, dividing them into lists in his mind, judging them as either potentially useful or unworthy of his attention.

When the waiter approached our table to ask if we required anything else, Holmes grabbed him by the sleeve, had him bend forward, and said to him, "If you would be so kind, I want you to ask several of the other patrons to join us for a moment. Please summon that one over there in the overcoat with the patch on the left elbow, the red-haired man with the spectacles, and the young woman in the green dress."

"Yes, sir," the waiter said, and walked off to do Holmes' bidding.

Moments later, there were five of us at the table.

"The three of you are musicians, I see," Holmes said. "A master of the flute," he stated, nodding to man in the overcoat, "a composer," as he waved a hand in the direction of the bespectacled fellow, "and a lovely young violinist."

"And you are?" asked the composer.

"I am Sherlock Holmes. My name is known quite well in certain circles of London. And this is my associate, Dr. Watson."

"The famous detective," said the violinist as she lit a cigarette. "But what do you want with us?"

"I want something from you," Holmes said, "and I have something I am sure you are all in need of, as I understand that the lives of artists are hard ones and we all must have food on our tables."

Holmes took a wad of bills from his pocket and spread the money on the table. "This is ninety-nine pounds, to be divided evenly among you as payment for the answer to a question, along with a demonstration of that answer if such is needed, although that may require one or more of you to take a short trip with Watson and me."

"What is the question?" asked the flutist with obvious interest.

"This," Holmes said as he fished Dr. Stewart's notebook from his pocket, opened it to the appropriate page, and set it down on the table, "is the question."

The composer picked it up, examined it.

"A piece of music or, rather, a small scrap of a song," he said. "I do not recognize it."

"Let me see it," the flutist said, taking the book from his fellow musician. He stared at the page for a moment, passed it to the violinist.

The young woman read the notation and closed her eyes as she took a long drag on her cigarette.

"It is quite exotic," she said, opening her eyes and putting the notebook down.

"Can you elaborate on that statement?" Holmes asked.

"A strange melody, an odd structure, as if it had been composed as part of an arrangement quite alien to typical European musical sensibilities. I cannot tell much from this small sample, but I suspect it would be quite beautiful, though unusual, if played."

"Interesting," Holmes said. He turned to the other musicians, each in turn. "Do you gentlemen concur with the lady's opinion?"

"I should certainly like to attempt to play it," the flutist answered.

"It never ceases to amaze me," the composer said, "the infinite variety to be found in music. Yes, it is quite, as you have just been told, exotic."

Holmes handed one third of the money to the composer. "Thank you."

"What about our money?" the flutist asked.

"Your part in this is not yet concluded. Fear not, there will be greater compensation for my use of your skills. If you do not mind, settle your payment with the restaurant and accompany Watson and me back to our flat."

The composer went back to his table, counting his thirty-three pounds as he went. A short time later, Holmes, the two remaining musicians, and I were on our way back to Baker Street after two stops so our companions could retrieve their instruments from their lodgings.

As Holmes showed the musicians in, I warned Mrs. Hudson of the noise that was soon to come from our flat. Our poor landlady shrugged and said something about having another cup of tea before bed, so the music would be fine.

Holmes and I sat and watched the musicians take their instruments from the cases. The flutist made the first attempt. The violinist held the notebook in front of him as he began to blow into his flute. The result, just a short sequence of notes, was, as they had predicted, exotic and almost magical in its essence, so far removed was it from anything that might have been included in the music Londoners were used to hearing. It sounded more like something I would have heard from the native musicians during my time in Afghanistan.

"Something from the Arab nations, I believe," Holmes said, putting into words what I had been thinking. "I am sure my friend Sigerson has heard such melodies in his travels."

Sigerson was, of course, the identity Holmes had assumed during the period when I, and everyone in the world other than his brother Mycroft, had believed him to be dead. Under that name, he travelled widely before finally returning to England and resuming his career.

"Let me have a turn," the violinist said. She handed the notebook to the flutist, raised her instrument and bow, and began to play. While the flutist had simply been trying to make sound from the bit of information contained in Stewart's book, the lovely young violinist played beyond the fragment, anticipating where the tune may have gone had more been written, and the room was soon illuminated by a mesmerizing song, music that almost made me forget the murders and the stolen blood.

"Enough!" Holmes shouted, and the music ceased.

"You didn't like it?" the violinist asked, looking hurt.

"It was … quite beautiful," Holmes said, "but we must not forget the business surrounding the song." He handed some money to the flutist. "You may go now. Here is forty-five pounds: the original thirty-three, plus another twelve for coming here to assist us."

When the flutist had pocketed his payment and left, Holmes returned his attention to the violinist. "If you will now be so kind, Miss," he said as he picked up his own violin from beside the fireplace, "as to teach it to me."

❊❊❊

How I managed to get any sleep that night, I shall never be able to explain, for Holmes' practicing, over and over again, of that strange song filled the air for many hours. But I did eventually rest and woke feeling quite refreshed.

Our plan for the morning was to visit Mrs. Harper at her mother's home. Holmes would bring his violin and play her the song we had discovered to see if she could verify it as the same melody she had heard at the cemetery.

That plan, though, was delayed by Mrs. Hudson's announcement that a policeman had come to see us. She let a young constable into the flat, and I saw it was the same man who had driven us to and from the scene of Dr. Stewart's murder.

"Yes, Constable," Holmes said. "What brings you to us this morning?"

"Mr. Holmes, sir, Inspector Gregson needs you immediately."

"What has happened?"

"Something has been found."

"Has another death occurred?"

"No, sir, but you'd best come with me."

"Watson, grab your hat and coat!"

The constable drove us in the direction of Dr. Stewart's home, passed that particular house, and turned left down a street that ran alongside Stewart's. He parked and led us on foot down a narrow path that ran behind the blocks of houses, the sort of route that would allow pedestrians to take a shortcut on which carriages would not fit.

There on the path, at a point where the narrow cobblestone trail took a slight uphill direction, we found Inspector Gregson. On the ground were shards of glass, some large enough to still be recognizable as broken bottles. Many of the fragments were stained red, and the spillage had also marked some of the path's stones.

Holmes shouted, "Blood!" and crouched over the pieces of glass, closely examining the wreckage.

"Some young boys were out playing yesterday," Gregson explained, "and came across this little mess. But they didn't bother to tell anybody until one of them mentioned it to his father at breakfast today. He had the sense to call the police. When the constable who came to look this spot over saw that it was blood, he sent word to me. It seems this path is rarely used, so nobody else noticed this until those boys, or, if they did, they ignored it, as Londoners often do."

"Judging from the amount of drying that had taken place," Holmes said, "this very well could have happened immediately after Dr. Stewart's murder."

"So the man who killed Stewart," I said, "did it for nothing, as he lost his stolen blood shortly after committing the deed!"

"The murderer," Holmes said, standing straight up again and facing Gregson and me, gesturing to various points on the ground as he spoke, "took this path from Stewart's house, hoping it would help him escape unseen. He was carrying the bottles of blood…I estimate four bottles, based

"Blood!"

on the amount of glass here...when he took a slight misstep there, which put him off balance, though not enough to fall, causing him to lose his grip on his precious cargo. He then, as we can see from the marks over there, just past the field of glass, ran from the scene, no doubt out of fear that the sound of the shattering bottles would alert someone to his presence."

"This makes matters worse, does it not, Holmes?" I asked.

"Indeed it does, Watson. With this supply of blood wasted...whatever its intended use may have been...there is sure to be another killing, and very soon!"

"But who ..." Gregson started to ask.

"I do not know, Gregson!" Holmes shouted. "Until we can determine how this person chooses whose blood to take, and why, we have no hope of getting to the next victim before he does! There must be an answer! There must!"

Holmes frustration was palpable. The case was wearing on him. He thrived on interesting puzzles and intellectual challenges, but when human lives were being lost and the solution would not come to him, he felt his failures deeply. Despite his often cold and calculating ways, Holmes hated to see tragedy occur if there was any chance, even slight, that he could prevent it.

❁❁❁

"Yes, that's it!" Elizabeth Harper squealed as Holmes finished scraping his violin bow against the strings. "I couldn't hear it in my mind before, but my memory had been awakened by hearing it now."

"Are you certain?" Holmes asked.

"I have no doubt that this piece of music was what I heard whistled after the funeral."

"Then you have been of great help today, Elizabeth."

"Mr. Holmes, are you any closer to finding out who took John away from me? And now poor Dr. Stewart...I heard about him late yesterday... why is this happening? My husband, and then a man who helped me when I needed it more than ever before; I can't help but think I am to blame in some way."

"That is nonsense," Holmes said. "This sequence of frightful events is entirely the fault of the man who has been committing these acts. Nobody else is to blame, and I urge you not to entertain such thoughts."

We stayed a while longer and drank tea prepared by Mrs. Harper's mother. When we were sure Mrs. Harper was as calm as could be expected under the circumstances, we said our goodbyes and returned to Baker Street.

❁❁❁

It was not long at all before the event we dreaded came to pass.

Both our Scotland Yard allies arrived together late that night, once again waking poor Mrs. Hudson. Superintendent Rawles looked exhausted. As much as I often disliked the man, I now felt sorry for him. Inspector Gregson was not faring much better, as he looked haggard and pale as he sat.

I poured drinks for us all as we waited for Holmes to emerge from his bedroom. I knew, from their faces, what they had come to tell us, but we all seemed to be acting under some unspoken agreement to not talk of it without Holmes, as if it was, perhaps, too terrible to have to be explained twice.

Holmes entered the room, fully dressed, as if he knew we would not linger long at our flat. "There has been a third killing, as I expected!"

"This is dragging on for far too long, Holmes," said Rawles. "We should have solved this by now."

"Yes, I truly wish we had, Superintendent," Holmes said, "but throwing criticism around the room will do no good tonight. Tell me of the crime."

"The victim was a visitor to London this time," Rawles began. "Professor Andrew Van Houten, fifty years of age, had traveled here from the United States to participate in some research in the field of psychology, some sort of study being sponsored by King's College. He had arrived a week ago and taken up lodgings not far from here, renting a second story flat quite similar to this one.

"The murder occurred only an hour ago. How the killer got into the building has not yet been determined, but the landlord, a middle-aged widower, says he heard noises coming from Professor Van Houten's rooms and went up to scold his tenant for being so loud so late at night. When he got to the top of the stairs, he was nearly bowled over by a large man carrying a big sack."

Holmes clapped his hands together once to make Rawles pause his narrative, shouted, "Did he get a look at the brute's face?"

"Unfortunately, no," Rawles said. "It was dark and the landlord is nearsighted and hadn't put his spectacles on. The intruder ran down the stairs and charged out the front door. The landlord then entered the apartment and found the professor dead."

"And how was the murder accomplished this time?" Holmes asked.

It was Gregson who spoke now. "A nasty business gets nastier," he said. "It looked like he just walked in and pummeled the poor professor with his fists first. Then he tossed him up onto a table with his head hanging over the edge, face down, and cut his throat. The blood...most of it, though there was a considerable amount spilled...dripped into bottles or whatever was used to collect it this time. From the amount of blood on the floor, I'd say he got more than he did from Harper but far less than he took from Stewart."

"Thank you, Gregson," said Holmes. "And now we shall have to see the carnage for ourselves. I trust you've left the place well guarded with instructions that nothing is to be moved."

"Of course I did!" Rawles roared, as if Holmes had just dealt him an insult.

"Good," Holmes said. "Watson, prepare for another excursion into the horrors man inflicts upon his fellow creatures!"

❊❊❊

The interior of Professor Van Houten's flat and the condition of his body were as Inspector Gregson had described them. A scene as utterly terrible as the rooms where Harper and Stewart had been killed, the floor was splattered with blood and the corpse had been savagely beaten and had its throat cut open almost from ear to ear. It was decided, based on the pattern of the blood that had avoided capture and now stained the floor that the killer had been in a great hurry this time, probably due to the presence of the landlord downstairs, as opposed to at Dr. Stewart's house, where the residence had been empty except for the victim and his assailant. Holmes agreed with Gregson's earlier statement that several bottles had been placed on the floor at the end of the table and much, but not nearly all, of the loosed blood had fallen into those containers, which had then been carried away in the bag the landlord had mentioned the fiend as having during his escape. There was not much more for Holmes to discover there, as Gregson and Rawles had thoroughly determined what had happened.

The landlord trembled as Holmes questioned him.

"At what time did you retire for the night?"

"About nine, I think."

"And was Professor Van Houten home at this time?"

"I do not believe so."

"He had his own key?"

"Yes."

"And his entering did not wake you?"

"It did not."

"When the large man who nearly knocked you down the stairs exited the building, did you hear him turn the latch to unlock the front door?"

The landlord thought for a moment, and then admitted, "No, I did not hear such a sound."

"Can you tell me anything at all of the appearance of this man?" Holmes asked.

"I'm sorry, sir, but I already told the inspector that he was tall and broad-shouldered, but I couldn't see his face."

"Thank you," Holmes said. "That will be all."

The landlord went back to his own rooms.

Holmes turned to Gregson, Rawles, and I. "So the door was unlocked when the murderer departed. Van Houten arrived after the landlord had gone to bed. Either the killer had a key, which I find unlikely, since, if he was known to Van Houten there may not have been such sudden violence to fell the professor before the slaying slash was administered, or Van Houten carelessly left the door unlocked, thus sealing his fate."

Superintendent Rawles was the next to participate in the conversation. "So we have the theft of blood again, but how does this American professor connect to the other victims. It started with Harper, and Stewart was connected in that he treated Harper's wife. The killer saw him with her at the cemetery, if not before, but how do we get from Stewart to this poor Van Houten?"

"That is the missing piece to this puzzle," Holmes said, "and its absence is having a devastating effect."

"What do you intend to do about this missing piece, Holmes?" Rawles asked angrily. "I can only suppress the details of these crimes from the public for so long before the news leaks out and panic erupts!"

"I intend to think, perhaps as I have never thought before," Holmes said. "There is an answer, and I will not rest until I have found it. You may have the body of this unfortunate man taken from here now, Rawles, for there is no more to be discovered in this blood-soaked room. Come, Watson, I require a full pipe and a chair in which to consider all we know and all we must yet uncover."

❁❁❁

Sherlock Holmes, true to his word, retreated into his mind immediately upon our return to Baker Street. He sat down, lit his pipe, and closed his eyes, occasionally inhaling deeply and letting the rich tobacco smoke drift back out of his mouth and flow upward to dissipate against the ceiling. When the pipe went out, he placed it on the table beside his seat, folded his hands upon his lap, let his head rest against the back of the chair and did not move at all for hours. I could only imagine what was going through his brain, how he desperately and methodically tried and tried again to put the puzzle's pieces together and fill the terrible gaps in the picture. I hoped he would hit upon the right solution and suddenly open his eyes, clap his hands, and shout something like, "Watson, I have it at last!"

But that moment did not arrive. By the early morning hours, Holmes was still lost in thought, so I retired and had several hours of sleep. When I rose at eight, nothing had changed, so I tried to occupy myself without making any noise that would disturb Holmes' process of analysis. The newspaper bored me and I had nothing else I strongly desired to read, so I sat at the table in the center of the room and took a sheet of paper and a fountain pen and began to slowly write down some of the particulars of the case, hoping something might occur to me while I waited for Holmes to reach a revelation. At one point, Mrs. Hudson opened the door halfway, stuck her head in through the opening, and asked in a voice just above a whisper if I would like some tea. I answered with a nod.

I was still at the table when our landlady returned and tiptoed in with her tray. She had brought two cups in case Holmes had come out of his trance but shook her head as she saw that he was still in the same position, still unresponsive to outside stimulae. She carefully put the teapot and all its accessories down and was about to make her exit when she happened to look down at my notes. All I had written so far was a list of the victims' names and professions:

John Harper, solicitor
Jacob Stewart, physician
Andrew Van Houten, professor of psychology

At that moment, the most wonderful, unexpected, joyously coincidental event took place. Our dear old landlady, the gentle and longsuffering Mrs. Hudson, who knew nothing about the string of horrific murders... for we made sure not to speak of the grisly details of our worst cases in her presence...glanced at the list of names and changed the course of our investigation with one simple sentence.

"Dr. Watson, I'd have expected better of you than to be reading that dreadful book!"

"What book, Mrs. Hudson?" I asked, confused. I glanced around, but there were no books on the table or close by. "I am just making some notes on Holmes' latest case."

"Oh, I'm sorry, Doctor," Mrs. Hudson said, picking up the sheet of paper and reading it more closely. "I misread. This reminded me of a book I read not very long ago, but I see now that these are different names, though similar."

Willing to explore any avenue for answers, no matter how flimsy the chance may have seemed, I decided to question Mrs. Hudson further.

"What book was that?"

"I would rather put it out of my mind, Dr. Watson, for it was not the sort of story I would like to revisit."

"I simply wish to know the title."

"It was called *Dracula*, and was a story of horrors."

"What sort of horrors, Mrs. Hudson. I'm sorry, but this may be of some importance."

"How could a silly book written to give nightmares be of any importance to you or Mr. Holmes?"

"Will you please just tell me about the book? I'm begging you, Mrs. Hudson."

"All right, Doctor," she said, sitting down at the table with me. "It was about this awful creature...a vampire, they called him...who wasn't really alive, yet wasn't truly dead either, and survived by drinking the blood of living people."

"Mrs. Hudson, do you still have this book in your flat?"

"No, I gave it to my friend Mrs. Maxwell. Such terrors suit her interests better than mine."

"I see, well I suppose it shouldn't be too difficult to find a copy. And these names, Mrs. Hudson, are like some names in the book, you say?"

"Yes, Doctor, though not quite the same. There is a solicitor named, I think, Harker instead of Harper ... and a Seward, not Stewart ... and there's a professor with a Dutch name beginning with Van."

"And what do these characters have to do with the blood-drinking creature?"

"Well, in the end of the story they hunted him down and killed him."

"Mrs. Hudson, thank you."

"You're quite welcome, of course, Dr. Watson, though I still don't understand for what."

"Holmes!" I shouted, turning toward the silent detective. "Are you close enough to the land of the conscious to have heard any of what just transpired?"

Holmes' position did not change, but his eyes opened and his lips moved.

"I heard every word. Mrs. Hudson, please take away that tea and brew us some strong black coffee. Watson, at what time does the nearest bookseller open for business?"

❁❁❁

By half past ten, I had acquired two copies of the novel, *Dracula* by Bram Stoker. The proprietor of the bookshop told me that the book had sold only modestly well in the two years since its publication, though it had received quite a bit of praise from critics.

I took the books back to our flat, gave one to Holmes, and sat down to read my copy. I read it in sequence, just as I would have read any novel. Holmes, however, went through the book in his own eccentric way, turning pages rapidly, and then pausing to read certain sections, and then rushing past whole chapters again, very much like a dog pushing aside great amounts of dirt to find a buried bone.

"There are indeed some striking parallels here, Watson!" Holmes said after a while. "In this book we find the characters of Jonathan Harker, a young solicitor; Dr. John or 'Jack' Seward, head of an asylum; and Professor Abraham Van Helsing, a Dutch doctor who seems to know something about many strange subjects. What do you think of it so far?"

"To be honest, Holmes, I am quite enjoying it. It is a thrilling tale, told in an interesting style, as the author has chosen to tell his story by means of journal entries and letters. I can see why Mrs. Hudson found it terrifying."

"Read on, Watson. I shall be back in several hours."

"Have you read it all already, Holmes?"

"Only the parts I found important. Reading for pleasure and absorbing all the details is an act better suited to you, my friend. Finish the book while I look into some other matters that may be of use to us now that the direction of this case has shifted, I hope, in our favor."

Holmes grabbed his hat and coat and hurried out the door. I returned my attention to the deepening nightmare of Bram Stoker's epic of fright.

❀❀❀

It was nearly dark when Holmes returned. He rushed in, tossed his hat and coat aside, sat down, lit his pipe, and asked, "Have you finished your reading, Watson?"

"I have," I answered, "and have even gone back and reread certain sections. It is a ghastly story, but well told."

"And do you agree that this novel may be the basis of our murderer's maniacal activities?"

"Indeed I do, Holmes. It seems quite probable that this man has read *Dracula* and formed an obsession with the story, which has led him to engage in these killings and steal the blood of his victims. Do you think he believes that he himself is the title character?"

"That is possible," Holmes said, "or perhaps he thinks it is his mission to avenge the slaying of the vampire."

"And he is under the illusion that his victims are the characters from the book, due to the similarity of names?"

"It would make sense," Holmes agreed. "He comes across the name of John Harper, who was, coincidentally, a solicitor like the Harker of the novel. After murdering Harper, he follows the widow, Elizabeth, hoping she will lead him to the others responsible for Dracula's demise. It happens that her doctor at Charing Cross Hospital bears the common surname of Stewart, which is quite close in sound to Seward. He overhears Elizabeth calling the doctor by name after the funeral, and so he chooses Stewart as his next victim. Then, having accidentally lost the blood he took from the doctor, he must have a new victim almost immediately, for it seems he cannot go long without acquiring a supply of the fluid of life. He then somehow hears of the visiting American, Professor Andrew Van Houten, who, again, has a name that resembles that of one of the book's primary characters.

"Before all this, he had begun his strange work by stealing the blood of pigs from that farmer in Shepherd's Bush, but animal blood, it seems, did not suit his purposes."

I thought Holmes' theory was quite sound, but I still did not understand one vital detail of the case.

"But what does he do with all the blood?" I asked. "Surely, even if he is under the impression that he is Dracula or another vampire, he cannot be consuming it, especially in such quantities. Human blood is, for the vast majority of people, an emetic, which means that attempting to drink it will cause one to vomit."

"I do not know what he does with it, Watson. I can only tell you that, as we have known since before learning of his apparent obsession with this book, he is bound by some urge to collect it, and has taken to killing his fellow human beings to do so."

"Yes," I said, "it is a question as yet unanswered. And I have another question on my mind."

"Then ask," Holmes said.

"While I have been here reading for all these hours, what have you been doing?"

"I have been walking, Watson, and pondering what he have learned today, considering ways we may use our new knowledge to find this crazed person before the need for fresh blood causes him to choose his next target."

"And what course of action have you decided on, Holmes?"

"It would be wise, I think,' Holmes said, "for us to consult the author of *Dracula*."

❀❀❀

"Where are we going, Holmes?" I asked as we rode along the streets of London.

"The Diogenes Club," Holmes answered.

I had been to that particular...and rather odd...gentleman's club on several prior occasions. Holmes' brother, Mycroft, was one of its founders and seemed to spend most of his time there. The Diogenes Club was a quiet place, with its silence strictly enforced in every area I had been allowed admittance to except the Stranger's Room. Talking was absolutely forbidden in most of the building, and any man who broke the rule would be told to leave. Most of the members seemed content to sit and read, often for hours at a time.

"And what do you hope to accomplish there?"

"Do you recall that trivially silly case a year ago when one of the club's members asked me to look into the matter of several books having vanished from the club's library?"

"Yes, I do. You solved the mystery within several hours if I recall. It turned out that one of the members, since expelled because of that matter, was a collector of rare editions and could not resist the urge to take the books for his private hoard. You were summoned on that occasion by a man called … Baxter, wasn't it? He was of the opinion that your brother could have caught the culprit in half the time it took you, but Mycroft was away at the time."

"Yes," Holmes said, "it was during the case that I had access to a directory of at least most of the club's members. I was not allowed to take the list from the building, and I cannot remember all its names, but I was fairly certain I had seen this Bram Stoker listed. I contacted Mycroft yesterday while you were still reading the novel and he confirmed my recollection."

"So we are going there to meet with this novelist?"

"Indeed."

"But how will we converse with him in the Diogenes of all places? You surely do not intend to use the Stranger's Room, where we might be overheard by anyone."

"Have you seen all the Diogenes Club's chambers, Watson?"

"Of course not, Holmes; I have been in only a fraction of the place."

"Would it surprise you that Mycroft has a private office in a corner of the cellar?"

"There is very little that would surprise me about your brother, Holmes. He is a most unusual man."

"That he is, and he has agreed to lend us his space for the purpose of interviewing the man who dreamed up Dracula."

"And what do you know of Stoker so far?"

"Abraham Stoker," Holmes said, "more often called Bram, is fifty-one years old and was born in Ireland. Although a novelist of some medium success, he is better known as a theatre man. He is manager of the Lyceum Theatre and personal assistant to the famous actor Sir Henry Irving."

"Several impressive accomplishments," I said as we arrived outside the Diogenes Club.

❀❀❀

An employee of the club led us inside and down a flight of stairs to the left of the main reading room. The underground area of the building was quite large, with corridors branching off in several directions. We were soon inside Mycroft Holmes' office, which contained an assortment of books, a large map of Europe on the wall, a sturdy oak desk with an accompanying chair I suspected had been specifically crafted to accommodate Mycroft, who was a very wide man, and a smaller desk upon which sat a typewriter. There were also three other chairs, of which Sherlock Holmes and I took two. When Bram Stoker was admitted to the room five minutes later, he took the third seat, none of us wanting to overstep a possible boundary and occupy Mycroft's chair, although Holmes' brother would not be joining us.

Bram Stoker was a sturdily built man with a full brown beard that had begun to show some gray. He nodded at us politely as he entered, though his face betrayed the fact that he was confused as to why he had been summoned to the Diogenes Club and brought to its subterranean level.

"Please sit, Mr. Stoker," Holmes said.

"What the devil is this all about?" Stoker asked. "Where is Mycroft? It was he who sent for me."

"He did so at my request," Holmes explained. "I am Mycroft's brother, Sherlock Holmes."

"The solver of mysteries," Stoker said. He turned to me and asked, "Who are you?"

"Dr. John Watson," I said, offering a handshake, which Stoker accepted.

"I know the name," the Irish author said. "You have written some accounts of your friend's exploits."

"Yes, I have," I said, "and it is Holmes' current exploit that has caused us to wish to speak with you, sir."

"I hope I'm not suspected of some wrongdoing!"

"None at all, Mr. Stoker," Holmes said. "We are here to consult you about some unintended consequences that may have been initiated by your novel, *Dracula*."

"What sort of consequences?"

"Three murders," Holmes said.

A look of shock came over Stoker's face. He was silent for a moment, then, "Tell me what has happened."

"I will," Holmes said, "but first I must insist that you share the details of what I am about say with no one, as certain facts have been kept quiet by Scotland Yard to avoid alarming the public."

"I know how to keep my mouth shut," Stoker said. "Let me have it, whatever it is."

"Please sit, Mr. Stoker," Holmes said.

With that permission, Sherlock Holmes gave a lengthy and detailed account of the murders of John Harper, Dr. Jacob Stewart, and Professor Andrew Van Houten, including all the facts and theories we had collected. Bram Stoker was visibly disturbed as he listened.

When Holmes had finished, Stoker shook his head sadly, stared down at the floor, and finally looked up at Holmes and spoke again.

"I somehow managed to grow up healthy enough, but I was a sickly child. And as I lay there weak and tired, my mother would lull me to sleep by telling me the dark ghost and fairy stories of Ireland. Her voice calmed me, but the content of the tales painted vivid pictures in my imagination and often induced nightmares. It shaped an important part of who I grew to be. I came to love the dramas that form in the mind when the right influences do their work. This drove me to work in theatre and it put me to work with a pen as well. I wrote *Dracula* to inspire such dreams, however dark they may be, in the minds and hearts of others…as well as to make some money; I'd be a liar if I claimed that wasn't a motivation as well… and I think, based on what readers have told me, that I have succeeded. But this … this saga of butchery, man killing his fellow man because of some obsession with a story I concocted!"

I felt sorry for the man. "You must not blame yourself, Mr. Stoker," I said.

"I am not an idiot, Dr. Watson!" he roared, his old accent becoming more apparent with his indignation. "But they were my words, the product of my imagination, and I now feel obligated to help end this series of killings in any way I can. Tell me, Mr. Holmes, what is it that you wish me to do?"

"I simply want to ask you some questions," Holmes said, "and you must think them through completely and do your utmost to answer honestly and include all details no matter how trivial they may seem."

"You have my word that I will try," said Stoker.

"Since the publication of *Dracula*," Holmes asked, "have you had much interaction with those who have read the book?"

"I have received a number of letters, some praising the book and others damning it. I have also been approached by various people at the Lyceum Theatre and elsewhere, even several times at restaurants and other such places. Short conversations regarding the book have taken place and I have occasionally been asked to sign copies of *Dracula*. It does not surprise me that readers can find me, as I am, and have been for some time, a public figure due to my work in the world of the stage."

"I understand," Holmes said. "I am now going to relate to you what I know, or at least suspect, of a certain individual. If any of these details cause you to think of a specific person, please tell me so."

Stoker nodded. Holmes began.

"We are looking for a man. He is not very old, for he is able to run and engage in other forms of physical exertion, including acts of violence. He is quite tall and broad-shouldered. He is right-handed. And he has a habit of whistling often, perhaps as if he is not even aware he is doing so."

Stoker sat up straighter in his chair, a look of excitement crossing his face. "Most of that could have described a thousand men," he said, "but the last part!"

"You mean the whistling," Holmes guessed.

"Yes," Stoker said. "Was it a strange song, something unlikely to be heard in London?"

Sherlock Holmes began to hum the song.

"Yes!" Stoker shouted. "What is it?"

"As near as we have been able to determine, based on the opinions of several musicians, it may have its origins in one of the Arab nations."

"And it has caused you to recall something, Mr. Stoker?" I asked.

"Several months ago," Stoker said, "I was leaving the theatre one afternoon…I remember being quite hungry after a rather intense argument with Henry Irving over the particulars of a production we were planning… when I was approached by a man I had never seen before. I was quite rude to him at first, due to my mood rather than anything he had done to deserve such treatment, but my attitude softened when he said, in a nervous stutter, that he had enjoyed my book.

"We conversed for a few minutes and he admitted to me that *Dracula* had made such an impression that it had induced dreams. But he told me this calmly…I took it as a compliment…not in any way that would cause alarm or make me suspect him of being dangerous. I remember he walked with me for a few blocks and told me something of his life. It seems he had just returned from some time in the army and was now looking for employment so he might afford to have his own flat rather than continuing to live under his father's roof. He seemed a polite, sensible young man and I even offered to consider hiring him to do some custodial work at the Lyceum. I suggested he come to see me at some point in the following days, but he never appeared. We parted ways before I reached the restaurant I was headed for, and as he walked away from me I heard him begin to whistle that odd song. I did not think of him again, except to assume that his search for work had led him elsewhere."

"And his appearance," Holmes asked, "did it match the description I just gave?"

"In that he was tall and strong, yes it did," Stoker said. "As for his age, I would estimate him to have been between twenty-five and thirty years old."

"What can you tell us of his face?"

"Not much, I'm afraid," Stoker admitted. "It was a brief meeting and I do not recall anything unusual about his look. It was a normal, average face, not strikingly handsome, nor unfortunately ugly."

"If you saw him again, would you recognize him?" Holmes asked.

"I believe so," Stoker said. "But how can you find him if all you know is his size, approximate age, and the song he likes to whistle?"

"The answer will come to me, Mr. Stoker," Holmes said. "It must come to me or more blood will be shed. You have been a great help to us."

"I have done very little," Stoker argued.

"You have confirmed some of the details surrounding our prey," Holmes countered, "and that is of immense importance. Thank you, sir, and good-bye."

With that, Holmes rushed out of Mycroft's office. I hurriedly shook Bram Stoker's hand and ran after Holmes.

Back on the street, Holmes rapidly instructed me, "Watson, go and fetch Gregson and Rawles. Bring them to Baker Street. I will meet you there in an hour."

❁❁❁

The four of us gathered in Holmes' and my flat, drinking Mrs. Hudson's always excellent tea. Holmes revealed to Gregson and Rawles everything we had learned during our interview with Bram Stoker.

"So still no progress has been made," Rawles complained. "You and Watson are just going in circles, Holmes, as Gregson and I follow along like dutiful servants. I've nearly had enough of this!"

"Superintendent Rawles," Holmes said, "we have a chance at gaining ground here if we pursue the few small clues provided by Stoker. We now know the approximate age of our suspect as well as the important fact that he was discharged from the army not long ago. This is the juncture in our investigation where I need you to use your rank to gain access to some information."

"What do you want?" Rawles demanded.

"Contact the army," Holmes said, "as quickly as you can and ask for records of any men released from service in the past year who have home addresses in London."

"But that could be dozens or hundreds of men!" Rawles protested.

"Not so many," Holmes argued, "if we eliminate certain specifications. Older men, such as those retiring after many years of service, can be disqualified. So can any who were sent home due to crippling or noticeable injuries. We know our man is not blind or missing any of his limbs. Also, as he was looking for a job when Stoker encountered him, we can assume he is of the middle or lower classes and not the holder of a high degree of education and therefore unlikely…though it is not outside the bounds of possibility…to be an officer, so we must concentrate first on the enlisted ranks. So, Superintendent, we are seeking a recently discharged former soldier in his twenties or early thirties, without physical handicap or deformity, who is tall and strongly built, and was probably a private or corporal."

"Well," Rawles sighed, "I suppose that will shorten the list a bit."

"It will," Holmes said. "Is it a task you are capable of handling?"

"Undoubtedly," Rawles spat as he stood. He stormed out of the flat and we could hear his loud footsteps as he descended the stairs.

"And what am I to do, Holmes?" Inspector Gregson asked.

"You will accompany Watson to King's College. There is a part of my plan to identify the murderer that I did not mention to Superintendent Rawles."

"And what is that?"

"It occurs to me that we still do not know how he became aware of the existence of Professor Andrew Van Houten in order to fall into the delusion that Van Houten was a character from *Dracula*. This leads me to wonder if he, perhaps, heard or read the name at the college, where Van Houten had come to engage in work in the field of psychology. Perhaps our blood-stealing killer had taken employment at the college or had even enrolled there. If we can acquire…using your police credentials of course, Gregson…a list of those associated with King's College, we can look for names it has in common with the results of Rawles research regarding the army. When that is done, see if you can find anyone working on the psychological study Van Houten was in London to participate in. Give them a description of the suspect. Perhaps casting that bait into the water will yield some sort of result."

"I understand," Gregson said. "Shall we be off then, Dr. Watson?"

"Indeed," I said, and grabbed my hat. "Holmes, what will you do?"

"I am going to sit and smoke," Holmes said, "and read this *Dracula* story more thoroughly than I did on my last perusal of the book. Lurid fantasy is of little interest to me, as there is sufficient evil in the world that I do not need authors to create more to fill my mind, but I believe a deeper knowledge of this tale and its central monster, this vampire, is vital to my forming a complete picture of the murderer's bizarre obsession with blood.

"One of the most frightening facts I have learned in my years in this profession is that the mind is such a fragile thing that a single book, if read at a time in one's life when one is most vulnerable, can completely distort a human being's understanding of reality."

❁❁❁

Gregson and I found the record keeping clerk at King's College to be quite cooperative. He was happy to provide us with a list of all low-level employees hired within the past year. This included janitors and other maintenance workers, as well as librarians, clerks of various kinds, and other jobs that required no complicated credentials or advanced education. We were told it would take some time to gather the information, so we agreed to return to his desk in an hour.

"One more question," Gregson said to the clerk. "There is, I believe, a project of some kind involving the science of psychology to be run at the college. Can you tell us the name of the man in charge of that affair?"

"That would be Professor Appleton," the clerk said, and gave us directions to the proper building.

❁❁❁

"And what do a police inspector and a physician need from me?" Professor Appleton asked after introductions had been made. Appleton was a slim man in his forties. He smiled and seemed full of energy. His office was a cluttered mess of papers, books, and other paraphernalia, and smelled of sweet pipe tobacco.

"We understand," Gregson said, "that you were leading a study in which the late Professor Van Houten was involved."

At that, Appleton's smile left his face. "Yes, Inspector, I am. It's a terrible thing, what happened to Andrew. He and I corresponded for quite some time. I finally had an opportunity to meet him in person and work with him on an important research project and then … so suddenly the man was gone, erased from the world almost as if he'd never been here at all. Are you working to catch his killer, Inspector?"

"I am," Gregson said.

"Well then I certainly hope you've come here to ask my assistance, because I would very much like to help you put a noose around the bloody bastard's neck!"

"That's what I'd hoped you would say," Gregson said. "I'd like you to answer some questions."

"Of course," Appleton said with a nod.

"What is the purpose of this psychological study?"

"To understand the changes in one's personality and behavior that can be triggered by an injury to the head and, by extension, the brain that resides within it."

"How many people are involved in this study?"

"Four professors; Andrew would have been the fifth. And twelve subjects, most of them patients referred to me by various sources."

"When is this study to begin?"

"Officially, in a fortnight, though I have already interviewed several of the subjects in some detail in order to plan certain aspects of the project."

"I see," said Gregson. He paused for a moment, perhaps to consider his next question. As he fell silent, I noticed a scrap of paper among the clutter on the professor's desk.

"Pardon me," I said, "but that small piece of paper there." I reached forward, tapped it with my forefinger. I had read the words on it, upside down from my vantage point. Written on it was, 'Prof. A. Van Houten,' followed by the address of the building in which Van Houten's body had been discovered with its throat cut and its blood drained.

"The address of the flat Andrew had rented," Appleton said, peering down at the desk. "What of it?"

"How long has it been sitting on your desk in plain sight?"

"Several days, I suppose, or perhaps even a week."

"By all that's holy," Gregson muttered, apparently seeing the same picture I had just imagined. "Ask him, Dr. Watson!"

"What?" Appleton asked, confusion painted across his face, then, as revelation struck, "Dear Lord! Have I … inadvertently …"

"It's not your fault, Professor," I assured him, "but I must ask you to honestly answer a series of questions. I understand your first instinct may be to avoid breaching the trust your patients place in you, but I must insist you tell us everything you can, for it may save innocent lives."

"Yes, yes," Appleton said. "Please ask me anything."

I decided to begin with the widest possible question and work to narrow the field as Appleton answered. "How many of the patients have been in this office?"

"Six of them," Appleton answered.

"Of those six, how many are men?"

"There is only one woman among them."

"Are any of the men under forty years of age?"

"Two of them are."

"Have either of them recently left the British Army?"

"Both have," Appleton said. "They were referred to me by an old friend, a colonel, when I happened to mention my study of the effects of head injuries to him over a drink one night."

"Is one of them a young man in his twenties or very early thirties, tall and strong?"

"Yes."

"Does he have a habit of whistling?"

"Indeed he does."

At that, I began to whistle the song that had become so familiar in recent days.

"Yes, yes," said Appleton. "That is the tune he whistled as he entered this room on the day I met him. And his constant urge to whistle it is one of the changes that befell him after his wound."

"How much can you tell us about him?" I asked, grabbing, without asking, a pencil and sheet of paper from the professor's desk.

"His name," Appleton said, "is Jasper Jefferson. Twenty-six years old, he was a corporal with a spotless service record until a year ago. While in Constantinople, Corporal Jefferson got into a fight, a silly brawl with some locals over some trivial matter. During the fight, a chair was picked up and smashed over Jefferson's head. The resulting injury, a severe concussion, seemed to heal, but Jefferson began to exhibit strange patterns of behavior. He was unruly, restless, easily distracted from his duties, as if all the discipline he'd possessed had been knocked out of him. And, on top of that, there was the whistling. That song, it seems, had been played by local musicians there in Turkey at the time of the fight. It must have been what he heard as the impact to his head occurred, and the music was somehow ingrained in his mind. He whistled it almost incessantly until his fellow soldiers nearly resorted to violence to make him stop.

"After some time, it was decided that he was no longer fit for military service, and so he was discharged when his regiment returned to England. Once back in civilian life, he took up residence with his father here in London and sought work, though employment was difficult to find as his habit of whistling and general personality are not easily overlooked. He was sent to me by the colonel I mentioned a moment ago and I conversed with him for some time, ultimately coming to the conclusion that his case would fit my study nicely."

I stood, as did Gregson.

"Are you certain Jefferson is the man you're looking for, Dr. Watson?" Professor Appleton asked.

"Almost absolutely," I said. "The facts fit quite clearly. How did he seem to you, Professor? Would you have judged him to be a dangerous man?"

"Not any more so than a thousand other former soldiers now living in London. He was a confused young man with unusual problems, but I'd never have guessed him to be a coldblooded murderer."

"Tell me, Professor, did Jefferson ever mention a novel entitled *Dracula*?"

"No, I don't believe he talked about books at all. Is it of some importance?"

"We have no time to discuss that now, Professor Appleton. I assume you have the address of Jefferson and his father on record."

"Of course," Appleton said.

"Then hand it over now," Inspector Gregson rather rudely said, "before this lunatic kills again!"

With an address scrawled beside the notes I'd scribbled while listening to Appleton talk, Gregson and I raced outside, boarded our carriage, and urged the driver on at all possible speed, headed to Baker Street to tell Sherlock Holmes of our success.

❁❁❁

Gregson and I stormed up the stairs, bypassing the usual greeting to Mrs. Hudson. At the top, I flung the door open and marched in, Gregson just behind me, to find Holmes standing, looking over the shoulder of Superintendent Rawles, who was tracing his finger down a sheet of paper, reading names aloud.

"Johnson, Private Percival; Elliston, Sergeant Edward; Simmons, Private George … there are too many, Holmes. We shall never find the right one!"

"Corporal Jasper Jefferson!" I shouted, startling Rawles and causing Holmes to spin about and stare. Gregson and I were out of breath with excitement.

"You have had success then, Watson?" Holmes asked.

"Indeed we have," I said. "Jasper Jefferson is the man we want. Everything fits!" I sat down to explain, as quickly as I could, all we had learned from Professor Appleton.

When I had finished, Holmes clapped.

Superintendent Rawles rose from his chair, scowled at us. "You sent me on a fool's errand, Holmes! You sent me to beg for that long list of names while Gregson and Watson were off getting to the root of this mystery!"

"I had to cover all avenues of investigation, Rawles, now please shut your mouth. Need I remind you that your duty is to apprehend this murderer?"

"Give me his address!" Rawles demanded, holding his hand out.

I glanced at Holmes.

"Give it to him, Watson. It does not matter who holds the paper. We are all going to this man's residence together … and armed."

❋❋❋

We reached the address as quickly as we could, the five of us…Holmes, Gregson, Rawles, the constable who had driven us, and I…with revolvers in hand, marched up the front walk of the handsome two-story house belonging, according to our information, to the father of Jasper Jefferson. We did not know what to expect. If Jefferson was home, would we find the confused but apparently harmless young man described by Professor Appleton, or would we meet the ruthless killer who had butchered Harper, Stewart, and Van Houten to satisfy a strange obsession with blood? And what of Jefferson's father? How do you explain to a man that his son is a monster?

"If it's locked, we're going to break the door down and storm the place," Rawles said. "Gregson and Constable Miller, the two of you will find the stairs as quickly as you can and search the top floor. Holmes, Watson, and I will take the downstairs."

We marched up the front walkway. Gregson tried the door. It did not open.

"Let us in, Miller," Rawles said.

Constable Miller took several steps back, ran forward, slammed into the door with his shoulder, and we heard the wood begin to crack. He repeated the act and this time the door split down the middle, both sides swinging inward. Poor Miller almost fell into the house, but managed to right his balance and stepped inside instead, his revolver at the ready. We followed him in.

Immediately upon entry, Gregson and Miller, as ordered, climbed the staircase that stood just to the left of the doorway. It was a small upstairs, for we heard, only a moment later, Gregson call out, "There are only some empty rooms. Nobody is here!"

As Holmes, Rawles, and I turned our attention to the first floor, we were suddenly assaulted by the smell.

It was the odor of death and decay, rancid and rank, worse than anything I had smelled in years. We followed the stench down the hallway, glancing into each room as we went, kitchen first, then a bedroom.

We found the parlor next and stopped in the doorway, stunned. When the worst of the shock had subsided, Holmes was the first with enough courage to step inside. I followed, with Rawles coming next. Gregson, who had caught up to us, entered last, ordering Constable Miller to remain in the hall.

None of us could have been prepared for what we found in that parlor. As horrific as had been the scenes of Harper, Stewart, and Van Houten's deaths, this was far worse.

The body of a man lay on the floor, in an open space where the furniture had been shoved aside to make room. He had been decapitated and his head rested a few inches from the point where it had been severed from his body. The corpse was badly decomposed and covered with flies and maggots. What made the scene even worse, and the slaughterhouse stench even more unbearable, was that vast amounts of blood had been poured over the dead man, spilling all over the body and the carpet, some of it splattering the nearby chairs and couch. Empty bottles and jugs littered the floor around the corpse.

"Nasty business," Gregson muttered.

Rawles said nothing. He took out a handkerchief, which he held over his nose and mouth.

I could feel my hands trembling.

Only Holmes seemed unaffected by the horror we now witnessed. "Watson," he said, "will you please examine the body?"

I stepped forward, my shoes sticking to the soup of spilled blood that covered the floor. I bent over the body and looked as closely as I could without kneeling. The decay of the corpse made it difficult to see what the man had looked like in life, but the state of what skin remained, as well as the condition of the teeth and the bones that showed through the diminishing flesh, made it clear that he had not been young.

"He was of the proper age to be Jefferson's father," I said. "And the cause

Upstairs... we heard Gregson call out, "Nobody is here!"

of death is obvious. His head was hacked off with a large knife of some sort."

"How long would you estimate this man to have been dead, Watson?" Holmes asked.

"Perhaps as long as two or even three months," I said. "This terrible smell, as well as the presence of all these insects, is due more to the freshness of some of this spilled blood, rather than the body, which has dried to a great degree since the beheading."

"So," Holmes said, "we can assume that this man, probably the elder Jefferson, was slain before the murders of John Harper and possibly even before the theft of the pigs' blood from the farmer."

"That is a safe bet," I said.

"So the maniac killed his own father," Rawles said, "and then started murdering other men to take their blood and pour it on his first victim. The man is truly insane. But even lunatics have reasons, even if normal men cannot understand them. What in God's name was he thinking?"

"Perhaps," Holmes said, "it happened this way: Jasper Jefferson, having returned from military service and taken up residence with his father, was already on the edge of insanity due to the head injury suffered in Constantinople. He was in London, looking for work, and reading the novel *Dracula*. He had some sort of argument with his father, went into a rage, and committed patricide by decapitation.

"Such an act, committed in a moment of blind, angry passion, would surely unseat the sanity of almost any man, especially one who may have already been suffering from delusions. Seeing the corpse of his father, his mind connected it with the final fight in the book, in which the vampire Count Dracula is beheaded by the knife of Jonathan Harker.

"Jefferson, in this moment of utter mental confusion, came to believe that this is not the corpse of his father, but that of the vampire. In the novel, the body of Dracula crumbles to dust, but as this body did not vanish in such a way, Jefferson decided that it could be resurrected. If it is blood that a vampire requires to remain alive, then it must be blood, the mind of Jasper Jefferson surmised, that is the key to such a being's restoration.

"At first, he tried animal blood, stealing it from the farmer at Shepherd's Bush. When that did not work, he decided that human blood was required. We do not know what human blood he first tried to use for this purpose. Perhaps he cut himself and let his own blood drip upon the corpse, or perhaps he murdered others we are not aware of. Then, at some point in the evolution of Jefferson's mania, he came to the conclusion that the blood of those responsible for Dracula's death must be used to resurrect him.

"He could have easily happened upon the name of John Harper, who, like Harker in the book, was a solicitor. Such firms do advertise, so the name could have caught Jefferson's eye. We know that he then most probably overheard Dr. Stewart's name at the cemetery and linked it, in his mind, with Dr. Seward from the novel. And we have recently learned how he came to know the name and address of Professor Andrew Van Houten, whom he identified, we believe, with the character of Abraham Van Helsing. The string of murders began here, gentlemen, with a slain father who may have taken on another role in the mind of his demented son!"

"It all makes sense, Holmes," Rawles said in a voice muffled by his handkerchief. "But where is Jasper Jefferson now?"

Suddenly, as if God, or perhaps the devil himself, had heard Rawles' question, Constable Miller, from the hall, called out, "Someone is at the door!"

We heard a ferocious roar next, then a scream of pain and the sound of someone falling, followed by running footsteps and a door being slammed shut.

We turned from the carnage in the parlor and headed toward the noise, the four of us almost becoming jammed in the doorway in our attempt at speed.

We found Constable Miller on the floor, his fingers over a bloody wound in his side. He was still conscious, his other hand pointing at the door.

"Watson," Holmes barked, "Help the constable! Gregson, Rawles, with me!"

As Holmes and the two policemen rushed out of the house, I knelt to see to Miller. The wound, though deep, would not, I thought, be deadly if I could stop the bleeding. I applied pressure to the injury with my handkerchief.

Though weak and in pain, Miller was able to speak. "It was him," he said. "He's as big as was said. Soon as he saw me, he drew a knife, took a stab at me before I could raise my hands. I'm sorry."

"It's all right, son," I said. "You did your best. Now relax. You'll be all right in a week or so."

At that instant, I heard the sound of a revolver being fired outside. There were two shots. I wanted, more than anything, to draw my own revolver and run out the door to see if Holmes required assistance, but the welfare of the injured constable had to be my primary concern.

The flow of blood from Miller's side seemed to be slowing and I did not suspect that any organs had been punctured. I instructed Miller to hold the handkerchief steady and stood to look out the door. As I began to open it, I heard the voice of Sherlock Holmes calling out with great urgency.

"Watson, if you can leave your first patient, another requires your attention!"

At that summons, I bolted through the door and rushed out into the street to find Holmes standing over Superintendent Rawles.

"Has he been shot?" I asked.

"No, he has collapsed," Holmes said. "I fear the strain of running has been too much for him."

I knelt to see to Rawles, but soon confirmed the worst possible development by checking for a pulse.

"He is dead, Holmes," I said. "His heart has quit."

As I stood, regretful of my inability to save the superintendent, Gregson walked back toward us shaking his head. His revolver was out, with smoke still wafting from the barrel's end.

"I took two shots at him," Gregson said, "but neither found its mark. The bastard's gotten away." He let loose a series of profanities, but stopped when he noticed Rawles. "What's happened to him?"

"His age and girth killed him, it would seem," said Holmes. "He was unfit for the demands of police work."

Even I, his closest associate, could sometimes be shocked by the coldness of Holmes' honesty. In this case, under the stress of what we had just been through, I felt compelled to scold the detective.

"Holmes, would you be so kind as to show some respect for the dead, regardless of your opinion of them in life?"

As I spoke that sentence, I could not have anticipated how deeply my choice of words would influence the next turn of events.

❋❋❋

Gregson summoned reinforcements and the scene was soon cleared. Rawles' body was taken away, as was that of Mr. Jefferson, although the two dead men would be taken to different destinations. Constable Miller, in no danger of dying, was transported to hospital. Several armed officers of Scotland Yard were ordered to remain at the house in case Jasper Jefferson should return, though Holmes thought such an event unlikely to occur.

Holmes and I were soon back at Baker Street, where we had promised to wait until Gregson joined us, the inspector having gone to Scotland Yard to speak with his superiors now that the lead investigator of the case was dead.

"Now that Jefferson knows he is being hunted," Holmes said as he smoked, "he will melt into London. A trained soldier will know how to hide. He has already demonstrated his skill at stealth, as he remained unseen, despite his size, at both the cemetery and the farm at Shepherd's Bush. It will not be easy to catch him."

"Do you think he will attempt another killing?" I asked.

"Driven by insane obsession as he is, Watson, I believe it is a certainty."

Holmes and I talked a while more. It felt as if we were wasting precious time, but there was nothing more we could do. After several hours passed, we heard the door downstairs open and close. Mrs. Hudson came in a moment later.

"Inspector Gregson to see you, gentlemen," she said, stepping aside to admit our friend.

Gregson, red in the face, sank into a chair and lit a cigarette. "A sound thrashing from the heads of the Yard I just got!"

"What did they say?" Holmes asked.

"What do you think they said? A high-ranking officer dead, a constable wounded, four civilians killed, and a murderer on the loose; that's what they said! They're just about as ready to put you in chains for obstructing this investigation as Rawles was at the height of his anger."

"But," Holmes said, "Since you have come here alone, Gregson, and I do not hear pounding upon our door, something must have been said beyond an expression of your superiors' rage."

"Conditions, Holmes," Gregson said. "There are strict conditions."

"What conditions?"

"Since you have been of great help to Scotland Yard on many occasions, and since they do not desire a public panic…accompanied almost certainly by a call to crucify the police for lack of results…of the sort that came with the Ripper murders of '88, it has been decided that you are to be given one more chance, a short chance, to find Jasper Jefferson. This does not mean Scotland Yard will not act while awaiting your possible success. They too will search London for Jefferson. They have, in fact, assigned Lestrade to that part of the investigation. You, Holmes, will be allowed two days in which to use your methods to seek a resolution to this debacle. When that time has elapsed, you will be arrested and held until Jefferson is caught. In the words of those who outrank me, you will either redeem yourself or pay the price for your impertinent disregard for those officially sanctioned to uphold the law."

"I see," said Holmes. "And what about you, Gregson, and any consequences stemming from your bringing us into this, as you called it, debacle?"

"My fate, Holmes, is tied to yours. I will continue to work alongside you and Dr. Watson, but reporting your activities to the Yard if they so request. If we succeed and Jefferson is caught before he commits another murder, I will suffer no punishment. But if we fail, they will demote me back into a constable's uniform, in which case I will probably resign."

"Then it would seem, Inspector," Holmes said as he rose from his chair, "that we all have much to lose if we fail, and we must not forget that any victims Jasper Jefferson chooses to pursue have even more at stake. We have not a moment to waste!"

"But where do we begin, Holmes?" I asked. "London is immense and crowded, and as you pointed out earlier, Jefferson has the training to survive on the streets and conceal himself from discovery. The old adage about needles and haystacks comes to mind."

"Yes, Watson, but solutions to that famous problem do exist. One would be to burn the haystack and sift through the ashes to find the needle. But we must not burn down London. So, we simply must find a magnet with which to draw the needle out of its hiding place."

Luckily for us, it was the needle himself who had chosen the magnet. Just as Holmes had finished his sentence, Mrs. Hudson announced another called to 221B Baker Street.

"A Mr. Stoker wishes to join you, gentlemen."

Bram Stoker's face was pale, his hands shaking as he entered our flat. I motioned for him to sit. "Tea for us all, please, Mrs. Hudson," I said.

"What has happened?" Holmes asked our new guest.

"He came to see me at my office in the Lyceum!"

"Jasper Jefferson went to you?" I asked.

"Is that his name?" Stoker asked.

"It is," Holmes confirmed. "We encountered him today after discovering that the first of his victims we are so far aware of was his own father. Unfortunately, he eluded us. At what time did he visit you?"

"Not an hour ago," Stoker said. "I came here straight away."

"Tell us what transpired."

"I looked up from my desk and there he was, staring at me. I had not heard him enter and do not know how he got past the doorman. He glared at me and said, 'Do you not know me? I am reborn.'"

"He thinks he is Dracula now?" I guessed.

"It seems his delusion has deepened," Stoker continued. "His voice was odd, as if he had adjusted his manner of speaking to try to mimic how he imagined Dracula's accent while reading my novel. He … he thanked me for making his story known to the world, told me he was grateful for my exposing the injustice that was done to him. He has it all backward, as if he thinks the vampire was the hero of the book!"

"Our interruption of his attempt at resurrecting Dracula," Holmes said, "whom he had come to believe his dead father to be seems to have caused him to slip further into insanity and assume that he himself is the vampire! Fascinating! Did he want something other than to thank you?"

"He appears to be seeking vengeance against yet another man. He bragged of having dealt with Harker, Seward, and Van Helsing, whom he thought the three men he killed were, as you guessed, Holmes. He asked me how he could find the fourth of his enemies, so that he could destroy him. He said he had seen him, had heard his name spoken, but had lost sight of him during a great battle. I was confused and did not know what to say. He told me I had one day to find what he wants, and that I am to leave him a message pinned to the door of the Lyceum where it can be seen by all who pass by. I assume this is to prevent a trap being set for him, as hundreds of people, perhaps even thousands, walk that way each day. I promised, mostly out of fear for my own life, to do as he asked, though I do not see how I possibly can, having been given so little information. Was he speaking from a completely delusional point of view, or does he, in fact, have a victim already chosen?"

As Bram Stoker asked that question, Sherlock Holmes burst out laughing. It was loud, powerful, victorious laughter, and I smiled to hear it. Such a noise coming from the detective could, I knew from long experience, mean only one thing. Holmes had reached a vitally important conclusion, an epiphany that would shift the balance of the game.

"What is so damned humorous?" Stoker demanded. "I see nothing funny about a butcher choosing his next piece of meat!"

"It is indeed quite humorous, Mr. Stoker," said Holmes, "for I am to be the next target of this madman! Now we shall see the prey turn the tables on the hunter!"

"How do you come to this idea, Holmes?" Stoker asked.

I, however, was beginning to understand. I listened as Holmes explained his theory to the startled author.

"In your novel, five men are members of the party directly responsible for Dracula's demise. Three of them, or, rather, three men Jasper Jefferson, through the twisted workings of his mind, identified as the characters Harker, Seward, and Van Helsing, are already dead. One character, the American called Quincey Morris, does not survive the final battle against the count, so we might assume Jefferson is not actively looking for an equivalent to him in his strange game of blood and death. That leaves one member of the group, assuming we discount Mina Harker, a female character, for Jefferson spoke of his intended victim as 'he,' and 'him.' The remaining man is called, in the story, Arthur Holmwood.

"We know Jasper Jefferson was in close proximity to us outside his father's house. Although he ran from us and we did not see him again once he seemed to have fled, he is a former soldier and so would have knowledge of how to move with little noise and hide from us. If he was not far away and was still listening when Gregson returned to the area in front of the Jefferson house, at which time I made what Watson considered to be a rude remark about the late Superintendent Rawles, he would have heard Watson say to me, 'Holmes, would you be so kind as to show some respect for the dead, regardless of your opinion of them in life?'"

"Good Lord!" Bram Stoker shouted as he understood. "The lunatic mistook the words, 'Holmes, would …' for Holmwood! His mind connected the pieces of the puzzle in the same absurd way it did when he learned the names of Harper, Stewart, and Van Houten. And now he thinks you, Holmes, are Arthur Holmwood."

"Precisely," Holmes said, and he laughed again. "Now, since Jefferson already knows Arthur Holmwood's appearance, all you have to do is tell him where to find him."

"But this little flat of yours will not suffice as a place to set the trap," Stoker argued. "In the book, Holmwood inherits the title of Lord Godalming when his father dies. This flat, charming as it may be, is unfit for the aristocracy."

"Quite true," Holmes said. "We shall have to make other arrangements."

"And quickly, Holmes," Gregson said. "Do not forget we have been allotted only two days to conclude this nasty business!"

"Yes, Gregson, I realize that," Holmes said. He closed his eyes for a moment, as he often did when searching for a solution or pondering a problem. He opened them and spoke to Stoker. "I have it. You will leave a message for Jefferson that will draw him to us tomorrow night. We must make it so that guns are not fired and no attention is drawn to our activities. We must avoid injury to the public despite the fact that this game will reach its conclusion in the heart of London. We must also minimize the number of police present, for we do not want circumstances to run beyond our control. We will need, Stoker, your theatre and the noted actor you have spent years working with. And from you, Gregson, we will need your presence as well as that of one more Scotland Yard man worthy of our trust. Lestrade will do, I think. The six of us will bring Jasper Jefferson to justice. If my plan goes as I intend the insanity that inspires him to kill will be what ends his reign of murder. This is how it is going to work …"

❀❀❀

Stoker, as per Holmes' instructions, pinned a note to the outer wall of the Lyceum Theatre the next morning. It simply said, "Lord G. will meet you onstage at midnight."

Holmes and I, along with those we had gathered, spent much of the day at Baker Street discussing what would take place that evening. When night fell, we travelled to the Lyceum and entered the building by way of a rarely used rear entrance to avoid being seen by any eyes watching the main doors.

At half past eleven, we were in the positions Holmes had assigned. I crouched behind the third audience row. I could see the stage through the spaces between seats. I had been instructed to not raise my head above the tops of the seats, for I had to remain invisible there in the shadows, where the light of the single lit lamp, which illuminated the stage, could not reach. I had my revolver, but Holmes had ordered that it was only to be used in the event of imminent, life threatening catastrophe, for he wished the affair to be as quiet as possible.

Bram Stoker, who knew the theatre's interior as well as any man alive, had climbed up onto the railways that ran along the ceiling above the stage with a few pieces of equipment.

Three of our number were in the backstage area, concealed as fully as possible and under instructions to remain silent until a certain signal was given.

Sherlock Holmes sat upon the stage in a wooden chair, facing what was, from my vantage point, the left. He was not armed, but did have a cane with him.

As twelve o'clock neared, we waited, all of us prepared for the worst, hoping for the best.

I do not know how he entered the theatre without making a sound, but his voice suddenly rang out from the darkness to the side of the stage.

"You are a brave but foolish man, Arthur Holmwood, to come here alone to face me!"

With those words, Jasper Jefferson leapt up onto the stage and stood staring at Sherlock Holmes. It was the first time I had seen Jefferson. He was indeed a large man, well over six feet tall and built like a boxer of the heavier classes. His hair was disheveled and his eyes wild. He wore an unbuttoned overcoat that, as he walked, swung behind him like a melodramatic cape.

"Count Dracula," Holmes said with a courteous nod.

"You stupid, suicidal Englishman," Jefferson growled, his voice rising in the strange accent Stoker had described. "You should have fled London and never come back. You know what I had my servant Jefferson do to your friends in order to resurrect me. Now, I will inflict similar ... no ... worse torments on you!"

"I do not fear you, Dracula," Holmes said, "for I have right and mercy on my side, while you are but a foul undead thing!"

"And you, Holmwood, are but a frail mortal whose blood will be consumed!" Jefferson shouted. He raised his hands, fingers bent as if he thought he had claws, and charged at Holmes.

I was terrified, afraid for my friend as the giant former soldier ran toward him. It took me every ounce of will to keep from standing and aiming my revolver at Jefferson, but I stayed where I was, determined to let Holmes see his plan through.

Jefferson reached Holmes, tried to grab him with his long arms, but Holmes stood from his chair, stepped to the side, and, with an outstretched leg, tripped Jefferson.

Jefferson stumbled, but did not fall; he regained his balance, pushed outward with an arm, and struck Holmes across the face. Holmes, skilled in physical combat, though smaller than Jefferson, raised a fist while wielding his cane in the other hand. They danced around each other for a moment, turning several times until they were facing in the same directions as when the encounter had begun, with Holmes to the left and Jefferson toward the right side of the stage.

"Surrender," Jefferson hissed, "and I will make your death quick! Continue trying to evade me and I will drain your blood slowly and you will die in agony!"

"No, Dracula," Holmes said, "I will not surrender. But I think it is time you faced a power greater than any of the mortal men you have slain."

With that, Holmes lowered his arm and tapped his cane twice on the floor.

The theatre went dark, completely enveloped in blackness.

Jefferson howled like a wild, confused beast.

There was a loud rumble, like thunder, as Bram Stoker, hidden above the stage, activated a phonograph.

Lightning seemed to split the shadows as Stoker manipulated the electric lights, causing a dizzying flashing.

When the manmade storm was over, a soft, steady light illuminated the stage. Jasper Jefferson, frozen in place, his face a dull mask of incomprehension, stared straight ahead.

Holmes, I was happy to see, was all right. He had moved to a few feet behind Jefferson, still holding his cane, ready to pounce if the next act went wrong.

Entering from stage right, England's most famous actor, Sir Henry Irving appeared. Known to many as a fine Hamlet, Macbeth, Iago, and King Lear, Irving was now dressed in a long white robe and wore a thick white beard.

Jefferson, not recognizing the actor in his disguise, stared but did not move.

"Dracula," Irving said in a firm, confident voice that echoed across the stage as if the speaker knew exactly how to manipulate the air currents that carried the sound, "you have defied death long enough! You are an abomination, a thing that spits in the face of all that is holy!"

Jefferson finally spoke again. "Who are you?"

"I am your creator, though your undead form offends me greatly! I am God! And no longer will you prey upon my children, you foul creature of the night! I am here to cast you into the pits of Hell! Kneel and repent. Beg forgiveness, or I shall have angels come forth and drag you to eternal torment!"

Irving's performance, I though, was marvelous, but Jefferson saw fit to challenge him.

"I will not kneel before any being, man or god!" Jefferson shouted. "Perhaps even gods can bleed!" and he raised his hands again as if to charge.

Holmes raised his cane, but Henry Irving, unshaken by Jefferson's threats, held up a hand, which I interpreted as being directed at both Holmes, to tell him to wait, and at Jefferson, as one last offer of mercy.

"Well, where are your angels?" Jefferson taunted.

"Michael, Raphael, your lord commands you to come!" Irving said in as bold and authoritative a voice as had ever roared from human lips.

Behind Irving, from stage right, appeared Inspectors Gregson and Lestrade. They wore robes of the same style as Irving's, though Gregson's was red and Lestrade's yellow. They carried swords, blunted for stage use, but still of hard, heavy iron.

The angels walked around God, Michael on the left and Raphael on the right, swords held high, robes flowing, anger on their faces.

Jasper Jefferson turned to run, but found Sherlock Holmes standing in his way. Holmes landed a swift punch to Jefferson's gut, and then struck him once in the side of the face with his cane.

Jefferson fell. He lay there shaking, stunned not only by Holmes blows, but by the effect the sight of God and his angels had on his unbalanced, delusional mind.

Holmes stepped aside as Gregson and Lestrade put down their swords, grabbed Jasper Jefferson by the arms, and dragged him away.

The man who thought he was Dracula babbled incoherently and began to drool as he left the stage.

In the balcony, the woman who had been hiding there since the performance had commenced stood and applauded.

"Take care with your prisoner, inspectors," Elizabeth Harper shouted, "for I want him to live many years in a very small cell, where he will think every day of what he did to my poor husband. Death is too good for a beast like him!"

Bram Stoker climbed down from the space above the stage. I came out from between the rows of seats and tended to Holmes' slight injuries.

With our two police allies having taken Jasper Jefferson from the theatre, those of us who remained spent a few quiet relieved moments getting used to the idea that no more murders would be committed by the madman, no more blood would be stolen in the night, and the chain of events Inspector Gregson called, "a nasty business," was finally at its end.

❋❋❋

Sir Henry Irving's career as an actor lasted until his death in 1905. During a performance of *Becket*, he suffered a stroke and died an hour later.

Bram Stoker would live for another twelve years. His novel, *Dracula*, was never enormously successful during his lifetime. His bestselling work at the time of his death was a biography of his friend Sir Henry Irving.

Elizabeth Harper, widowed so young, married a second husband several years after the death of her first. As far as I am aware, they are still quite happy together.

Jasper Jefferson, a few weeks after his apprehension at the Lyceum Theatre, was sentenced to spend the rest of his life in an asylum for the criminally insane with no opportunity for release. It was only due to his obvious madness, said the judge, that he was not hanged.

Sherlock Holmes put the affair of the murders committed by Jasper Jefferson out of his mind as soon as the case was concluded. He was never the sort to dwell on past events, no matter how dramatic. Instead, he eagerly anticipated the arrival of our next client.

For me, it was a different matter. Despite having seen many terrible things done to one human being by another, both during my military service and my years at Sherlock Holmes' side, I found the Dracula murders especially disturbing, and they haunted my dreams for several months after their finale at the Lyceum. But the nightmares ceased naturally, for time heals most wounds, and it was not until I sat down to write this account of that lurid case that I relived those dark and bloody days.

The End

Blood Oath

"The two shall never meet," I swore. I made this promise to myself years ago, shortly after I had the great fortune to become a published writer of Sherlock Holmes stories. I have kept this promise, though I'll admit to dancing around the edges from time to time, coming close to breaking it, but never quite giving in to the temptation, for doing so would, I think, pollute two characters I've held very dear for a very long time.

What I'm talking about is, of course, writing a story in which Sherlock Holmes literally faces Dracula. It will never happen!

The world of Sherlock Holmes and Dr. Watson must be one of cold, hard logic. Science must prevail. Knowledge and observation are the keys to solving crimes. The laws of physics must hold up. Throw the supernatural into the mix and you get chaos. If matter doesn't behave as it should, and if spirits and ghouls and gods and monsters enter the equation, what good are Holmes' powers of deduction? A detective of Sherlock Holmes' kind must exist in a world where chains of events follow the laws of nature, not spit in their face. Inserting Dracula into that world would be a very, very bad idea. It is something I will never do when trying to write Holmes' stories that stand comfortably alongside the canon created by Sir Arthur Conan Doyle.

But, that doesn't mean I haven't occasionally bent my own rule, though not to the point of snapping it in two. In my short novel *Season of Madness*, published a few years ago, I had Dr. Watson team up with Dr. Jack Seward to solve a mystery, uniting the doctor from the Holmes stories with the doctor from *Dracula*. In the world of that book, Dracula was indeed real, though permanently dead by the time of the story's events. But Holmes did not appear in the story and certainly did not come face to face with the vampire.

I've also written stories featuring British Secret Service Agent Quincey "Hound-Dog" Harker. Although the adult form of the character (whose adventures take place in the 1930s) is my creation, he is the grown up version of the son of Jonathan and Mina Harker of Bram Stoker's novel. In some of Harker's stories, he is aided by an older version of Jack Seward. In an as yet unpublished Harker story, I used an elderly Sherlock Holmes and Inspector Lestrade, which, I suppose, puts *that* Holmes into the same world in which Dracula existed, which means he can't be the same

Holmes who appears in my regular Holmes tales, including the one you've just read.

Anyway, the point is that I have not and will not insert Dracula or other supernatural elements into any Holmes mystery I write for this series of anthologies. But we can have the people within the stories believe in all sorts of bizarre things as long as Holmes is there to put superstition to rest in the end.

In previous essays in this series, I related how I first became fascinated with Sherlock Holmes. It was a combination of seeing the great Jeremy Brett portray the detective on television and being given by my grandfather, as a Christmas gift, the massive old hardcover edition of The Complete Sherlock Holmes he'd first read during his own boyhood in the '40s. From then on, Holmes was my favorite fictional hero and I'm still thrilled by the idea that people pay to read stories I've written about him!

Count Dracula, on the other bloody hand, is easily my favorite fictional villain. I'm not sure what my first encounter with Dracula or with vampires in general was. Vampires scared me when they appeared on a few of my favorite TV shows when I was a kid. They showed up on *Thundarr the Barbarian*, and also in the "Space Vampires" episode of the late 70s Buck Rodgers series. As for Dracula specifically, it was probably either one of the old movies being shown on TV on a Saturday afternoon or a heavily abridged, illustrated version of the book I found in my grammar school's library. Whatever it was, it made me a lifelong fan of the count. I've read Stoker's novel many times and have made it a point to see most of the Dracula movies made over the years.

If I had to pick my favorite versions of Dracula, I'd start with the novel, of course. I also have to mention my three favorite film versions: the 1931 Bela Lugosi movie with its wonderful atmosphere; the 1958 film *Horror of Dracula*, which has my favorite cast, including Christopher Lee as Dracula and Peter Cushing as Van Helsing; and finally, the most faithful adaptation of the novel to ever make it onto film, the 1977 BBC production *Count Dracula*, starring Louis Jourdan in the title role. And there is also the great Marvel Comics series *Tomb of Dracula*, which ran for 70 issues in the 1970s and featured stories by Marv Wolfman and art by the great Gene Colan.

So considering how long I've been a fan of both Sherlock Holmes and Dracula, and how I've sworn never to have them meet in a story I write, maybe it seems natural that I'd do a story like the one in this book, where one of Holmes' cases is connected, intimately and horribly, with Bram Stoker's novel.

But I didn't plan it. It was a complete and sudden accident of inspiration.

Writers are often asked where they get their ideas. In some cases, the roots of our stories are easily traceable. We remember exactly what triggered the thought that led to the tale being born in our imagination. For example, with one of my previous Holmes stories, "The Adventure of the Stolen Centennial," I heard a news story on the radio about a village in Japan that was about to throw a big party for the first man there to reach his hundredth birthday. I started thinking about how sad it would be if he died just before reaching that milestone. That thought led to another and I began to ponder why someone might want to murder a man just before he turned one-hundred. So it's clear where that story had its origins.

But "The Adventure of the Vampire's Vengeance" was different. I had just finished my previous Holmes story, "The Adventure of the Last Biscuit," so I was still in the Baker Street frame of mind, but I wasn't planning on starting a new one right away, as I had other, non-Holmes stories planned. Yet there I was, driving to the day job early one morning, when the premise of "The Vampire's Vengeance" sprang fully formed into my head, flashing like a bolt of lightning! I hadn't been thinking specifically of Dracula or vampires or anything related to them, but something simmering under the surface of my conscious mind suddenly pushed the story to the top of the heap and I knew I had to write it, beginning that very same day. Sometimes writers just can't explain the workings of their own imaginations, and maybe that's a good thing.

The story came together quite easily, as it united two things I'm very familiar with: the world of Sherlock Holmes, and the novel *Dracula*. And I had a great time writing it. It is, so far, my longest Holmes story, and my darkest.

A few things that set it apart from my previous tales of the great detective:

This was the first time I've used actual historical figures in a Holmes story. Bram Stoker and Sir Henry Irving were, of course, very real.

Inspector Tobias Gregson plays a large role in this one. I had used Lestrade, the most well-known Scotland Yard man from the Doyle canon, in several previous stories (and he does play a small part toward the end of "The Vampire's Vengeance"), so I thought it was time to give Gregson his fair share of the attention.

I also had fun giving another supporting member of the traditional Holmes cast a bigger role than I had in previous stories. Mrs. Hudson truly contributes to the eventual resolution of the mystery this time, which was more satisfying than limiting her to occasionally walking into Holmes' and Watson's flat and announcing, "There's a gentleman here to see you," or "Your tea is ready, sir."

I also believe this is the first time I've had Holmes and Watson visit the Diogenes Club. I suppose it was inevitable that I would eventually set a scene there, as it's a mysterious, interesting place that's been the subject of much speculation among Holmes' fans for many years. But Holmes' brother Mycroft still hasn't actually made an appearance in one of my stories. He's been mentioned often enough. His name pops up in this story, in my very first Holmes story, "The Massachusetts Affair," and in the novel *Season of Madness*, but he's never actually shown his face or spoken a line of dialogue. I'll get around to Mycroft eventually, but only when he insists on being included.

Overall, I had a tremendous amount of fun writing this novella. It was a pleasure to show my favorite detective reacting to the consequences of an unbalanced mind reading one of the greatest horror novels of all time. I hope readers of this book, some of whom are bound to be fans of both Holmes and Dracula, enjoy it.

I have no plans to ever have the world's most famous detective meet its most feared vampire, but it's nice to come as close as I can without breaking the promise I made years ago.

AARON SMITH - is the author of over 20 stories for Airship 27 Productions, including 7 Sherlock Holmes mysteries. His other work includes the Richard Monroe spy novels, *Nobody Dies for Free* and *Under the Radar* for Pro Se Press; the vampire novels *100,000 Midnights* and *Across the Midnight Sea;* the zombie horror novel *Chicago Fell First*; and numerous other stories in anthologies, magazines, and comic books.

More information about Smith and his work can be found on his blog at www.godsandgalaxies.blogspot.com

CPSIA information can be obtained
at www.ICGtesting.com
Printed in the USA
LVOW08s2253040517
533319LV00010B/647/P